PENGUIN BOOKS

MIDNIGHT FREEWAY

Vivaan Shah is an actor and writer from Mumbai. He was born in 1990 and published his first novel *Living Hell* in 2019. He also published a horror short story for the *Hindu Businessline* titled 'Entombed', and one for *HT Brunch* called 'The Reptile Kind'. He has acted in movies and shows adapted from literary sources ranging from *7 Khoon Maaf* and *Bombay Velvet* to *A Suitable Boy*. He has been acting and participating in theatre since he was a child, and has adapted works of Edgar Allan Poe and Ambrose Bierce into a play he directed, entitled *Comedy of Horrors*.

MIDNIGHT FREEWAY

VIVAAN SHAH

PENGUIN BOOKS

An imprint of Penguin Random House

PENGUIN BOOKS

USA | Canada | UK | Ireland | Australia
New Zealand | India | South Africa | China

Penguin Books is part of the Penguin Random House group of companies
whose addresses can be found at global.penguinrandomhouse.com

Published by Penguin Random House India Pvt. Ltd
4th Floor, Capital Tower 1, MG Road,
Gurugram 122 002, Haryana, India

First published in Penguin Books by Penguin Random House India 2021

ISBN 9780143453239

Typeset in Plantin MT Pro by Manipal Technologies Limited, Manipal
Printed at Thomson Press India Ltd, New Delhi

www.penguin.co.in

ONE

I was taking a leak on the corner of the service road off the Western Express Highway when I got the call from Khar police station. One of my clients, a Bharat Morwani, had been detained by the duty officer on charges of vehicular assault, disturbing the peace, and disorderly conduct. He was considerably intoxicated, as I could tell from his voice which quivered over the phone, crackling with bad network as accompaniment, as if his predicament wasn't bad enough.

'Now, just take it easy!' I yawned into my Samsung S6. 'And tell me exactly what happened.'

He'd gotten into an altercation with the driver of a silver Volkswagen Jetta MK6, Licence Number MH02NA536, 2018 Model. The sedan had overtaken his maroon Honda Civic in a rash and reckless manner at the turning of Reclamation and S.V. Road. He caught up with the car on the flyover and smashed into the right mudguard, denting the entire door and busting a tail light. According to the passing patrol jeep that had picked them up, he'd even been pulled over earlier at a checkpost and had been let off with a warning. But he was obviously in the mood for trouble. Morons like him always like to push their luck. They like to see how fast they can go before they have to pull the brakes. They live for the kicks and the law of the passing moment, taking each step too long for their own good.

He'd been pulled over dozens of times, mostly for driving under the influence—once for breaking the speed limit, twice for exceeding the decibel limit, thrice for not wearing a seat belt, and another time for just having long hair. That was the most heinous of his offences as far as I was concerned. The rest are just routine. When it comes to one's personal conduct, the measuring tape begins at the profile—hair, scars, birthmarks, beards, moles, skin colour, etc. There's nothing worse than an unkempt, dishevelled monkey who doesn't look like he belongs out on the street on a working day. Not that I have anything against the uncouth, it's just that the hours between nine to five belong solely to those committed to earning an income. It's not like I myself am not prone to idle hours of distraction during the daytime, but that's because my clock runs through the night. I'm on call 24/7. Kind of like a doctor, only, I service souls, not samples.

Being a criminal lawyer is like being a shepherd. You hold the hands of the misguided and try to navigate them across the stone wall of procedure. It takes hours . . . years, sometimes. The wheels of progress move slow and steady.

After he told me what happened, I asked him to sit tight with one eye open, and his mouth sealed shut. It was 2 o'clock in the morning; not an ideal time to give the area's Additional Commissioner of Police a call. I had a couple of names stashed away for such occasions, but I didn't want to waste them on him. He wasn't worth it. He'd be back again tomorrow with a smashed headlight for an alibi. He couldn't keep himself off the road, not with all the indiscriminate gangs hovering about his neighbourhood—spray-painting their initials on crumbling walls and abandoned hideaways, blowing up their parents' hard-earned money on full-tanks, spare parts, sub-woofers, spoilers, and souped-up growlers that woke up any respectable resident with a bedtime past 12.30. Not to mention the bikers doing wheelies on Carter Road with torn silencers, putting their lives and twelve others at hazard in the process. It was an all-night free-for-all roadside wrestling match for two-wheelers and four-wheelers alike: a royal rumble.

Like most members of the peer group devoted solely to the expanse and pursuit of leisure, Bharat had nothing better to do than cruise around looking for trouble. He lived for a fight. It was the one consolation life offered him on many a dreary day, practically the only thing for him to look forward to. He relished the adrenaline rush of a confrontation—the blood boiling to a steady degree, all the warmth and pulsation, the stadium soar of passions—like the sensation one derives from the dive of a roller coaster or in the thick of the cricket field. There was nothing purer than a fight to determine his personal capabilities, nothing more direct than a little face-to-face human antagonism. Conflict was his sole companion and the only thing in life that made any sense to him.

'Never mind Bharat,' I calmly reassured him as I entered Khar police station. 'It's okay. It's all over now.'

I wiped the hair off the side of his forehead, caressing his swollen eyebrows—two black eyes, both of which sat like goggles over his lids. His chin had been bruised and his entire lower jaw dented, whole—swivelling left and right as if it were holding back a mouthful. Blood trickled out of his left nostril, curling down his upper lip like one side of a handlebar moustache. This face wasn't accustomed to these kinds of beauty spots. Ordinarily, it'd be the one doling them out, not the receiving end.

They'd worked him over nicely, given him the special treatment. What else do you expect if you can't put your money where your mouth is? The way he was talking, they must have thought he was stacked with a bundle. When they found out all he had in his wallet was his driver's licence, they shoved him in remand and beat the living daylights out of him. It had probably been an uneventful day at the station. It was practically empty at this hour of the night save for a few derelicts passed out on the waiting room benches. The night duty officer frowned behind his desk, looking down into the register—lost in thought, sticking his finger into one ear and wriggling out a scab to be flicked upon the tabletop. He didn't look like he was in a charitable mood; on the contrary, he appeared downright hostile. I pushed aside one of the hawaldaars that had been assigned to Bharat, and took him to the corner, away from everyone. According to the head constable, he had been talking big, taking all kinds of names, some that he'd dare not repeat. Serves him right. All his ball-talks had degenerated into the slobberings of a snivelling delinquent.

Bharat was still a kid, but acted twice his age as if it were his birthright. He still liked to think he was bigger and brighter than anyone else in the room.

'What are they booking us for?' I asked.

'They're booking me, not you!' he whined. 'You still get to go back home to a comfortable bed.'

'We're in this together! Remember, what did I tell you? We're one and the same person. A team. You follow?'

'That son of a bitch belted me one in the eye. There's pus coming out . . . I'm gonna go blind!'

'There's no pus in that black eye, and you're gonna be seeing fine. Now pull yourself together, shooter, and let's see a smile on that pretty face of yours.'

He winced.

'That's good. See, you look better already. There's nothing wrong with that face save what's behind it.'

He looked away from me, avoiding eye contact. Two hard-nosed hawaldaars stared at him from both sides of the duty officer's desk. It was getting to be their off-duty hour any minute now. He stared them back. The thought escaped them.

'You look fine from where I sit,' I said.

'You sure?' he slurred at me.

I noticed another gash on the top right corner of his temple, shaded by his parting—this one looked like the permanent variety.

'Well . . . nothing a few nights' rest won't fix.'

I lent him my handkerchief to mop up his nose.

'You know what . . .' I bent over, closely examining him redden my brand new shiny white Kamal Vihar napkin. I'd nicked it off a fast food restaurant in Bhandup and knew it would come in handy. 'I'll tell you something . . .'

'What?' he sniffled, inspecting the napkin to see how much damage he'd done.

'There's nothing wrong with the way you look. You look fine to me.'

'Then?'

'It's your soul that's mixed up, not your mug.'

His eyes narrowed.

'You ever hear of a thing called a conscience?' I asked him.

'No. What's that?'

'It's this tiny little thing at the back of your head. Thrives in there like a ringworm, feeding off your brain cells; takes up a hell of a lot of your time, making you think about things there's no reason to think about in the first place. Things like right and wrong and what another person feels like. It's tough enough feeling what you got inside yourself to have to bother with someone else's worries. That's what I like about you. You skip all the bullshit. You got no scruples. The only thing you got on your mind is number one. That's the only person you're looking out for.'

His eyebrows shrivelled up together, trying to follow my drift.

'You see, I'm trying to save you all that time!' I explained. 'All those wasted years thinking about this and that, and what you did and didn't do, or what you should have done. Now me, I got no conscience—sold mine off a long time ago with a second hand Sony Trinitron and a busted down Maruti Suzuki. You weren't around back in those days, when all we had were

Midnight Freeway

800s to pass the time. You're young. You've got your whole life ahead of you. What do you want with all this aggravation? Haven't you got any friends? Chill out with them, go out and enjoy yourself. Grab a drink with some folks. Where'd you guys hang around? Sheesha?'

'I don't go to Sheesha anymore.'

'What about snooker? Go hit a couple of frames at CrackJack. I bumped into a couple of your buddies out there. Go hang out with them.'

He leaned back in his chair, shoving his head aside as if he didn't know me. Crumpling his forehead with his thumb and middle finger, he forced out an exhalation, looking down hopelessly over the chipped tiles that spread across the waiting room.

'What does it look like?' he asked.

'By the looks of it, there's no telling who's in charge here,' I whispered, glancing around. 'Now, you just stay seated and have a drink of water. There isn't a thing in the world to worry about. It's all good. You following me?'

'I follow.'

'That's good. Alright, now take it easy. I'll be right back.'

TWO

I didn't want to spend any more time there than I had to. It was getting late, and I had a hearing at 11 o'clock in the morning. I had to report to the sessions court at 9.30. It was a matter concerning an old lady who had allegedly slit the throat of her ex-husband. Just my meat, and infinitely more rewarding than what I was faced here with.

The duty officer, a Sub-inspector Naresh Saawant, was hell-bent on putting him in the slammer. He said he'd have to spend the night in lock-up and would be eligible for bail come morning. I promised him I'd drop the kid home and talk to his parents, but he wouldn't listen. He said Bharat had spoken rudely to one of the constables and had threatened him. I informed him that the kid was a little soft in the head and meant no harm. I assured him that he wasn't like everybody else and that I would take personal charge of his rehabilitation. I offered to pay for the damages to the Volkswagen and slip in a little something extra for his troubles.

Sub-inspector Saawant started to look towards Bharat with a bemused stare, tilting his head sideways to get a better look at him. He couldn't size him up. Not by a long shot. People like my client can never be fully comprehended at face value. With officers like Saawant, they're about as likely to inspire empathy as a mosquito is to attract hospitality.

'By the looks of him,' he mused, 'I'd say this kid is worth one and a half.'

'One and a half? The kid drives a Civic.'

'Looks like he's from a good family.'

'Well . . . depends on your definition of "good".'

'Well-to-do.'

'He isn't as loaded as he looks.'

'Nowadays, it's the ones from *good* families that look the *worst*.'

'Believe me; he just talks big.'

'Well, if he can afford to go smashing up his car every time someone cuts him at a signal that isn't his in the first place . . . then I'm sure he can afford to arrange a reasonable sum of money at such short notice.'

'Look, the kid's stupid. I told you. He may be trashed. But he doesn't exactly have spending money spilling out of him. It's me that's going to be footing the bill for now, and if you want to know anything about my background, I'd be more than glad to supply you with the necessary details. You can have my whole life story, for starters.'

'What's your name?' he snarled at me.

'Pranav Paleja, friends call me Pannu, colleagues call me P.P., strangers call me Pranay, and those who wish to antagonize me simply refer to me as Paleja.'

'Well, let me tell you something, Paleja.'

He turned. 'He was doing 120 at the turning.'

'110.' I corrected him.

'He broke the signal, the speed limit, was driving under the influence, and crashed his car deliberately into a moving vehicle. That's four fines. It means we'll have to suspend his licence. Government of Maharashtra regulations. You get three chances.'

'Oh come on . . .' I pleaded. 'Look . . .'

'It isn't the Volkswagen guy's fault.'

The Volkswagen guy stood outside at the entrance with a morose look on his face, leaning over the front railings, arguing with the head constable about how the signal had turned red. According to my client, it was still yellow. The head constable kept trying to console him, promising that there was nothing he could do about it at the moment and he would have to go through the routine procedure to file an NC. Bharat silently arose from the bench on hearing the man's voice grow louder and his accusations more distinct. I noticed this from the corner of my eyes and instantly went after him, leaving Saawant's desk. The man started yelling about how he was going to see to it that Bharat went to jail. He pulled out a brand new Motorola Razr flip phone from his chest pocket and started making some phone calls.

'Just you wait . . .' he told Bharat. 'I'm going to break your arms and legs.'

'Ehh . . .' the head constable stopped him, his voice stiffening up. 'No threats here now. I'll have none of this. Both of you'll please conduct yourselves with decorum; otherwise, we'll have to call our superior.'

'Come on, you chickenshit . . .' Bharat riled him on. I reached him before he could start foaming at the mouth. 'You don't know who I am! You don't know who you're messing with!' he hollered.

'Bharat!' I shouted, trying to pull him back. 'Take it easy . . .'

They both went at each other like a pair of stray toms. I leapt in between, trying to tear them apart, but they had already gotten a firm hold of each other's throats. The Volkswagen guy started clawing at Bharat's face, writhing in agonized contortions like a wild animal. He grabbed Bharat in a headlock and started strangling him with his full-sleeved forearm and bicep, his heels scraping the gravel underfoot, throwing off bits of dirt at us as we attempted to stop him. His otherwise ordinary demeanour couldn't contain his escalating hysteria. He had to literally be dragged away from Bharat, and be restrained by two naiks that were crossing the outside corridor. With the able assistance of the head constable who was charitably endowed, we were able to separate the two of them. I dutifully reprimanded Bharat for his unreasonable behaviour and took him back inside the station, away from the Volkswagen guy.

'Who the hell does he think he is?' he fumed.

'It's nothing,' I said, 'Take it easy. Just forget about it. He's an idiot.'

I sat him down on a bench, telling one of the hawaldaars to fetch him a glass of water and a cup of tea if possible. The head constable was doing the same for the Volkswagen guy. We each tended to our respective specimens like seconds at opposing corners of a boxing ring. Once I was certain the Volkswagen guy had taken a couple of deep breaths and was willing to reconsider the proposition, I went back out to the front porch where he was standing with the head constable inspecting the damage on his car. His name was Yogesh Moolchandani, or at least, so he claimed. He was about twice Bharat's age and at least four times his size. He looked like an upmarket businessman, the creases of whose shirt had long worn out their welcome. He was dressed like he was coming back from a yuppie conference, had on a pair of brown leather square-toes, an original Gold Rado strapped to his wrist. His starched collars had now been nicely ruffled up by all the action.

'I'm extremely sorry about the . . . uh, belligerence of my client, sir,' I said, calling him 'sir' just for the heck of it, knowing it'd do more good than anything else I could do or say. 'He is a bit troubled at the moment. He's got a hell of a temper.'

'Yaa, well so do I,' he groaned, looking me up and down with his ivory eyes, calculating whether or not I was in the mood to tangle with him.

'I would look upon it as a personal favour,' I said, 'if you considered dropping the charges. I'd be eternally grateful and am willing to compensate you monetarily.' I took out a visiting card for Anmol Auto Works Mechanics and Spare Part Supply, a small service centre and repair station in Tardeo for foreign cars. It was right next to the GCube showroom and supplied all original parts straight from the factory. It was owned by an acquaintance of mine, had at one point even been a client owing to an unfortunate set of circumstances, but he was a reliable man and would take care of the repairs for me on credit. I told Mr Moolchandani to send the Volkswagen Jetta there first thing in the morning, promising him it would be fixed up and as good as new.

'If you want, I can even have them come and have it picked up.'

He put the card inside the chest pocket of his full-sleeved rayon shirt and looked at me absolutely still, the agitation pouring out of his face.

'Are you trying to be funny with me?' he said softly, 'You think I'm stupid?'

'No . . .'

'You think I don't know you're making fun of me, taking my case, so to speak. Yanking my chain!'

'I guarantee you I am not doing anything of the kind; I'm dead serious.'

'I don't need to take that to the factory; it's a Jetta, not a GTI Roadster. I can get it fixed anywhere. Stop trying to patronize me; I know what I'm driving.'

'It's a beautiful car. I didn't mean to offend you . . .'

'What do you drive?' he asked, glancing out to where the cars were parked next to the pavement. 'What's that you got out there, an Ikon?'

'That's right. I am proud to say I am the owner of a 2004 model Ford Ikon, with brand new licence plates. Just got the polish done yesterday. Had sent it for my monthly servicing.'

'To Anmol?' he laughed, pulling the card back out.

'No, I have a separate concern that looks after automobiles of my price range.'

13

'I'd like to see his mechanic,' he spat, pointing towards Bharat, 'he must be used to these kinds of jobs.'

'Ohh . . . he uses the services of a certain garage in Chimbai.'

'Well, I don't intend to send my car to either one of those places. I've got my own mechanic. And he takes cash upfront, which is what you're going to have to give me. That's eleven grand for the tail light, twelve for the fins, eighteen for the rims, eight for the mudguard, and I'm gonna have to change the door. That's at least half a peti (lakh) worth of damage, not to mention that scratch on the spoiler.'

'Well . . . you see . . .' I smiled, 'as you can imagine, I don't have that kind of money on my person, but as I said before, if you send it over to Anmol Auto Works, he will have your car fixed up in two or three days max.'

'I don't want to send it to Anmol. I want the cash upfront for the damage, so I can get it repaired at my own leisure . . .'

'I'm afraid . . .'

'Never mind what you're afraid of . . . if you don't want your client to be sitting in a jail cell for causing a potentially life-threatening accident, I suggest you cough up the dough.'

'There was nothing life-threatening about it. He just tapped you.'

'You call *that* a tap?' He showed me the door on the right side. It wasn't shutting properly, and had been bent entirely out of shape. The mudguard protruded out, touching the floor, as did the back bumper that was nearly about to detach itself from the rear.

Midnight Freeway

'Look, Mr Moolchandani, it's going to be tough for me to arrange that kind of money right now. My office is shut, as is the bank, and the maximum withdrawal limit at an ATM is 30,000. I'm telling you, I'll get the car repaired for you tomorrow morning.'

He yanked my shoulder literally right out of its socket and pulled me away from the head constable, guiding me up towards the main gate. Bharat's smashed-up Civic was parked right outside.

'You see *that*,' he smirked, pointing at Bharat's car. 'That's nothing. Twenty grand tops . . . with difficulty, twenty-five. It's only a Civic, after all, but what I got there is going to set me back a hefty amount. I can't take it to any old garage.'

'Why's that?'

'. . . 'cause it's an unregistered vehicle.' he snarled, tightening his lips firmly over his teeth. 'Do I make myself clear?'

'I see . . .'

'Which is why your client has put me in an awkward position, as you can see, for no fault of my own. I wasn't the one who wanted to come down to the police station, but you know what this guy says . . .?'

'What?'

'He says he's personally acquainted with DCP Narayan Panth, Bandra police station, ex-Crime Branch encounter specialist. That he'll get me buried in the Aarey Jungle.'

'He's talking nonsense . . .'

'Then he takes Mateen Lakdawaala's name. Now I know who Mateen is, and there's no way in hell he's going to lift a finger to save this idiot's neck.'

15

'What's your line of business?' I asked, suddenly interested in how he was acquainted with the said person.

'Property real estate consultant.'

'Builder?'

'You could say that!'

'Where are the bodyguards?'

'On vacation.'

'Look,' I breathed faintly, 'taking care of an unauthorized job of this sort isn't exactly alien to Anmol.'

'They've done it before?'

'On several occasions, once even at my behest,' I winked.

'I see,' he smiled, 'Then I take it you're not exactly alien to this kind of a situation yourself.'

'Far from it. In fact, I'd say I'm pretty well acquainted with it.'

'About as well acquainted as your client is with the Deputy Commissioner of Police.'

I laughed, not knowing whether he was serious or fooling around with me.

'Why don't you just take my phone number and give me a call if anything . . .'

I exchanged phone numbers with him, and that seemed to settle things, at least temporarily. But he still kept hurling all kinds of abuses at my client as I walked back inside. Once I was certain he had put the card back into his chest pocket and had his last spit, I went back inside to Saawant's desk. I took a seat after regaining my composure. I was liable to slip up with the appropriate aggravation.

Midnight Freeway

'Sorry about that. My client tends to be a bit . . . uh . . . childish.'

'Should probably stay that way. Doesn't need to work for a living. Lowlifes like him don't deserve to drive a Civic. Don't have "civic" sense.'

'One and a half?' I exhaled, leaning over his desk.

'That's right. Otherwise, he's going to have to wait inside with all the others for a date. You can go to court, pay the necessary fines, and wait another year before you can get to process a new licence.'

'You filed the case?'

'Nothing's gone on record yet.'

'Then I'd like it if we can keep it that way. One and a half is a bit too much, in my estimation. Not a practical amount.'

'Not one rupee less.'

'I haven't known too many people, not even of the Volkswagen variety, to be able to cough up that kind of bread to break out of a jam. Let's talk sense.'

He opened up his register and began to note down my client's name and car number.

'Wait a minute . . .' I tried to stop him, putting my hands over the book. He stopped writing and looked up at me, seemingly displeased at my obstruction.

'50,000,' I said.

He looked back down and continued writing, pushing my hand aside.

'Please . . . look, that's all I got in my account,' I told him. That was far from the truth. All I had in my bank account was nothing to speak of. I had less than five grand in my pocket, and that's what mattered.

'Don't waste my time . . .' he groaned, starting to file the case.

'Look . . .' I began, now with a change of tone, 'please don't put anything on record. I request you,' I told him calmly without breaking into hysterics, 'My client has an ongoing case currently up for dismissal.'

'What for?'

'Hit and run.'

He glared back at me, his eyeballs tilting up from his downward stare.

'So you see,' I continued, 'another case of this kind would simply finish him. He won't be able to leave the country.'

'Not my concern. You make mistakes, you have to face the consequences.'

'I'm willing to give you how much ever I can withdraw from the nearest ATM; you can even come with me, or send one of your constables. He's a young kid. Why d'you wanna ruin his life? Give him another chance. Come on . . .'

'The saahab is on his way here.'

'We don't have to let him know anything about it,' I said, softening up my voice as I closed in towards him. His three-star superior didn't look like he was going to show up anytime before breakfast. I called his bluff. 'We can take care of this just between the two of us. You wouldn't want to get him involved, I mean, after all, then what would you get?'

He sat upright, his left eye tightening sternly on me. He proceeded to write, ignoring me now altogether.

Midnight Freeway

'Look please . . . I will talk to your saahab personally, please . . .' I kept going on, but he wouldn't listen. 'Please saahab . . . please . . . don't write this down. We can take care of this. How much do you want?'

He was adamant. It took a lot of work to get him to close the files and settle the matter off the record, unofficially, without anything going into the books. It wasn't easy, given their enthusiasm for wielding a pen and paper as if it were a sword. It's basic common sense. The second they begin to note things down and put them in the register, it changes the entire complexion of the circumstance at hand, and the offender automatically starts to sing a different tune. I say Bharat shouldn't have let them drag him down to the station in the first place. He should have asked them to clear it then and there, on the spot. But he didn't know how to talk to them. First, you have to start nice, like he's your grand uncle. Then once you get the formalities done with, and you're really starting to get through to one another, you've got to take it to a first name basis, playing it tight like you know the rules and aren't there to take in the scenery. There's no point scavenging broken bits of Marathi from here and there to get on the same team, and expecting 'bhau' (brother) as a term of addressal to have the power to cure even arthritis. There's nothing a cop hates more than a person trying to fake his mother tongue, and getting caught at it once the words lose coherence. They'd rather you speak your piece the way you're inclined to in other circumstances, so that you don't scramble up your judgement, let alone theirs. If they don't listen to reason, then patience is the only recourse.

Sooner or later, they're bound to break. After all, if it's a matter of making their job simpler, then why not? Paperwork has always been my arch enemy. I tend to prefer the one-to-one contact of straightforward talk.

At first, Saawant wasn't willing to speak my language, but all it took was a bit of small-talk to get him to open up. First about the weather, then about the match, or about the traffic, or worse still, about the coming Municipal elections. Having to go there meant he wasn't interested or conversant in any of the former. Bargaining with a police officer is kind of like trying to get the liquor store to keep the shutter open for one last drink. They can entertain your request only as far as hospitality dictates. When it comes time to pull the plug, there isn't a chance of squeezing a drop out of them unless you have the persistence to stick your foot in to keep the shutter from hitting the ground.

THREE

It was 5.30 in the a.m. when they let us go. They'd impounded his car and slapped a 185 on him for drunk driving. I had to drop the stinking son-of-a-bitch home in my own car. The entire car reeked with his presence of Antiquity, Imperial Blue, and God knows what else. I had to keep the AC on for him as a show of companionship. And why not? I could afford to burn some fuel. It was getting hot even at midnight; it was that time of year. A corny old remix was blaring away on 93.8. Bharat was in a mess. He was looking out the window in a daze, like a child who'd come to the city for the first time. He hunched his shoulders, his mouth agape, his eyes drooping aside in a motionless glare. He looked like he was about to collapse any second, but the seat belt held him up. I insisted he wear it. I'd spent every buck I had on me to get him off. I managed to get Saawant down from 1.5 lakhs (which is what he had initially started with) to 4,500. It wasn't for nothing that they called me the Snake Charmer of Santa Cruz. I no longer lived there, of course. I had to lug my Ford all the way back to Chembur, where I put up. Bharat had to be dropped at his place in Bandra on 15th road, which wasn't far off from Khar police station. I kept the AC on all the way up to his building.

'You sure you'll be able to make it up in one piece?' I asked, as he kicked open the door of the passenger seat. 'You want me to drop you upstairs?'

'Naa . . .' he groaned. 'I'm okay.'

'I bet you are.' I grinned at him. He slammed the door shut on my face.

I lowered all four windows and turned the AC off now that he had vacated my vehicle.

'Take it easy!' I yelled at him as he sauntered down the driveway of his compound. 'I'll seeya tomorrow.'

He didn't even bother to wave back. I'd collect my fees when he was sober. I didn't like to work on credit. Usually, I liked my payments upfront, but in his case, I could afford to make an exception. The total charge came to something like Rs 6,400 for the fees, plus Rs 1,200 for the RTO, and another Rs 500 for conveyance. Total of about Rs 8,500, including tax. More than what the cop had made off him.

I pulled out of his lane, straightening out onto Waterfield Road after taking a right from China Gate towards Moti Mahal. The roads were practically empty; I had them all to myself at this hour. I didn't stop at a single red light, just zipped through all of them, racing back towards Reclamation. I hadn't eaten anything since the dinner I took in at 8 o'clock last night. My stomach was starting to rumble. I kept a lookout for a 24×7 as I ran along the street parallel to Hill Road. Once I reached the jeweller's lane where Tavaa and Fab India sit side by side, an assortment of establishments surrounded me on all sides with their shutters pulled down. Gymnasiums and grocery stores, hair and beauty salons, opticians and men's clothing shops with lounging bright-shirted mannequins; covered street stalls and storefronts, without a trace of welcome. Even the roving late-night cyclewaalas had cleared out of the path to Carter Road.

A little up ahead, though, next to an HDFC ATM, I could faintly perceive what appeared to be a 24×7 chemist resting alongside the corner of a four-way crossing. I slowly wheeled out towards it, pulling up next to the kerb. I parked the car outside the ATM and stumbled over to the closed-up glass door only to be told it was out of service. There was another one across the road, a Kotak Mahindra branch which appeared to be working.

I went over to it and swung open the door noisily, nearly dislocating it off its hinges. It made a hell of a racket before it screeched to a standstill. The guard was rolled up in sleep on the floor next to his chair using a stack of folded newspapers as a cushion. He was lying in his vest and had hung the shirt of his uniform over the backrest of the chair to be fanned by the AC vents. The panelled tubelights were harsh on the eyes—accustomed as they were by now to impoverished illumination—and would have done better at a McDonald's outlet than at an ATM. It smelt like a fungused five-star hotel. It was bright as daylight, a glowing beacon of cool air and shelter from the gloom of the night. I stuck my card into the receiver. The machine stalled on registering it, making a succession of beeping noises and proceeding onwards to ask for my PIN. I entered it, and placed a withdrawal sum of about Rs 500, but much to my astonishment, a slip rolled out from the receptacle informing me that the machine was unable to process my transaction. I tried again, but this time the screen just hung up, and kept whirring without a beep, making me wait another five minutes before declaring: 'Transaction timed out'. The machine was either out of cash or just in a plain bad mood. I banged on the side of the monitor a few times before scrabbling at the keys, pressing them in no apparent order, just trying to get a reaction from the catatonic screen. I kicked at the base, shaking the guard out of his sleep with its 'THUD'. He momentarily raised his neck at me, and opening one lid just to be sure I wasn't doing any damage, turned back to the pile of newspapers, letting out a snore.

I guess the machine was just trying to spare me the embarrassment of spelling out in so many words that I had depleted my remaining balance. The last time I checked, it was still there. Perhaps it had been deducted for my Vodafone bill. I checked my phone; there was a message from SBI informing me of a payment made to my service provider the day before yesterday. I didn't realize all I had left in my account was Rs 1,250. Before picking up Bharat, I was making my way back from the airport. Another one of my clients had been detained by customs for carrying a shipment of 18-carat solid gold bracelets in cargo. Five grand was all he could spare me for getting him out, and that's all I could spare Sub-inspector Saawant for getting Bharat out. Since I did most of my business in cash, I often neglected to deposit the proceeds of my income in the bank, as is customary. I would instead end up blowing up a substantial portion of my earnings on indiscriminate expenditure, such as I had done just earlier, and hence often find myself in such a situation.

There's no sense in the way the economic food chain works, especially after-hours. To whom the money goes, why, and for what. There's no justice in it either. If hard work really paid off, it must be on the instalment plan. To make a buck without lifting a finger was something that was far more remote to me than I thought it was. I always figured myself to be wise in matters of trading my wares to my advantage. I thought I was smart, but there stood the truth before me at 5.45, in the morning, staring back with unblinking eyes. I was broke—plain and simple. I hadn't picked up a case in quite a while that wasn't devoted to the milk of human kindness—each job I took upon as a sort of favour without taking into consideration any monetary prospects.

I slipped the card back into my wallet, staggering out of the ATM, bewildered. The guard inside turned the other side as I exited. I walked across the road again—it was completely empty—the neon lights of the 24×7 hovered invitingly over my car. I clicked open the passenger seat and dumped the wallet back inside, popping open the dashboard. Behind the folder containing the car papers, registration, and other official paraphernalia, I had a small 9mm standard semi-automatic stashed away someplace. I had procured it from one of my clients as remuneration. It was worth up to ten grand on the grey market. I tore open the dash looking for it, running my hand all through the inside. In one of the corners, I managed to get a hold of what felt like a metallic object. It could have been a screwdriver as far as I was concerned, but once I managed to yank it out of the glove compartment and held it tight in my clutched palm, I could be certain of what it was.

I slowly walked over to the 24×7, stuffing it into my back pocket. The front door was locked, and a shutter was bolted all the way across it. There was a square slit in the middle of the door through which transactions were intended to take place. It was barely enough space to stick your hand in through. The kid behind the counter was fast asleep. There wasn't a watchman in sight for miles. The CCTV footage that played on a monitor next to the cash register looked blurry. I whistled out to the kid, waking him out of his nap. He shook his head on realizing he had a customer to attend to, and got up from his stool bleary-eyed and walked over to the front door peering out through the open square.

'Hmmm?' he asked.

'You think you could open up the shutters?'

'Sorry, not allowed to.'

'It'll just be a minute. Plus, it's gonna be six any second now,' I lied, glancing at my watch. 'You're going to have to open up during daytime hours.'

He checked his clock. It said 5.45 a.m.

'There's still time. What do you want?'

'Well, you see . . . I don't think I'll be able to find it standing out here. If you could let me in for just a minute, I'll go over to one of your shelves and be out of here in no time. Just gimme a minute.'

'Sorry, not allowed,' he insisted. 'Can't open the shutter. What do you want?'

Midnight Freeway

'As I said before, I'm not quite sure what I want, but I know where I'll find it. You've got it stacked up there in one of the corner shelves. It's a particular type of shampoo that I want, but I don't know the name.'

'Herbal Essence?'

'Something like that. Lemme just have a look. All I wanna do is check.'

I encircled my scalp with my right index finger, emphasizing a bald patch right on top, demonstrating to him how badly I needed whatever it was that I supposedly needed. I said it was a special shampoo, plus a bottle of chocolate milk. One of the imported brands, a name he probably wouldn't be able to pronounce.

'What's it called?'

'Why don't you just let me come in and have a look for myself? You know there's nothing more a customer hates than to be made to feel like an outsider. If you came over to my house to deliver supplies, I wouldn't make you wait outside at the door while I fetched my wallet. I'd have you in, get you a chilled glass of water, let you play with my dog while you're at it. I wouldn't make you stand outside with the latch on. It's not good manners.'

'I'm sorry, we have to. It's compulsory during night hours. We haven't even got our 24×7 permit as yet. The cops keep telling us to keep the shutter pulled down. If we did, we wouldn't get any business.'

'Just like a booze shop. Well, I'm standing out here, aren't I? I'm giving you all the business you want right now. If it wasn't for me, you'd still be out there behind the counter listening to your radio. Come on . . . let it open. It isn't gonna hurt anybody.'

The kid looked at me a couple of times, before finally giving in to my persuasiveness. He unenthusiastically unlocked the shutter, slowly cranking it up with a lever on the other end, and unlatched the door. Once it was open and his hands were clear, I rolled out my 9mm and stuck it straight in his mouth. His hands lifted involuntarily.

'Okay, now slowly move back and go over to the last shelf on the top right corner.'

I tip-toed into the shop, pushing him forward. His eyes started to bulge out of their sockets, and his drowsy face was now suddenly overcome with alarm. I kicked the front door shut, and glanced behind to keep an eye out for a patrolling police jeep or any innocent bystander that could be possibly coming our way. The coast was clear. The kid pulled out a shopping basket and started to empty out everything I instructed him to place inside it. Cheese balls, Cheetos puffs, Five-Star Crunchy, Tobasco sauce, Jim-jams, facial tissues, Senor Pepito, liquid soap, Chana Jor Garam, aloo bhujia, Kinder Joy, Fruitella, Schweppes ginger ale. He wrapped it all up nicely in a fresh oversized polythene bag and handed it over to me, trembling with disbelief.

'Thanks!' I nodded. 'Now you just go back and sit right where you were sitting.'

He stumbled back over to the counter and planted himself on the stool, motionless and also somewhat bewildered at my intrusion.

'You're going to have to give a written statement for the police, with the list of the items that were stolen. I can help you with that, I know the law. If you'd like, I could write it down for you; it'll make life easier.'

'No thanks!' he shook.

'If you need an advocate, I'd be glad to lend you my services at base price. They're going to think you stole the stuff, so you're going to have a fair bit of explaining to do. The CCTV footage isn't going to be worth shit. With that black and white pixelated video, they wouldn't be able to spot a buffalo if it pranced in here with a bazooka.'

I promised the kid I'd be back the next day to straighten things out for him, but I had nothing more than my own word to go on. He tried to spot the number on my licence plate as I pulled out, but his neck wasn't long enough to peer out of the store from behind where he was planted.

I tore open a pack of nachos and started the ignition to swerve off in the opposite direction, even though I was going the wrong way. I took a left up ahead at the crossing and decided to go via St Andrew's. I had a couple of hours to kill before reporting in court. The office would be closed, and no place this side of town would be open for breakfast just yet. I had two options, either to go home or wander the streets like a hobo looking for a place to park my rear end. The first option certainly seemed the more agreeable, given the circumstances. I wasn't in any condition to show up for work without sufficient recuperation. They'd be able to tell I was up all night and hadn't freshened up. That wouldn't paint a pretty picture. An office-going man like myself ought to get a good eight hours sleep every night and show up in the morning fresh, with a pressed shirt, and a clean-shaven smile—the hair parted sideways, leaving off a trail of fake cologne. It wasn't becoming of a man in my station to harbour craters beneath his blinds, cigarette stains on his teeth and a pair of cheeks pricklier than a cactus' behind. A man second-in-command to the eminent Adv. Lalith S. Mangharam, who headlined our quiet little Chamber of Mangesh & Mangharam, which lay tucked away in the back quarters of Ballad Pier. We handled all kinds of clients—violent offenders, recidivists, thieves, some out and out scamsters, even some criminal types about whom the less said the better. But I still liked to believe there's some good in all of us. I'd try and make them see sense, make them change their ways. I liked to take a personal interest in my clients; in their moral compass. I was one of the few lawyers at our office who had a pretty good track record. I hadn't lost a single case as yet and liked to keep it that way, even if it meant not having ample employment. Not having a blemish or a black spot in your resume is about as far a man with my disposition can come to true fulfilment. Genuine satisfaction; the kind you get after scoring high in an important paper, or knowing you made it through the entire term as a model, upstanding student. Or when you get the first glimpse of your marksheet after spending long hours in line at the University. There it is, neatly divided into clean sets of rows and columns—your entire future, past, and present right in front of your eyes.

Things looked pretty bright as far as my academic prospects were concerned, but it was outside the classroom that most of my worries lay.

FOUR

They say home is where the heart is. In my case, it was where the heart, soul, and mind resided in their more sanitary moments. The sanctuary it provided from the uncertainty of the outside world was the only reward I enjoyed from my daily labours. There aren't too many sensations that compare with the relief of returning to your grounds after a hard day's work, with your dog slobbering all over you at the door, and recreation—the fruit of honest toil, God's gift to mankind. I had a Windows 7 desktop with a Core 2 Duo Processor, a Tata Sky cable set-top box, and a Sony surround sound music system with a Panasonic subwoofer, along with a light-brown stray mongrel I had picked up from the Vashi bridge and called Moti. He was strolling around one rainy night with a bum leg. I put him in the car and took him to an animal shelter. Got him his rabies shots, fixed up his hind leg and christened him.

I was emptying out all the contents from the treasured plastic bag when the phone rang. Moti browsed through the merchandise, seemingly uninterested yet vaguely curious about what I had brought home. I laid it all out on the floor, inspecting each item and doing the mental mathematics of how long it would last me. It took a couple of rings to make me sit up and take notice of the phone. The call was from an unidentified number. I picked up.

'Hello . . .' I spoke softly into it.

'Hello . . .' the voice trembled from the other end of the line. A timid, restless voice, that of an elderly lady. 'Yes . . . am I speaking to Pranav?'

'Yes, that's right. Who am I speaking to?'

'Hi . . . I'm . . . uh, Bharat's mom.'

'Oh . . .' I sat up, quite literally.'Hello, yes . . . uh . . . what can I do for you?'

'I . . . uh, believe he was with you last night?'

'That's right. I even dropped him home. Is everything alright?'

'Well, you see, that's the thing. He never came back up. When you dropped him home, he asked the watchman for his father's car keys and took the big car out.'

'The big car?'

'Yes . . . it's a CRV,' she said.

'Okay. Did he say where he was going?'

'No. According to the watchman, he was . . . uh, quite . . . uh . . .'

'Quite . . .?'

'He was . . . how would you say . . . uh . . . in a state of intoxic—'

'He was sozzled?'

'According to the watchman, he was quite drunk.'

'Have you tried his phone?'

'He's not picking up.'

'Okay . . . uh . . . Ma'am . . . aunty, sorry . . . you don't mind if I call you aunty do you? After all, I do look upon Bharat as a friend. He's more than a client, you know, and I have some outstanding bills that'll attest to that.'

'How much does he owe you?'

'Well . . . uh . . . Ma'am . . . uh, sorry . . .'

'You can call me aunty, beta.'

'Aunty . . . uh . . . that's a matter that doesn't concern you right now. You don't need to worry about it. He's a grown-up boy; he can handle his own affairs. I'm sure he's good for the money.'

'What about his car?'

'It's at the station. I'll get it back to the building by evening.'

'In what condition?'

'Just a minor accident. Nothing big. The damage on the other guy's car was worse . . .'

'What other guy?' she asked, a hush building up in her voice.

'Just some guy. No one. In a Volks.'

'How much is he asking for?'

'He was quoting some stupid amount, but the damage didn't look all that bad. I think I can get it done for less at Anmol Auto Works. I spoke to them just now and gave them the details of the car; they should get back to me with an estimate around . . . uh . . . 11.30 or so . . .'

'Anyone get hurt?'

'No.'

'Thank God!' she let out a breath like a jet of steam.

'Was there anyone else with him last night?'

'I don't know. He's been cruising around with these friends of his . . .'

'What friends?'

'Bobby and all . . .'

'That Bobby and all are no good, I told him not to hang out with them . . . they're punters.'

'Bobby, Hiteish-Lokesh, Gabba, Rishabh, Saket . . . even that Gagan "Sardar". They've apparently been getting into a lot of fights . . .'

'Have you tried Bobby's number?'

'I tried Bobby's mother. She's not picking up. According to one of the mothers, they play cards all night at Bobby's garage, sometimes even up till morning.'

'Look aunty, just leave it to me, don't worry about it. He's probably passed out at a friend's place or something. He'll be back home in no time. I personally guarantee it. You have nothing to be worried about. Your son will be safe and sound, and as good as new.'

'He borrowed five grand from me last Wednesday; and the day before yesterday, again he was asking for ten.'

'Okay . . .' I masked my alarm. The news came as quite a surprise to me. 'I . . . uh, was not aware of that.'

'Beta . . .' now her voice began to really quake. 'I think he's in trouble . . .'

'In debt, do you mean?'

'I don't know.'

Midnight Freeway

'Well . . . don't worry . . . I'll get him home. Any phone numbers would be of huge help,' I informed her.

'Sure. I'll keep you posted.'

'Thank you ma'am . . . aunty.'

'Thank you, beta. Gob bless.'

She hung up. I didn't know what to make of it. He didn't look to me like he was in the condition to make it up a flight of steps, let alone be capable of handling an SUV. I dialled his number. It rang a few times, but there was no answer. There was the remote possibility that he might have crashed somewhere else. I knew he'd show up by lunchtime, so I paid it no further heed at the moment, knowing I had more on my mind than could fit on my plate. I popped open a can of the Schweppes ginger ale, lighting a cigarette to spill into the fizz. The doorbell rang. I thought twice before opening it. The shop was shut, and I was well past working hours. Thinking it would be the newspaper guy, I went for it. But as I peeped out the keyhole and unlatched the door, I was a bit taken aback on noticing two policemen slouched at the doorway. I promptly stubbed out the cigarette and opened the door.

'Good morning!' I greeted them.

'DCP Narayan Panth, Bandra police station, Motor Vehicle Theft,' the one with his cap on proclaimed. The other one was a three-star named Naveen Kenkre, his deputy, as I was later to find out. They stepped into my house and asked if they could have a word with me.

'Sure,' I promised them, smiling one of my crack-toothed grins in the face of adversity.

DCP Narayan Panth gently lifted his police cap off his scalp and tucked it into his elbows as he scraped his soles clean on the doormat. He was a swarthy, well-built, middle-aged chap with a determinedly non-Maharashtrian look about him. The trip down from North India had whitened his sideburns a tad. There was no moustache or facial hair of any kind, just a cleanshaven courtesy that crinkled out with the slightest facial gesture. The hairs from the other guy's moustache poked out uniformly like the needles of a porcupine. A punch on his upper lip was likely to send a splinter into even the sturdiest of knuckles. On entering, they both gave Moti, who came out of the kitchen, a nod as if acknowledging a manservant. He acknowledged it, and slowly slunk off, not wishing to disturb us. He plonked himself next to the bathroom and dozed off before they parked their footwear at the shoe rack.

DCP Panth pulled out his mobile phone from his chest pocket and hurriedly tapped at a succession of keys, opening some folder to put a photograph on display.

'Do you know this man?' he asked, showing me a younger picture of the man from last night—Yogesh Moolchandani, dressed in a dark grey double-breasted blazer, posing with a brass trophy at some business convention.

'I can't say I do,' I said, studying the photograph. 'At least, not *this* version of him.'

'Do you know him or not?' the other one snapped.

'I met him just briefly last night at Khar police station. One of my clients had had a run-in with him on Reclamation.'

'What client?'

'Chap by the name of Bharat Morwani.'

'Bharat Morwani?' DCP Panth asked, folding his arms up and queasily rotating his shoulders.

'Yup.'

'Lives at Le Chateau?'

'15th Road, near Shiv Sagar.'

His head started to squat sideways on his neck. He looked up at the ceiling in recollection of the specified individual. 'Hmmm . . .' he let out. 'Son of Deepak Morwani?'

'Wouldn't know about that,' I smiled. 'You see, mine isn't a familial connection. It was socially that I became acquainted with Bharat, and merely circumstantially that I came to represent him from time to time in matters of a legal capacity. The family lawyer is someone else, a Mr Sandesh Prabhakar, if I'm not mistaken, from a separate law firm—Karmchand and Karamchand Associates. They handle his father's affairs, do his dad's work whenever necessary. They're into . . . uh . . .'

'Speakers,' he said.

His deputy looked at him, half-dazed.

'Sound systems. They've got that place on Ambedkar Road,' DCP Panth told him.

'Nirmala?' the deputy nodded.

'That's his mom's name if I'm not mistaken . . .' I said.

'I know him,' said DCP Panth. 'His father's an old friend of mine. He'd gotten in touch with me recently to recommend a security system for their new showroom on Pali.'

'Well . . . it's a small world,' I sighed. 'That's probably why he tried taking your name last night to scare off the duty-officer.'

'That's what he did, huh?' he asked, his voice deepening with each successive syllable.

'That's what he did.'

'Did it work?'

'I'm here to tell you that it didn't. At least, not after what he said you'd do.'

'Where is he?'

'I don't know. I dropped him home after picking him up from the station. Must be somewhere or the other,' I told him. 'What's the matter?'

'You seen him since last night?'

'It was nearly morning.'

'What time did you say you dropped him home?'

'I didn't say. We left from Khar police station at around 5.30 a.m., so we must have been at his in the next five to ten minutes.'

'You sure you dropped him all the way home?'

'Right inside the door. Even tucked him into bed.'

'That's mighty considerate of you,' Naveen Kenkre smirked.

'It's my job to take other people into consideration,' I told them, taking the liberty to flick a match and light up another cigarette now that we had five degrees of separation. For all I know, Naveen Kenkre could have turned out to be a distant cousin. 'I'm not too different from a doctor, you could say . . . but after a point, there's not much else I can offer but moral support.'

'Where did you go after dropping him home?' DCP Panth asked, slightly adjusting his change of tone even further to match the breadth of his query.

Midnight Freeway

'Where else, officer? Home. I have a hearing this morning. I have to be at the sessions court by 9.30 . . .'

'Is there anyone who can attest to your whereabouts from 5.30 a.m. to just now?'

'Uh . . . I'm sure there's plenty of people; take my watchman for one.'

'Where is he?' Naveen Kenre snarled.

'Downstairs. I mean . . .' I laughed, spinning my wrist around to detect the needle on my Timex. 'That's a mighty slim margin of time officer . . . I mean, after all, what is it?' I twisted at the dial to enliven some activity in the seconds hand. 'Quarter past eight?'

The two of them looked at each other like I was blind, or just dumb, more likely.

'It's 8.30!' Naveen Kenre informed me.

'Ahh . . . thanks,' I smiled. I set my watch accordingly.

'More like quarter to nine.' DCP Panth checked his phone.

'Well . . .' I chuckled, 'you don't give people much time to get from place to place . . .'

'You seem to have a rather . . .' DCP Panth reached for a word, stretching his arms up in the air and leading his back into a slow crackle. 'Laidback approach to time, for someone who claims to be so punctual,' he exhaled, briefly alluding to my approaching appointment. That was all the thought it was going to get from these two. If they had it their way, they would have gladly taken me out for tea and bhajias.

'I never claimed any such thing!' I protested.

'And especially for someone who charges by the hour,' Naveen Kenre added.

'I don't charge by the hour, and I have no higher a regard for other people's time than you do right now.'

By now, Moti had been awakened by the vigorous chatter in the living room. He came moping along, half asleep, and went up to Naveen Kenkre's feet. Kenkre kicked him away, and pulled out his mobile phone, a navy blue Vivo Y91i.

'Accident on tollbooth of Bandra–Worli Sea Link,' he read from it. 'Single male driving. Dead on impact, identified by driver's licence as Yogesh Moolchandani, resident of Tardeo. Car of imported make, Volkswagen Jetta MK6, Maharashtra number plate. Crash happened at 6.25 a.m. CCTV footage shows car crashing into the tollbooth at speed close to 200 kmph. Tollbooth attendant dead on impact, gate-check man critically injured.'

He even had a picture of the crash site. The silver Volkswagen Jetta was smashed left, right and centre. The windscreen had cracked right open, shards of webbed glass clung on to the edges, the crossbars of the roof rack dangling unsteadily over. The bonnet had been displaced almost right off its hinges, and protruded over the bent bumper at an angle of 40 degrees. By the look of the frontal section of the sedan, it appeared that the point of contact was more likely to have been on the front right-hand side of the vehicle—the driver's seat, which was squashed up sideways looking like a deformed nose—probably rubbing him out instantly on impact.

'Hmmm . . .' I studied it, scratching a nostril.

Half of Yogesh Moolchandani's upper torso spilt out of the driver's seat window, his arms terribly mangled, and his forehead smeared with glass. It was a most distressing spectacle, and must have nauseated many unknowing passersby, most certainly the swanky South Bombay-bound traffic.

I put it away before the image had the chance to settle on my psyche. It was the sort of sight my fancy had the tendency to dwell on, involuntarily, of course. The mucus that had been clogging up my sinuses from lack of sleep started to solidify into the dark green snot that starts to pour out in a viral infection. I shut one nostril and blew out a booger which landed—'splat' on the tiles.

'That all you have to say about this?' Kenkre asked. 'A snort? If you want to blow your nose, you can go to the bathroom.'

'I guess I don't have much to say about anything,' I sighed.

'I can imagine,' DCP Panth began. 'Seeing as you were trying to settle a fight with the person involved only a few hours before the crash.'

'What's that got to do with it?'

'Was Bharat in any way acquainted with this Mr Moolchandani prior to his unfortunate encounter with him on Reclamation?'

'I don't think so, seeing as he was nearly gonna tear Bharat's head off last night at Khar police station. You can ask anyone who was there.'

'Were you acquainted with him prior to this incident?'

'Of course not.'

'You never met this man before?'

'I haven't . . . honest to God,' I insisted. 'I just saw this chap there at the station last night. I barely had a word with him. I just went to apologize.'

41

DCP Panth slid his hands into his back pocket and flipped open his wallet, holding it apart for me to get a good look at. It was like a longish rectangular woman's wallet with enough cardboard visiting cards in it to give my travel agent a heart attack. From it emerged a ziplock plastic bag with a Motorola Razr, which he held aside, continuing to rummage through the inside flap in order to unearth a large plastic envelope filled with an assortment of restaurant menus, home delivery joints, and more visiting cards. He picked out one from the heap and laid it out on my makeshift dining table, placing it next to a stack of coasters and a pen holder.

'We found this on him, in his chest pocket,' he said, presenting the visiting card for 'Anmol Service Station' I had given him last night. 'Look familiar?' he grinned.

'Oh yes,' I added. 'And I forgot to mention that I'd given him that in case my client had caused him any automotive harm.'

'They ran a check on the car he was driving last night . . .' he mentioned, taking a long pause.

'Who?'

'The nightdogs at Khar police chowki. In particular, Naresh Saawant, at whose urging I made this long trip down here.'

'And?'

'It's an unregistered vehicle, hasn't shown up in any of the files at the RTO.'

'I didn't know about that.'

'It's imported, perhaps illegally.'

'Then why'd he crash it?'

'That's what we're trying to figure out. All the signs say suicide, but the officer in charge of the case just spoke to his business partner Avnish Murpana, and according to him, there wasn't anything remotely wrong with his life. On the contrary, things were looking hale and hearty for him. He had just cracked a deal in New Bombay and collected a down payment of Rs 1 crore.'

'Was he drunk?'

'Was said to be a teetotaller according to Avnish Murpana. In all likelihood, if his statement is correct, the autopsy will report him as not having a drop of alcohol in his system.'

'And was he known to be such a racer?'

'Should ask Bharat; he'd know.'

'Look . . . what does any of this have to do with Bharat?'

'Well . . .' he cleared his throat, 'To me, it seems only logical that someone else had something to do with it. Since Mr Moolchandani didn't crash the car deliberately, the entire catastrophe could have only been orchestrated by someone who had been there at the police station last night, someone with an axe to grind, someone who could have followed him out from there . . .'

'If you're suggesting . . .'

'I'm not suggesting anything as yet. All I'm saying is that you and Bharat were the last two people to have had anything to do with him.'

'Bharat's car has been parked at Khar police station since last night. It's been impounded.'

43

'Then you're the only one who could have been racing with Yogesh Moolchandani on the Sea Link, instigating him to go faster than his capabilities would allow.'

'I drive an Ikon, officer. It wouldn't be able to keep up with a Volkswagen Jetta.' Maybe a CRV would. Just then, it dawned on me. 'Did the CCTV camera pick up another vehicle coming through at the same time?'

'There was an Indigo, taxi,' said Kenkre. 'But he was in a separate lane.'

'What about civilian vehicles?'

'Two Innovas, an Optra and an Accord,' he rattled out. 'We picked up a screenshot.' Here he showed me a huddle of cars bunched up at the EVC lane beside the yellow plastic BDI-stencilled boulders. 'Also a Skoda and a Corolla Altis waiting in another line, if I'm not mistaken. But they all slid on through. The only eyewitnesses we've got are the other tollbooth attendants.'

'Well . . .' DCP Panth groaned, 'I gave a call to this Anmol service centre when we found the card.'

'So?' I shrugged. 'What of it?'

'When I described the . . . uh . . .' he scratched his temple with a wink, 'specifications of the automobile to them, they claimed that they had just gotten off a call with a person who had described the exact same car, not a moment ago.'

'What a coincidence!'

'Coincidence?' A slyness crept into his tone.

'What else would you call it? I told you that I had given Yogesh Moolchandani the card to Anmol Auto Works. I was merely informing them that he was going to be getting in touch with them regarding repairs. What's wrong with that?'

'Nothing's *wrong* with it,' DCP Panth spat. 'Provided you can come up with an alibi for where you were from 5.30 to 6.25 this morning.'

There was just one alibi I knew of, and I had no intention of using it.

'How 'bout we do one thing, officer?' I suggested. 'Why don't you let me have a word with Bharat, and I'll get back to you in the evening. How about that?'

Naveen Kenkre exchanged an indiscreet look with his saahab, twirling his right shoulder blade and tilting his head towards me. 'I'm afraid that's not going to be good enough,' he laughed. 'You see, right now, you're the only lead we've got.'

'What about the guy who sold Moolchandani the stolen car?' I protested.

'Who said anything about it being stolen?'

'Yaa . . .' DCP Panth added. 'I never said it was a stolen vehicle, merely unregistered, and imported.'

'Perhaps illegally.'

'Where'd he get it from?' I asked.

'Car dealer by the name of Pawan Hiranandani,' DCP Panth declared. 'According to his partner Avnish Murpana.'

'He's the one who has that garage on S.V. Road with all those imported cars lined up, spilling onto the sidewalk.'

'I know that one.'

'We're going to go visit it right after we're done with you,' Kenkre croaked.

'Sounds like a good idea,' I snickered. 'I'll tell you what's an even better idea . . . how about you get done with me right now while there's still some breath in you, and go and catch the real criminals for a change. Like that scumbag Hiranandani, I know all about him. The whole of Bandra does. He's a thief.'

'Careful about the kind of statements you make in public,' DCP Panth warned.

'This guy's a real comedian,' Kenkre said to his saahab. 'We've got a special place for comedians. You know what they call it?'

'Naa . . .' I breathed faintly. 'Not unless it's in the telephone directory.'

'Remand. Do you want us to take you there? Right now, we've got a pair of twins performing to a cartload of clowns from the nearby waadi (slum).'

'Boys from Mahim,' DCP Panth murmured.

'Rough and tumble kind,' Kenkre continued. 'There's an eight-year-old kid with knife marks all over his abdomen. They're good company, provided you can put up with the noise. They make a hell of a racket about this time of day. Right before breakfast. We like to serve it to them late, sets up an early morning mood.'

'Look, I happen to know the law . . .' I started.

'That's just what the jokers at Anmol service centre told us,' Kenkre snarled. 'That you're one of the brightest lawyers in town.'

'They wouldn't know the law if they had a head-on collision with it,' I said. 'That's why they need comedians like me. To take care of all the fancy Beemers and Mercs that land up there, totalled beyond recognition. They'd rather you wouldn't file for insurance on a total loss, after all . . . that would be a stab at their stomachs. Some people live for cars, and some live off car crashes. Provides many a mechanic with able-bodied employment. If they had anything to say about me, just remind them that I have plenty to say about them too.'

'That's not why we're here,' said DCP Panth. 'If you want to point the blame at each other, do it on your own time. Right now, I just want to know what happened two hours ago on the Sea Link.'

'And if you find any answers in here, let me know.' I pulled out a crumpled up Sea Link return pass from my pocket, and handed it over. 'Maybe this will help.'

Naveen Kenkre examined it carefully to check the time it was issued at. It said '6.45 p.m.'

'If you crossed the Sea Link at 6.45 in the morning,' he speculated. 'Then you would have definitely gotten sight of the accident. It usually takes about twenty to twenty-five minutes for the tow van to show up.'

'6.45 in the evening, genius!' I grabbed the slip out of his hands and spread it against his chest. 'Read the slip, ACP Pradyuman. It says, "p.m." I got this yesterday, when I was on my way back from the office. I don't take the Sea Link in the morning on my way to work. I go by the old route.'

DCP Panth nodded at him in shame, closing his eyes softly as if to say, 'Naah, it's okay.'

'If these are the kind of deputies the state appoints you,' I said straight to DCP Panth. 'No wonder you have to go around doing encounters.'

His eyes flung open in a flash. 'What did you say?' he closed in.

'Nothing,' I giggled. 'I just . . . uh . . . heard something . . .'

'*What*?' he grabbed me by the scruff with the inquiry.

'Nothing . . .' I promised him, winking as if to say, 'it's okay, nothing big.'

'If you're referring to my stint in the detection unit of the Crime Branch, then just know that that's behind me. I'm dealing with cars now.'

'With or in cars?'

'Ehh . . .' Kenkre finally blew his fuse. He had been holding it alight like a lantern since he had entered the house. It only took an inference to get him to flare and fumble his way up to my collars. If I was wrong, he had no business getting aggravated, unless I wasn't, which of course, was something I could not accurately determine at the moment. You never know with a cop, whether he's got something on his mind, or in his pockets. Something to keep the mind occupied off-duty. Narcotics officers deal drugs, ATS officers spin arms, those on the Cyber Crime Cell have plenty of spare time to xerox mails and transcripts. The Liquor and Excise department has no shortage of bottles to peddle on the side to the dopes in the duty-free. It's only natural that the MVT (Motor Vehicle Theft) unit has the ability to facilitate the underhand sale of any and every vehicle confiscated by them, even those imported from overseas.

'We don't do anything we're not authorized to do,' DCP Panth told me. 'We don't deal in cars or in deaths. Maybe the odd bribe here and there, but that's only natural given the state of things.'

Kenkre concurred with a slight shake of the head. 'You have no business suggesting otherwise, just because you've got on that black lawyer's suit you parade around like a police-proof armour.' He let go of my neck, taking a pause to think of what to add to that. 'Sure, I'll admit,' he looked at his saahab as if expecting affirmation, 'we all stray from the straight and narrow path every once in a while. After all, we're all human, aren't we? And we've got our families to feed.'

'Not me!' I straightened out my collars. 'If you're looking for sympathy, you've come to the wrong place.'

FIVE

I was well within my rights to ask them to get the heck out of there. They left without much trouble, knowingly fully well that I was a lawyer and that they didn't have a thing on me yet. The statement I'd graced them with was about as far as their rights extended to. It was more than enough of what they were going to get from me for the time being, until they had something more substantial than a visiting card. If it came down to a summons, that's a different matter, but here I was merely a suspect in their eyes, and none too plausible at that.

I knew why they'd come here, probably to size me up and see if I was a rough customer, given I was their first lead at the crash site. I told them to give me a call when they really had something; in the meantime, I'd conduct my own little investigation into last night's proceedings, or today morning's—however one wants to look at it. As the saying goes at the office— 'a Sunday night for some and a Monday morning to the rest'.

I got word from Bharat at around six o'clock in the evening when I was standing in line at the registrar's office on the third floor of the annexe. His tea break was on, and closing time was only half an hour away. The sessions courts were most punctual when it came to matters of personal convenience. I knew I'd be back again at the next hearing doing the same thing, but it didn't stir me. I kept on in line, hoping to get at least my client's medical certificate submitted to the department. An assortment of all sorts of types assembled behind and in front of me. Some tall, some short, some fat, some old, some young, mostly Muslim. A Khoja family of bright burkha-clad geriatrics with white-frocked toddlers were sitting on one of the few benches that graced the third-floor waiting room. Black coats roamed the corridors, the sun reflecting off their dark glasses, and their convicts wagging deliriously behind them like shrivelled up tails. A hunchback in a white kurta–pyjama with mehndi-ed red hair wearing thick-framed spectacles cut through the queue in order to walk over to the water cooler, causing a succession of shrieks in protest. The line didn't look like it was going to budge anytime this century. All I could do was take in the scenery and put on my shades to put me at par with my fellow opponents. My common instinct was to skip a line. It was almost a pathological inability to submit oneself to the inertia of congestion, be it at the RTO, the train platform, a ticket counter, or even with having to grab a token at the bank. I'd usually pull some strings with the supervisor to just get me to cut through. It wasn't that I thought myself to be more equal than others; on the contrary, I'd always carried myself with the presumption that I was less than everyone else. It was merely a nervous predisposition on my part that prevented to permit me from standing in any kind of assemblage of citizens for long

51

lengths of time—convicts I had no problem with, especially in crowds (the more, the less threatening)—I had a tendency to turn uncooperative, perhaps even neglect all civility for personal advancement; a defect that could prove fatal in my profession. It was an anxiousness that usually managed to get me through a long slog at many an airport. But here I couldn't—I had to do as I was told, and join the ranks of those embarrassed enough to be present for their respective hearings.

Of course, the old lady couldn't wait with me. She'd had enough trouble standing in line to get her documents xeroxed and attested by the peon at the photocopy booth. It cost two bucks, but she could afford to spare the dough.

I got her bail application notarized at 9.30, numbered her documents and got them verified by an officer from the filing department at 10.45; the judge only showed up by 11.45. We were handed the chargesheet, which specified: 'Attempt to commit premeditated, culpable homicide of the first degree.' The public prosecutor had irrefutable evidence of her presence at the time of her ex-husband's death. It was cast in stone. We stood no chance of filing for remission in the event that it was an accidental death—which is what I then thought, and still think it was.

Third degree was the safest bet—the least I could bring it down to, considering my client's near-catatonic condition. She was nearing seventy, and had not the requisite physical stamina to appear in court quite as often as would be required if multiple cross-examinations were to ensue, as per my original plan. Even though my field of operation encompassed mainly interactions with public officials—police officers in the middle of the night, worn-out customs officials of a sort, at the most, magistrates—I'd still mastered the jargon necessary for conducting legal intercourse with a sessions judge, even in the additional capacity—all those roundabout sentences and sub-clauses, which you'd have to start again from the beginning once you'd made it up to the end. Scarcely would I let speech escape my lips in court that wasn't measured, almost to the point of abstraction. It was the good old sub-literate act of circumlocution, taught to us by faulty school teachers in grammar class: the art of saying as little in as many words as possible.

As the boss used to say, 'Keep the clock ticking, stretch time out as long as you can, possibly even beyond death.' That's the trick to winning a worthy warrant-trial—convoluting incidents as far as the tongue can tangle them, and confounding not only impressions upon the jury committee, but also instances upon the audience as a whole, of aberration in the proceedings there witnessed in the courtroom. It was to attack the very fibre of the case, and berate the necessity of having to drag everyone down to the courtroom in the first place, and waste the state's time and money on something that can be settled with the toss of a coin. And with the absence of entertainment, and the sullen looks on everyone's faces on a dim Monday morning, it wasn't unlikely to extract indifference, even to a murder charge.

My opening statement went something like this: 'I'm no somnambulist. The only time I've given it some thought was when this client, right here . . .' here I emphasized the old lady, just in case they thought I was referring to the bespectacled bailiff who was half asleep under an unfolded register. '. . . came to me with a case regarding a sleepwalking murder. Now, you see, your honour . . .' I addressed the court. 'That's a part of the law that's probably well outside the realm of the prosecution's understanding.'

'Wait a minute!' the public prosecutor interrupted, 'May I remind the court that according to Justice Hariprasad Gokhale, a person is to be held accountable for all acts committed by him or her in the conscious or semi-conscious state, that includes being drunk and being asleep.'

He was right, at least theoretically. If a man kills someone in his sleep, he's killed him plain and simple, whether or not he wanted to. It wouldn't be counted as premeditated murder, but it'd be murder just the same. Maybe they'd get a lighter sentence; maybe they wouldn't. It all depends on the vagaries of judicial circumstance, which is just about as vague as it can possibly get.

'Well, that depends, you see . . .' I cut him right back off.

The Additional Sessions Judge S.N. Solaskar sat up from his slouch.

'I knew someone,' I continued, now issuing declarations to anyone who was free to listen. 'Who once got off with armed robbery, because he claimed it was a water pistol, and then again I knew someone else obviously from the lower stations of society who had been tried and acquitted for "dacoity" (banditry) because he held up an autorickshaw with a pencil.'

Just then, I noticed the proceedings hadn't as yet swung into motion fully, and I was thinking out aloud. The public prosecutor just looked at me strangely, as if I'd had a late night. The chattering of mobile phones and empty comments slithering back and forth across the room had not ceased. The court was waiting on the appointed stenographer, who had been taken ill on that particular day, so the date of the hearing was pushed, in a matter of two anecdotes, to the 4th of the next month (subject to change), which was another two weeks from now. My client wasn't allowed out of Arthur Road till then. She had two female volunteer police escorts with her at all times, plus the jailer who had to be slipped a 500 so that he could let her out of his sight for at least five minutes, with the aim of a private audience with my client. I had to get her transferred to judicial custody after her preliminary hearing. Her bail was probably going to be set at nothing less than one to one and a half lakh, minimum.

At 12.50 p.m., we lined up outside the courtroom to get a glimpse of the causelist where the handwritten dates and schedules for the postponed hearings were hanging from a peg in the wall. I submitted a copy of her latest medical records to the clerk at the back-office of the old building at one, and made her have her lunch in the canteen downstairs at two. They gave us two soggy idlis drenched in sambar, and a glass of room temperature, potentially jaundiced, tap water. I asked for a tissue paper to write down the old lady's PAN card number, but they didn't have one; they served their wada paaos wrapped in newspaper. I'd already procured her bank account details and filed an invoice. The total charge came to something like Rs 4,28,000, including taxes. She claimed she had some nephew who could straighten things out, but I didn't buy it. Something seemed suspect.

'Who's this nephew, then?' I asked out of idle curiosity.

'My sister's son,' she replied courteously, but in a decidedly flat monosyllabic tone, like she didn't care and was doing me a favour by having lunch with me in the first place. She didn't like to talk much. As a matter of fact, she didn't have much to say. I suppose two divorces and a murder charge would be enough to shut a person up for good. Her name was Bhairavi Naraina, and she lived all alone in a plush high-ceiling 3 BHK overlooking Marine Drive with an off-white pomeranian named Fluffy.

'What does he do?' I asked, this time more inquisitive than curious.

'Owns a company.' She looked away, and then down into her greased plate, her thoughts swimming in the cold sambar before her eyes. It was a prettier sight than what was sitting at the other end of the table.

After processing her medical certificate and getting it attested at the registry, then transferred from peon to clerk to chapraasi and eventually by way of water-carrier, straight to the assistant registrar's office, we had to stand in line for another hour to meet her. The assistant registrar was tough to pin down. She seemed to be doing an awful lot of wandering about the place, cackling in falsetto and back-slapping her subordinates—her wobbly elbows resting on their desks—playing with the piled-up paperwork, giving dog ears to some of the pages. They all paid her due attention. After having filled in each other on how the day had been progressing so far, they were back to work—making those of us standing in line feel like we had been the ones faffing around and they had been immersed in arduous rigour.

Midnight Freeway

'State your name and case number,' she barked at me, once I had the privilege of her attention.

'Pranav Paleja,' I dutifully informed her. 'Case number 654. P.W.'

'654 . . . hmmm . . .' she frowned into Ms Naraina's files, her spectacles seesawing over her nose. She didn't even cast a glance at my client, just pretended she wasn't there, referred to her in the third person. I couldn't sense what energies were being exchanged by these two grumpy old women, but she seemed most certainly to have a bee in her bonnet about a lady my client's age committing such a vile atrocity. Murder had no place in the hands of an old woman. It was expected of the young and wilful, not those sedated by experience, those that ought to have more on their minds than themselves. She seemed to be unduly inquisitive about whether or not my client had any biological offsprings. It probably clarified her assessment of her character. When told that my client didn't have any children, she nodded in agreement, almost as though she had half suspected it herself. 'That's why!' she probably thought. After having given us precisely three minutes and fourteen seconds of her time, she asked us to carry on to the third floor of the annexe, where a line that reached practically halfway across the courthouse was assembled with increasing enthusiasm to be blessed with the registrar's acquaintance. Apparently, the offender was not required in most cases, and given her age and ill health, a dispensation could be made for her sake, so I informed her that she was free to leave and that I'd let her know the date and time that was to be set for her hearing.

It was exactly 6.05 in the evening when I got the call from Bharat's number.

'Hey buddy,' I hollered into the phone. One of the passing peons reminded me that I wasn't allowed to speak on the cell phone, which made me momentarily lower the phone in deference, only to raise it back against my ear once he had cleared out of the corridor. 'How's it going?'

'What happened last night?' Bharat grumbled.

'You crashed into an imported car.'

'Whose?'

'Some guy's. Claims it's stolen.'

'Lucky for us.'

'Not when you see the vehicle.'

'How much is the damage?'

'Still being tabulated.'

'What do you mean?'

'Well, that's the thing . . . Bharat . . .' I didn't know how to say this to him, 'the guy's dead!' I laid it out flat.

'What the hell are you talking about!?' he snapped back as if it was my fault.

'Where the hell have you been? Your mom's been looking all over for you!'

'I'm at Bobby's.'

'What the hell are you doing there?'

'Look, if my mom calls, just tell her I'm at Gabba's.'

'What if she calls Gabba's mom?'

'Look . . .'

'Listen to me, Bharat! There's been a bit of an accident.' I lowered my voice, yet kept it loud enough to pierce through to his end of the line. 'The guy you bumped into last night on Reclamation is no more.'

'What nonsense.'

'I'm telling you . . . two cops showed up at my house today morning. They showed me a picture of the totalled Volkswagen. Apparently, he crashed into the tollbooth of the Sea Link this morning at 6.30.'

'Should have seen him last night on Reclamation. He was zipping past the signal like Michael Schumacher.'

'That's not what I heard.'

'I was driving in my lane minding my own business, when all of a sudden this son of a bitch overtakes me right at the turn . . .'

'I don't wanna hear about that Bharat; I don't care. This isn't just about who cut who; the guy is dead . . . a tollbooth attendant went with him.'

'Holy shit! What the hell was the matter with him? Why'd he crash into the tollbooth?'

'Well . . . it's too late to ask him.'

'Well . . . uh . . .' he searched for what to say. 'God bless his soul,' he said, with an air of sudden solemnity. I could hear him kiss his index finger and wag it between his nose and forehead.

'The MVT unit is out asking questions about the car and what happened last night, and your name has come up . . .'

I could hear him start to sweat over the phone.

'Just pray to God that Sub-inspector Naresh Saawant doesn't give his honest impression of you. Hope to hell the forty-five hundred was money well spent in service of your forgiveness.' Forty-five lakh wouldn't wipe out all the collective damage he'd done in his lifetime.

'Uh . . . uh . . . muh . . . aa . . . I don—' he grew unintelligible with gratitude.

'Now I want you to tell me something, and I want you to speak clearly, none of that "chal to-ta-ya-leta, ba . . .!"'

'What?' his voice stiffened up.

The queue started to move, and I was getting ahead a good two and a half metres with the sudden shuffle, which lasted only about as long as a breath, when I got caught in the range of some official eyes. I lowered the phone, Bharat's muffled voice still trickled out all the way down to my shoulder. A stream of black coats poured out of the brown wooden batwing doors leading into the registrar's chamber.

I pressed the phone against my cheekbone and rested it on my left shoulder blade, shielding it from the sight of the inside—clipping open my briefcase and rearranging the required files, hoping that would divert the notice from my ear. 'Where did you go with your father's CRV after I dropped you home last night?' I whispered.

'Whaa?'

'You still smashed?'

'You're mad a'what?' he took offence. 'It's six o'clock in the evening . . .'

'Then why are you still sounding as if you just came out of a root canal?'

'I don't know what you're talking about . . .'

'Your mom told me that after I dropped you to your building, you took the big car out for a spin.'

'Big car?'

'The SUV, it belongs to your pop, in case you've forgotten.'

'Oh . . . ya, it's parked downstairs.'

I heaved a sigh of relief. 'That means you went straight to Bobby's house in that condition? Didn't take it anywhere else, right? Certainly not the Sea Link; Bobby doesn't live in town from what I know.'

'Bobby lives at Khar Gym.'

'Let me rephrase the question: Did you manage to make it there in one piece? And do you remember anything? Your place to Khar Gym is a five-minute drive you can do blindfolded, with both hands tied behind your back.'

'After you . . . uh . . . dropped me home from the . . . uh . . . police station . . . I think I went to Gabba's.'

'You *think* or do you *know*?'

'I picked up Gabba from his building and . . . uh . . . from then on it's all a blur . . .'

'This is not helping me, Bharat!'

'W-w-w-whaddayaa wan-me to do yaa?' he stuttered. 'I didn't kill him, you mad a'what? I never meant to kill anybody . . . that guy on Haji Ali just came out of nowhere . . . it wasn't my fault.'

'Gimme Gabba's number,' I instructed him, losing my last thread of patience.

'He's here, he's in the middle of a hand.' I heard the phone shift hands, before a low whine came out in reply. 'He's saying he can't talk to you right now.'

'You mean to tell me you're out there *gambling*!?' I nearly shrieked out across the courthouse. Spectacles from all corners shot at me with a 'Shhh . . . please be quiet.'

'When you owe me 8,500 and borrowed five grand from your mom . . .'

'Listen, man, can I talk to you later . . .?'

'You were the one that called me, shithead! Now listen up, and don't miss a word. Otherwise, it's going to cost you. If anyone gets in touch with you regarding this, just tell them you've been at Bobby's since last night. Keep the CRV parked there under the building. Don't move it. Say you came straight there from your building after I dropped you home . . .'

'What about Gabba?'

'Forget about Gabba, you fool. Don't get him involved. Just do as I say, and tell them what I told you.'

'How much did you say I owed you for your troubles?'

'As I said,' I took a long pause, scanning the vicinity for unfriendly eyes and then murmured. 'Eighty-five hundred.'

'Can't reduce it a little? For friendship's sake?'

'That's the going rate on damaged goods.'

'You or the car?'

'I'll let you be the judge of that.'

'Right . . . well . . . actually . . . uh . . . listen, is it okay if . . . if I sort you out with the money in a couple of days?'

'Uhh . . . just how many days we talking here, champ?'

'2–3.'

'2 or 3?'

'I'll give it to you day after.'

'Day after when? Day after today, or tomorrow?'

'Day after tomorrow as in . . . day after today . . .'

'That's tomorrow.'

'As in from tomorrow onwards . . . day after tomorrow. The day after the day after today.'

'I see, as in you mean two days from now?'

'One–two days.'

'I thought you just said two–three.'

'As in one, two . . . three.'

'Look, man, what I did for you was a big favour. I went way above and beyond the call of duty. I was on my way back home from the airport, had to be in court by 9 a.m. Having someone who'll show up at a moment's notice in the middle of the night isn't exactly the kind of thing all your friends can boast of.'

'I'm sorry about this man, but you see . . . I'm a bit light as of now. Just wait for a little bit, I'll have it for you in no time.'

'Which is 2 or 3 days, depending on my luck.'

'It's just a matter of eighty-five hundred.'

'I don't have eighty-five rupees on me right now. I barely have enough to make it past the Sea Link. I've got some big cases coming up, and you know it takes time to process the payments. These days with the taxes and all, you know how it is.'

'Look P.P., just wait one–two days. That's all I'm asking you.'

'Can't you take a loan from someone, ask one of your friends, Gabba perhaps?'

'I'm afraid that's currently not an option.'

'Well then think of something that *is* . . . or else I'm not going to be showing up for your hearing on the 8th to represent you for the hit and run.' I cut the call.

SIX

The court closed up for the day as the clock struck 6.30. The registrar arose from his desk, compiling a set of documents that had been submitted to him, and stuffed them piece by piece into the top right compartment of a foursquare of footlockers. The peons switched off the lights and fans, and the back quarter of the queue began to disperse, heading hurriedly to beat those of us at the front of the line to the stairs.

On the way down, I bumped into the chief solicitor from our office, Ms Nalini Hegde, on the second floor—standing outside one of the courtrooms like she was there for a doctor's appointment. She had a yellow docket, thick as a phonebook, folded up in her arms like someone was trying to get at it. As soon as she'd near anyone, her grip around the bloated spine would tighten almost involuntarily.

'What you doing here today, Pranav?' she intercepted me as I attempted to breeze by.

I stopped to shake her hand; normally, just a nod would do. She could talk up a storm and wipe out an hour before she got to the weather.

'Just dropped by for Ms Naraina's hearing,' I told her.

'Hear anything yet?'

'Just that it's been pushed to next month. What about you?'

'Here on the Hiranandani trial,' she muttered, chewing on her fingernails like she couldn't speak any further on the subject.

'Oh yaa, I heard about that one. Something about a Lexus, am I right?'

'Hmmm . . .' It was taking all the restraint in the world for her to be tight-lipped. It made her mouth swim in uncertain circles, before she decided to open it— 'I'm just . . . uh . . . here for the hearing,' she leaked. 'Part of Mr Mangharam's staff on this one.' She just looked at me blankly, the reflection of the spinning ceiling fans dancing on her spectacles.

'What are you looking at?' I asked.

'Your hair,' she said, her expression beginning to crawl in concern. 'Are you sure everything's alright?' she asked, unduly curious as to my state of being.

'Why, what's my hair got to do with it?'

'Everything. It's falling off.'

'As in?'

'As in, I heard some of the others at the office talking about it.'

'Is Mr Mangharam here?' I inquired, rotating my neck to peer into the courtroom.

'Just left. Probably going down the stairs with Mr Hiranandani.'

She looked over her shoulder, then did a swift tilt left and right before closing in. 'Well . . . it's good that you're here. I've been meaning to talk to you all day.'

'What about?'

She caught hold of my elbow and began to walk me down the stairs. 'I . . . uh . . . got a call this morning,' she began, 'from Bandra police station, Motor Vehicle Theft unit . . .'

'And?' I stopped to wonder for a second.

'They called on the office desk line, chap by the name of Naveen Kenkre. Deputy. Wanted to know if you work for Mangesh & Mangharam.'

'What did you tell him?'

'That you're the pride of the chamber. One of our top lawyers. A real prize. The undisputed paperweight champion of Ballad Pier. And that we've had no record of malpractice from your end, whatsoever.'

'Caught you in a charitable mood.'

'Not exactly,' she sighed. 'Can't argue with your files. They're as spotless as your teeth.'

'Ahh . . .' I scrubbed clear a black speck from my incisors. 'That I can't be sure about . . . don't exactly boast the pearliest pair of whites on this particular floor.'

'The last time you lost a case, you were probably in Government Law College.'

'I didn't go to GLC, remember . . .' I tapped at my forehead. 'I went to Rizvi.'

'Ohh . . .' she circled her mouth in mock astonishment. 'That's right. I forgot. I suppose that's the equivalent of an Oxford degree in these parts.'

'At least it's better than K.C.' I gestured at her, insinuatingly.

'Now, that is a matter highly contestable, my friend.' Her eyes twinkled with sporting mischief.

'Ask anyone . . .' I boasted, waving at a set of familiar faces from a herd of policemen that passed us by.

'Which way you headed?' she asked.

'Home.'

'Can you give me a lift up till Altamount?'

'Nope.'

'Why?'

'Because I'm not going that side.'

'You'll have to cross Pedder Road on your way to Chembur.'

'I'm not taking Pedder Road. I'm going via the inside route from Bombay Central, straight to Heerapana.'

'Ahh . . .' she whined. 'I can get a taxi anyway.'

'Then why'd you ask?'

'Because I thought you were going that way.'

'Well . . .' I cleared my throat. 'I'm not.'

'Plus . . . uh . . . perhaps I was wondering that maybe there's something you'd like to tell me.'

'What about?'

'. . . 'bout how the MVT was furnished with our landline number.'

'How am *I* supposed to know? As if getting a hold of the number to the Chamber of Mangesh & Mangharam is such a big deal. It's probably in the classifieds.'

'I know, but why were they asking about *you* in particular? What cause did they have to inquire about whether you were under Lalith Mangharam's employ?'

'Look,' I stopped once we reached the ground floor and moved her aside from the mouth of the stairway to make way for the descending crowd. 'I don't know why the MVT unit was asking questions about me. Perhaps it has something to do with the car I'm driving. You still want to take a lift with me now?'

'Gladly,' she shook her head solemnly, guiding me to a corner of the corridor. 'Straight to the Tulsiwadi RTO.'

'You wanna come and have a look at my PUC and Insurance?'

We walked on towards the opening archway.

'You look like you haven't slept all night . . .' she said.

'I haven't.'

'Pranav, are you sure you haven't gone and done something you shouldn't have?'

'What are you talking about!?' I squawked, baffled and also somewhat exasperated at her insistence.

'Don't forget, I draw up your contracts,' she continued. 'I know what's been going in and out of your account, and off-late it's been just a one-way street.'

'I've got a pending four lakh twenty-eight thousand that thinks otherwise.'

'If it arrives, that is.'

'When it does, I'll be sure to let you know. I'll give the whole office a treat.'

'Jalebis and samosas like your last birthday! Naah . . . thanks, but no thanks. I don't intend to leave this life by way of cardiac arrest.'

Midnight Freeway

'You see, that's your problem, Nalini.' I elongated an index finger at her. 'You spend too much time thinking about the next one.'

'Just remember . . .' She kicked a chit on the ground, pausing right before the front steps to the courthouse. 'We've got a reputation to uphold. That comes first and foremost. Always has. What you do in your own personal time is none of our business, at least as long as it doesn't land you in any kind of soup with the Motor Vehicle Theft unit. It might not reflect so well on the establishment. I don't like to pry into your clientele, but as far as I can tell, we're known to represent upstanding citizens. And we stand for excellence in all endeavours.'

'I can see that.' I spread my palm around the open daylight, a manic horde of undertrials pushing and shoving with black briefcases acting as blinkers, guided to and by their representing advocates.

'We're used to, uh . . . you know . . .' she gaped around. 'Businessmen, pillar-of-the-community type fancy five-star jobs that come in platinum coating, pouring out of old papers and index files, usually for some minor financial malfeasance or the other.'

'Well . . . I've always thought about the good of the client. For me, that comes first and foremost. It's through the client that I can serve the Chamber to the best of my ability. And if the client isn't happy, that reflects badly on our reputation too.'

Two white open-top Gypsies stood lined up inside the front gate, covering a quarter of the compound. The crowd cascading down the front steps parted into three separate files as the engines turned on. One could undoubtedly sniff the presence of a person of considerable significance, even in the cautious demeanour of the bodyguards cramped up at the back of the vehicles: amateur strong-arm types all of them, who'd never quite made the grade with a legitimate security outfit, and were loaned out by the dozen from Dongri, Malwani, and Bhayendar by underhand rental organizations specializing in safety. Even though they didn't wear a uniform, they made a pretty tight security detail. They carried shooters, all of them.

A gallant black Cayenne pulled up outside the driveway to the front entrance, and a burly chap in a grey safari suit, with a white walkie-talkie sticking out of his chest pocket, got out of the front seat, opening the back door for his boss Pawan Hirandandi, who was descending the steps with my boss Mr Mangharam—his gait drooped down into a deliberate hunch, furtively trying to dodge familiar eyes. Both donned casual work-suits, Hirandandani's bordered on the recreational, nestling the kind of blue floral shirt more suited to a cocktail party. Mr Mangharam had on a grey Raymonds pinstripe—not the fit he'd usually slap on in this kind of weather. It was in honour of the esteemed company he had for today that he'd taken the trouble. They were both hurried into Hiranandandi's Cayenne by a pair of bodyguards that leapt out of one of the Gypsies and the doors clamped shut before I could even pay my respects.

Of late, members of Pawan Hiranandani's security team had become frequenters of our office for various litigation and solicitation work here and there, mostly from Nalini, who was their patron saviour in the form of a paperwork queen. She was a sweet lady, kind and nice to everyone. She greeted them politely as we got down from the courthouse, knew how to say the right things and calibrate the right smiles in proportion to the predicament. It only made me all the more ill at ease. All her chronic niceness and agreeability of temperament, that ray of efficiency that lit up her path—a brass halo spinning over her head like a helicopter—I could change that in a heartbeat.

'So . . . uh . . . tell me something,' I said, as we stepped out into the sunlight. 'You said you were assisting Mr Mangharam on the Hiranandani case?'

I could make a dishonest person even out of Mother Teresa, given the right circumstances. The potential for treachery is right there, tucked away behind the wall of obedience that shackles us all.

'What about it?' she snapped back, as expected.

'Well . . . I, uh . . . happen to be acquainted with someone who purchased a Volkswagen Jetta from Mr Hiranandani.'

'Client?'

'Not exactly. I just met him last night. Either way, he's not with us any longer.'

She swiped a quick cross in the air before crinkling up her lips, then with a light nod, let out a 'Heh?'

'A guy called Yogesh Moolchandani. Builder from town.'

The name flickered like a half-lit match before her eyes.

'It's turned out to be an unregistered vehicle, too,' I informed her. 'That makes two for your client. A Lexus and a Volkswagen.'

'He's not my client.'

'Okay . . . Mr Mangharam's client.'

'So what?' she questioned, not a glimmer of refutation in her voice.

'The cops paid his showroom a visit this morning in regard to the man's death.'

'I see . . .' This got her transfixed.

As last night's story tumbled out right there beside the main gate to the courthouse, she started to listen, in earnest.

'Hmmm . . . Moolchandani . . .' she thought to herself in an indecipherable murmur. Her eyes fluttered all about the late evening scenery of Kala Ghoda as we walked onto the pavement. So lost was she in casual contemplation that she got nearly hit by a car as she strolled out onto the main road. I brought her onto the footpath, away from the traffic of the roaring thoroughfare.

'You ought to be more careful,' I told her. 'Crossing the road like that, in a city like Bombay of all places. You ought to know better.'

'Hmm . . .' she took off her spectacles to polish them on her black waistcoat; her lower lip rolled up over her chin, pondering the possibilities of engaging in confidential ex-curricular conversation with a colleague. She was calculating it in strictly mathematical terms, not whether or not it was the right thing to do, but instead, whether or not it made sense, which was the more immediate concern.

SEVEN

'Wait just a minute!' she lowered her voice, looking around to make sure the sing-chanaa waala and hawkers on the pavement weren't eavesdropping. 'You mean to tell me that the guy just killed himself accidentally?'

'Not accidentally. There was a deliberate precision in the way he went about it. The camera caught him coming into the tollbooth at over 200. An unregistered vehicle, probably stolen, knowing your client's reputation. It's bound to raise some distressing questions.'

'He's not my client.' She clucked her tongue in annoyance.

'But they've put you to work day and night on the case. Maybe you should get your hands off it. You don't know what you're in for. It isn't going to do you any good in the long run as a solicitor, that is, if you intend to remain solicitor.'

'I don't.'

'Then . . . how 'bout you do one thing? How 'bout you let me enter into the proceedings at present? I don't have to take your post; we could assist Mr Mangharam together.'

'Eh-eh-eh . . .' she started to rattle her head. 'Why would I wanna do that!?'

'Listen to me at least . . . ' I persisted. 'I happen to know that old Mr Pawan Hiranandani, "Pops" to Mr Mangharam, has been recently granted the Mitsubishi dealership for Bombay, as well as that of Volkswagen and Toyota.'

'So?' she repeated, this time through clenched teeth.

'And with the able assistance of our employer, he's currently trying to beat an unlawful car sale charge on a bleached yellow Lexus, shipped down from Abu Dhabi. He must have tampered with the chassis number to avoid paying the customs duty, in contravention of Transfer of Residence. An old trick . . . one of those fake TR certificate scams. Half of Bandra knows this . . .'

'None of my Bandra contacts told me . . .'

'The person he sold it to filed an injunction. He needs to get this case dismissed in order to facilitate sales; till then, their dealership license is suspended. With this minor mishap on the Sea Link added to the litigation backlog, you're going to have your hands full for the next couple of months.'

'So, what do you intend to do about it?'

'Help you out.' I shrugged my shoulders and bowed my head in a light gesture of sincerity. 'Lighten the burden.'

'By doing what?

'If you could get me a meeting with Pops Hiranandani . . .'

'Out of the question . . .' She turned her head elsewhere.

'Listen to what I have to say first . . .' I nudged her shoulder. 'I don't think there's anyone better equipped to handle this matter than me right now, given my personal involvement with the case, if it becomes a case, that is! Right now, it's just a hunch.'

'You just said the cops came to your house,' she turned back, '. . . 'cause they counted you as a suspect.'

'That's what they think. I know I didn't have anything to do with it. I'm sure of that much.'

'What about your client?'

'With him, I can't be so sure, you see. He's prone to a reckless temperament. He could have done anything after I dropped him home, even gone on an all-night bender, which is probably what he did. Right now, he doesn't have the memory to speak for much.'

'Then why don't you give me his number, and let me have a word with him . . .'

'Ah-ah-ah . . .' I smiled and tilted my head at her. 'I wouldn't dream of doing such a thing! Why should I just hand over such a painstakingly cultivated client?'

'Either way, I only represent people from town. When I do represent, that is. As I said, Hiranandani, I'm only assisting.'

'There's a chance here for both of us to take a crack at representing old Pops. Swell gig it could turn out to be. If you could have a word with Mr Mangharam, and recommend the possibility of a pre-emptive measure in the event that this crash on the Sea Link turns out to be an inconvenience for Pawan Hiranandani's dealership, which it won't and shouldn't, and isn't, to begin with, but still . . . you know, it's better to be safe than sorry . . .'

She squinted into the overhead sunlight, paying no heed to my sputtering proposition that followed her all the way up to a stationary taxi.

'Well, the way I see it, Nalini . . . it's plain and simple . . .' I slowed down and explained myself with a meaningful nod.

'What?'

'Right now, all that stands between these hands,' I pointed at her ringed mitts clawing at the folders, 'and an under the table "khokha"(crore) bonus to be collected from some safety deposit box in Surat, is our boss. How about we make a deal? If the sale of that Volkswagen to the late Yogesh Moolchandani turns out to be a full-fledged case, then I think you should suggest to Mr Mangharam that he take the auto licensing department and leave any seedier suspicions the police might have regarding the crash to us. We'll split the fees right down the middle . . .'

She cut me off before I could even frame another fragment of what I was about to offer.

'Tell me honestly . . .' she looked me firmly in the eye. 'You think Hiranandani could have had something to do with what happened on the Sea Link today?'

'Not unless the cops decide to make something out of it. It doesn't take a lot for an unlicensed car sale charge to escalate to culpable homicide, and in the event that it does, he might need someone to intervene and associate with the concerned proceedings.'

'How about we wait and see where the matter goes first? If the cops paid his showroom a visit, Mr Mangharam would be aware of it; perhaps you could have a word with him and ask him to fix you a meeting with Mr Hiranandani.'

'Out of the question. I have neither the tact nor the time, that's why I'm asking you.'

The corner of her mouth curved downward into a compassionate grimace, betraying the fleeting impression that she'd caught on to what I was trying to con her into. She gazed at me blankly, again, like there was hope for me yet.

'Well, Pranav,' she began, her company woman stance stiffening. 'At Mangesh & Mangharam, we try not to pre-empt a case before it fully crystallizes into fruition. That would be tantamount to a libellous effort. Plus, I don't see any credibility as of now in the information you're offering.'

'Have it your way. That's fine by me . . . only, in the event that something goes wrong for old Hiranandani, you might need to call upon my services. And in that case, I'll be more than just a phone call away.'

'Hmphh . . .' letting out a faint laugh, she coughed up enough phlegm to turn her face red. 'I'll see you around . . .' she drew on a breath.

'Take it easy!' I tipped her a half-hearted salute.

She turned around, and started to head back into the courthouse, pulling out her phone from her coat pocket and poking away at it as she ascended the steps.

I headed towards my car at the pay 'n park, distantly acknowledging some of the vultures that hung around the civil courts most evenings around closing time—pouncing on everyone that left the premises, leaping on car windows, begging for a case, even creating one out of thin air if they had to.

The parking attendant expected a tip as I hurled on the ignition and opened out the side-view mirror so that I could reverse out, but all he got was a handshake and a polite nod.

'Take it easy,' I told him, rolling the window up on his outstretched palm.

I twisted the ignition around with a jerk, managing to dislodge my housekey from the circular ring of the keychain. It dropped under the seat, and wasn't easy to reach. I had to pull my seat all the way back in order to clear an arm's length. I stuck my hand in over the seat belt hold to get a grip of the floormat. Pressing the back of my head against the horn and making it scream, I slid my palm under the driver's seat, scrabbling aimlessly for the key in the deepest recesses of the footwell. I could feel the tiny oval base, but the jagged serrations of its tip still seemed stuck in the grooves of the floormat. Just then, it occurred to me: I had heard of instances where the accelerator of a car gets jammed against the floormat and is stuck in place, refusing to react to the brakes. It goes out of control and keeps accelerating of its own accord, not responding to the commands from the driver. The vehicle is said to be in a state of motion paralysis. There's nothing that can be done to save it or anyone in it. It's like a wild elephant trampling through the bushes, knocking down every tree in sight, nothing an obstacle . . . until it comes in contact with something burlier than itself, possibly a banyan, a cement slab or even a concrete tollbooth.

EIGHT

The evening traffic was merciful to me on my way out of town; it only got bad after the Sea Link. I took the highway up to Milan Subway, opting again (as per custom) to go via the inside routes—crawling under the bridge with the suburban crowd, which was considerably less dense—rather than wrestling for space with the homeward-bound rush-hour traffic on the main roads. The petrol meter was reaching reserve, so I couldn't have the AC on. All I had was the occasional wind for company, and the fellowship of morose faces on either side. There was nothing of any consequence on the radio. I flicked hold of my phone from the dash once I got stalled at a signal.

Talking on the phone while driving is never advisable. I'd been guilty of it on numerous occasions and had even once been pulled over for it, but somehow it always seemed second nature so as to not even qualify as a matter for contemplation. It was as natural as the setting sun.

I tried calling the old lady client's nephew, rolling down my window with one hand and placing my phone between my shoulder blade and cheekbone with the other. His name was

Kartik Bhoparai. I saw it on the old lady's passbook. My only visible means of support. If he didn't pick up, it was either Bharat's parents or the police. The only other sources I could count on to nourish my next couple of days. The beeping sounds froze as the dial tone took shape. After a couple of uncertain seconds on account of the bad network, it connected. It rang. I rested the phone against my chin as the puny ring, flirting on the narrow boundary of inaudibility, slowly began to trickle out of the phone. When it seized, I stumbled into speech with a start. 'Uh . . . hello . . .' I coughed.

'Haa . . . hello . . . yes?'

'Hello . . .'

'Who's speaking?'

'I got this number from Ms Bhairavi Naraina Madam.'

He immediately cut the call on hearing the name. I tried calling again, double-checking the number I had taken down from the lady just in case it matched the one I had dialled, even with the preceding zero whose presence I had ensured in the event that it was an out-station line. He didn't pick up. He was probably dodging my call, knowing damn well why I was calling. It's a rule of thumb: when people don't pick up your calls, the only calls you get back in return are from the ones whose calls you yourself don't want to pick up in the first place. And such was my luck. Just as soon as I managed to overtake a BST bus that had long been blocking my path, I noticed my phone glowing on the dash. I answered it before it had the chance to utter a ring. It was someone from the State Bank of India, informing me that the call was being recorded for internal training purposes.

Midnight Freeway

I kept steering through the openings, trying to keep my mind on the road and not bump into anyone on my immediate left, but it was impossible. Even the left side-view mirror was not open. I didn't know whether to reach for it or turn my upper torso backwards to keep track; I was shackled to the seat belt even. Normally I'd never wear it as a rule, but there were paandus on the lookout at this time, especially in Vile Parle.

The 'PEEP-PEEP-PEEP' of the squalling horns was beginning to bore holes through my brain like a red-hot sieve. I rolled the window back up as I revved sternly into motion, trying to cut through the traffic with the assured manoeuvring of a two-wheeler. The operator from SBI was still giving me her introduction. I cut her short once she got to the point. Up ahead, I could see a long line of lorries moving truculently amid a herd of autos. The signal had given way, and as usual, I was stuck in the wrong lane. I took the expected insults and abuses from my fellow road companions as I moved aside, letting them pass through, stuck in the middle of the road like some idiot child in the midst of a stampede. Once I made it past the signal, having taken the intended left, I pressed down hard on the accelerator—since the road had narrowed down and was less thronged with vehicles—and kept an eye out in the diminishing daylight for a glitzy compound stocked with an imported array of sports cars and superbikes, on the right-hand side of the road; an oblong structure some forty feet in height, plated with a sheen of blue mirrored glass baring the metallic insignia of 'Hiranandani Horsepower'.

S.V. Road was noisy as hell—even though night was approaching, none of the storefronts seemed even remotely keen on closing up for the day. It took half an hour to make it past the gruelling traffic, congested crowds, and shrieking hawkers before I could find 'Sayonara', an ex-electronics shop that now specialized in suitcases, opposite which the showroom was located.

I tossed the phone aside onto the passenger seat after numerous attempts at reaching Bhairavi Naraina's nephew and crawled along another jammed signal at a sure pace, nudging the car into brief tortoise motions through a clearing in the middle lane. When I got the chance, I swept a curve at the end of the divider, seizing the oncoming passage long enough for me to complete a U-turn, thereby annoying a line of motorists barricaded by a yellow light on the left-hand side of the road.

Pawan Hiranandani's jet black Cayenne overtook me on my turn, not deigning to halt at my manoeuvres, as did the rest of the traffic. Mateen Lakdawaala's monster truck rolled on obediently behind, its wheels elevating it to a height of four feet above the ground, its blinkers nearly palpitating with authority, and its engine exhibiting the sonorous drone of the dispossessed. I recognized it instantly from the number of times I'd seen it parked at the entry of Shopper's Stop under Sheesha, when Mateen used to still roam with a convoy and had his face plastered on all the hoardings around Bandstand with his hands joined together in a public-certified idiot grin of approval.

He liked to tell people it was Z-Security. Well, it was Z-grade; that much was for sure. I never had the occasion to know him personally, but I had always watched him from afar . . . with his pack of punters, always the same faces crowding the same places, and the same cars nurtured through the better part of an adulthood.

He wielded considerable influence in the area and could get any file closed with the flick of a phone. Which is probably why Bharat had tried using his name last night at the police station, in vain. Obviously, my powers of persuasion proved more effective than a measly citation.

As I happened to recollect the man from last night, I also happened to retain his having informed me that he too was acquainted with Mateen Lakdawaala, perhaps to give me the impression that it wasn't highly unlikely that he himself was a person of considerable significance. And given his demeanour, the brief outburst certainly bespoke authority inflicted on some poor sod or the other.

I tailed them for the next two signals.

As I closed in on the stretch of 4th and S.V. that possibly contained his real estate allocated to the smuggling of foreign cars, I rolled down the windows, putting the radio on and turning up the dial, to make everyone take notice of my presence.

From about a block away, I could see the two behemoths cut into gateless premises, the yellow curvature of a Nissan GT-R bonnet adorning its entrance. The place seemed to operate after-hours. Apparently, the showroom would stay open all night with the front shutter pulled down. They'd take calls from any car dealers with more than a crore to their name. Not exactly disreputable, but about as far from the pale of decent society as one could possibly get in the automobile trade. Hiranandani and Mateen Lakdawaala had a partnership with a car dealership in Abu Dhabi, which they were probably using as a tax shelter. They'd ship sports cars, McLarens, Maybachs, the works, also all that fancy merchandise you see on the cover of Top Gear. Lakdawaala had sunk more than a crore into that business.

On the side, Pawan Hiranandani also ran a garage on Linking Road—a private parking lot for imported cars and unlicensed vehicles. They'd rounded up every rich kid they could possibly lay their hands on and milked them for every rupee they were worth, consoling them with the self-fulfilling notion that it was all for a good cause—Upgrade, that inadvertent clarion call of time. Just as the gullible child hopes to stay up-to-date by requesting the latest cellular device or computer application from his friends and other sources, so does the full-grown adult when it comes to that holy grail of personal possessions: the anointed vessel of daily transport.

I screeched past the Hyundai showroom, blasting some random song with the sole intention of making a spectacle of myself, and bent an impolite halt right outside the gate of an adjoining building, managing to scare off a couple of elderly pedestrians with the roar of the engine. It could have been parked with more decency, but I wanted it to stand out like a sore thumb so that the passing punters would take notice.

I hopped right out of the car with my briefcase, slapping on a pair of shades even though night was approaching, and slamming the door shut as hard as I could, my entire body language and code of conduct drastically altering on account of the surroundings I was in.

Midnight Freeway

'Uh . . . hello!' the seated nightwatchman of the building Madhu-Sheela, just before the showroom, called out to me. 'Excuse me.' He waved his hands forward in an indefinite motion of complaint, and shook his head vigorously at my car.

I went back in and reversed the car a few metres, so as to clear the path for a vehicle to pass through the front gate. I placed it at the curve under a No-Parking sign beside a double-parked Innova with its blinkers on. Unloading the 9mm into my pant pocket, I managed to camouflage its bulge by placing it beneath my empty wallet. The watchman seated on a steel chair near the yellow Nissan asked me what I wanted.

'Pops,' was my response.

He let me through with a barely detectable nod that carried the faint scent of disapproval, his or his employer's, I couldn't rightly tell; either way, it didn't matter one way or the other. The preferred pet name indicated my familiarity with the proprietor of the establishment. The Cayenne and the Monster truck stood on either side of each other like a pair holding hands discreetly. The Gypsies, with the contingent of bodyguards, were probably still stuck in traffic. The two monstrosities were stowed away in the back of the compound in an abandoned garage, an empty two-car parking space that could fit in three SUVs and a children's birthday party.

A parade of glistening bonnets glided by me on the way to the steel-blue structure. Thankfully the oppressive halogen head beams from the line of fancy cars had been turned off, but one of the engines was still running with a passed-out driver resting inside of its AC enclosure. I recognized the number plate at once. It was my employer's.

A poster plastered to the glass door had 'Hiranandani-HorsePower' printed diagonally across, silhouettes of urban high-rises poking the lettering from down below. An Ambuja Cement beefcake was drawn on the brick wall that stood beside the front entrance. The glass door was mounted on a burly 10-by-4-foot frame under an aluminium beam that gave the mistaken impression of a high ceiling. Inside, the office wasn't as opulent as its entrance promised.

A stained-glass board over the front desk said in big, bold capital letters—'HIRANANDANI HORSEPOWER—A MATEEN LAKDAWAALA ENTERPRISE—09878678670', under which was emboldened, in what unmistakeably carried the damp glow of fresh paint, 'A SHEETAL HIRANANDANI EXERCISE'. I didn't know if it was a joke or if they were serious. I took down the number, noting it had more 786s in there than would be deemed auspicious by even the most hard-headed maulvi. There were two bikes parked right outside the glass door. They obviously belonged to some of the salesmen working inside the office, so I took the liberty of helping myself to one of the helmets dangling from their window stands. I wondered what it'd be like if I stormed into the place wearing a motorcycle helmet and started kicking over the desks, generally scaring the place, knocking off the alarm system, disabling the CCTV camera, shoving all the employees into the back room with the vault.

The office didn't look like it was in the best shape, and I guess I wasn't helping it any with my presence. There wasn't even anyone behind the main counter, just a Sai Baba Calendar (also a Mohammedan one) and an obsolete red cordless telephone receiver. All kinds of electronic monitors, CCTV cameras, biometric hand scans, and numbered audio intercoms were set up at different corners of the office lobby. In fact, it felt less like an office, more like the reception area of an abandoned three-star hotel. A tinkling chandelier flickered from the mouldy ceiling, probably installed there during the last renovation to add a touch of class. There were two lifts, one for visitors and one with a silver panel above the dial which said 'MEMBERS ONLY'.

At length, the same bodyguard wearing the grey safari suit came lumbering up to me from inside a corridor, brandishing his walkie-talkie. He was a somewhat stocky, well-built Maharashtrian lad of about 35, and asked me what business I had there.

'I'm . . . uh . . .' I thought. 'Here for a meeting with Pops.'

'Pops?' he sputtered. 'Who's Pop?'

'Mine or yours, what's the difference? They're both in there!' I said, pointing towards the ominous corridor from which he had emerged, that branched out into what unmistakably appeared to be an area of some prominence. 'Our bosses, I mean.' I handed him a visiting card. 'I work for Lalith S. Mangharam.'

'Lalith who?'

'Look . . .' I laughed. 'You'd save us both a great deal of trouble if you'd just let me in. My employer will explain everything to you.'

He tore up the visiting card into four separate bits and backed one leg behind the other without the slightest exertion to reach for a dustbin. I followed him up to the counter.

'I'm an advocate,' I informed him. 'Here on the Hiranandani trial.' I opened my briefcase on the marble slab to produce some documentation that could vouch for my presence.

The guy ignored my explanations altogether, and looked at me funnily, the corner of his mouth crinkling up into a one-sided grin. He gave one look at the motorcycle helmet in my hand and knew something was off. Before he'd turned to his right, he'd already let out a whistle to one of the staff. A flabby waterboy in a grimy white half-sleeved shirt sounded back with a return whistle. Once he presented himself, the message was loud and clear.

'Please escort this gentleman out, Ganesh.' He told the gopher.

'With pleasure.' Ganesh smiled.

He caught hold of my arm and grabbed me by the elbow. 'Listen, big guy . . .' I shrugged my shoulder out of his grasp. 'I don't want any trouble. All I want is to have a word with the boss.'

'The boss isn't here,' he muttered, gently walking me to the door to give me a slow shoulder out the premises, without his grip getting too firm. He took the motorcycle helmet from my hand and stuck it back onto his Yamaha. He pulled down the shutters in front of the big glass doorway—they emerged from the aluminium archway, falling smoothly downwards—leaving it open ten inches from the ground.

If I gave it just a tug, it would pull right back up on its own.

NINE

In no less than five to ten minutes, the bodyguard popped his head out from under the shutter to see if I was gone. To be sure, I wasn't. Holding the shutter all the way up with one hand, he whistled out to me demeaningly. In a somewhat whimsical turn of events, I strolled back inside Hiranandani Horsepower—its doors had miraculously flung open to my arrival, on account of perhaps, a sudden revelation.

'What do you expect in a joint like this?' I told the chap as I re-entered the place. 'Couple entry?'

'I thought I'd seen you someplace.' The guy just looked aside and led me down through a dim corridor—most of the tube lights had been turned off—it was still swanky and marbled-up though, carrying the faint scent of turpentine, with carpeting you could do somersaults on. The varnish over the walls had probably dried up from the annual repainting that most establishments of this sort had to undergo around the holiday season. Towards the end of the corridor, past countless rows of cabins and cubicles, desktops, and restrooms both male and female, lay Pawan Hiranandani's office. It was a cosy little bunkhouse you could spend a couple of nights in and not complain about the weather—the air conditioning was that strong. It had pictures of Pawan Hiranandani with his family, Pawan Hiranandani with youth minister Matin Lakdawaala (when he was youth minister, that is), Pawan Hiranandani at school, Pawan Hiranandani at work behind the desk trying his damnedest to look studious, Pawan Hiranandani at his brother's wedding, Pawan Hiranandani with the kids, Pawan Hiranandani with an elephant in Kenya, Pawan Hiranandani wearing a sherwani, Pawan Hiranandani doing social service, Pawan Hiranandani wearing a garland, Pawan Hiranandani lined up alongside his friends in shades, elbows folded and all, and Pawan Hiranandani in a sportscar. Pawan Hiranandani, however, was nowhere to be seen. All I could see was a crowd of corpulence gathered around a plywood six-tier bookshelf: four large imposing-looking men, all attired in white full-sleeved collared shirts with what looked like their waists all collectively tucked into a pair of black formal trousers. Also Mateen Lakdawaala in a pair of bright white keds that slipped out from beneath a white acrylic desk, seated in a squeaky swivel chair with a pint of Pepto-Bismol next to a water canteen. He was the only one in casuals.

The bodyguard promptly exited the office once he had successfully ushered me in, closing shut the glass door behind me as delicately as he could. There was a different department of security personnel present in that room, if not exceeding him in post then at least in bloat.

He had a gentlemanly bearing though that was most becoming of his station, with just a whiff of clumsiness to compensate for his imposing bulk. A vague wobble still escaped his handling of the steel doorknob, and a crackle of walkie-talkies went off from behind him when he turned off into another corridor. Mateen Lakdawaala had his right arm in a sling, and had some difficulty getting up to wish me.

'Please be seated,' I insisted. 'I have no wish to intrude.'

'No . . . no . . . on the contrary, you're most welcome here,' He grumbled, almost sarcastically. With him, one could never be certain.

My employer sat in front of him and spoke with his back turned. 'What are you doing here, Pranav?'

'Well, you see, sir . . .' I explained.

'Save it.' A voice croaked away from a corner of the office-space. In a distant sofa lodged at the farthest end of the room, reclined Mr Hiranandani himself, in person. His work suit hung on the backrest of an adjacent armchair near the bookshelf. He was sprawled out on the green-velvet tapestry of a divan that curved up into a serpent-swell towards the edge, where he placed his right elbow to rest his upper torso against its cushioned support.

'Nalini just called!' he spoke, drawing up a blotch of phlegm to dispose of into a spittoon which doubled up as an ashtray. The string of his spit dangled from his lower lip as he cast it away, and invariably handed it over to one of his white-uniformed flunkies who stood by the side of the sofa with a glass of water and a Sinarest. When offered to him, he flicked his fingers at it disapprovingly and commanded the man to take it away with the spittoon.

'Throat infection?' I inquired.

Mr Mangharam still didn't turn his neck. Mateen Lakdwaala glared at me from behind his desk, still as a cushion-cover. Pawan Hiranandani just batted his head in reply, as if he had seen better days.

'Yaaa . . .' I nodded. 'It's been going around. It's that time of the year. I had a bad cough myself just the other day. By the way, what happened to your hand?' I swung around to address Mateen Lakdawaala.

'Heh?' Mateen leaned forward to hear again.

'I asked what happened to your hand. You had some kind of an accident?' My teeth started to show over my lower lip; I could catch their reflection gleaming in the glass cupboard standing right astern the desk.

'What happened to your face?' Mateen asked, all expression evaporating from his starkly mounted features. There was still a certain malice rolling about in the eyes that hovered over those deliberately deadened jowls.

'Huh?' I turned one of my ears to him.

'What happened to your face?' he asked again, this time more certain of what he was trying to get at.

'Nothing I can think of . . .'

'Why is it so shrunk?'

'Cause I didn't sleep last night.' I finally took off the shades. 'I don't get . . . the gist of the, uh . . . question.'

'Why are you so concerned with my fracture?'

'Oh, so it is a fracture . . . I just wanted to check.' I folded up the wayfarers and clipped them onto my collar.

'What happened to your hair?' he went on. 'Why is it so bald?'

'I don't see what that has to do with your right arm.'

'Am I asking you why you look like shit . . . and probably feel like piss . . .?' That, right there, was the reason they referred to him, in parts of Band Stand, at least on Mount Mary in the days before he became a politician, as Mateen 'Magarmach'.

'No?' I shook my head.

'So then mind your own goddamn business.' The freaking Crocodile. He had an alligator trap that could ensnare, and snap shut on anyone's head with the flick of a switch.

'Nalini just called, Pranav!' Mr Mangharam spoke, quickly changing the subject.

'So I've been told . . .' I said, leaning towards Mr Hiranandani.

'She told us . . .' Hiranandani coughed again, a ruffled heave of a breath—this time the guy wasn't there to collect it. 'That you were with Yogesh Moolchandani last night at Khar police station.' He cupped his palms across his mouth, momentarily grasping the man's absence. Mateen looked at Lalith Mangharam uneasily.

I offered him a fresh handkerchief. This one was from Mainland China, a quality item. He wiped his mouth with only the felt tag, pretending he wasn't dirtying the entire thing, and handed it back to me lathered in saliva. I folded it up as delicately as I could, and put it into the side pocket of my trousers that didn't contain my wallet.

Matin Lakdawaala leaned back and yawned at this display of chivalry, or—sycophancy, more likely. He kept fingering his right nostril with his left good hand, as he studied me with marble eyes. 'You know him?' he blurted out.

I thought about it a moment and shook my head. 'Nah! Never met him before in my life.'

'Never met him before?' Hiranandani reconfirmed.

'Yup!' I nodded in full certainty. 'Neither has my client.'

'You don't know about the road?' Mateen asked, scrutinizing my boss's every response.

'What road?' I asked.

His eyes swished over to Hiranandani's sofa and came back confused.

'*His* road.' Hiranandani specified.

'What, Moolchandani Marg? I don't know what you're talking about!?'

Mateen shut his eyes to the point of distraction. 'You see, by a curious set of circumstances,' he rambled, 'our friend, and associate, your acquaintance—Mr Yogesh L. Moolchandani, happens to own a road. A two-and-a-half kilometre stretch off Palm Beach Road, on the old CBD Belapur Bypass route, currently shrouded with weeds on the peripheries and unusable for any kind of organic farming, save for the most basic forms of brick-baking.'

'Mmmm . . .' I thought of what to add that would be worth their while. 'What does the 'L' stand for?'

'Land . . .' my boss declared.

'Oh . . .' I turned to him. 'I simply thought his old man was your namesake.'

'It's a clear four-lane, ex-toll-road,' Mateen continued, 'initially constructed for a link to a now-defunct Super-Freeway proposed in the late 2000s to connect Vashi with the Greater Mumbai mainland. It was once all marshland, blotted with mangroves and creeks—reclaimed sometime in the mid-90s before New-Bombay's initial reconstruction programme began to take shape.'

'What interest is that of to you?' I asked.

His eyes squirmed open— 'I happen to have made the first bid to purchase that particular strip of open Freeway.'

'Ahh . . . I see . . .' now my eyes almost dipped shut.

'Only thing is . . .' here he looked to my employer as if he had something to do with it. 'Moolchandani beat me to it. He's a bit of a real estate magnate, if you know what I mean.'

'So he assured me.' I said. 'You know, he even happened to mention that he knew you!'

Mateen's eyes sparkled with trouble, his knuckles twitched spasmodically. 'Yaa?'

'Yaa . . .'

He looked me now dead in the eyes. 'You gonna tell me why and how my name came up, or want me to extract it out of you?'

'Look, Matin . . .' Mr Mangharam started. 'There's no reason to get upset; he's merely a part of my staff you see . . .'

'He doesn't know anything about Yogesh Moolchandani from before?' Mateen asked him.

'He doesn't!' Mr Mangharam stated. 'I guarantee it.'

'Well . . .' Mateen leaned back, somewhat relieved, and addressed me from the corner of his mouth. 'I got a call from this Moolchandani at around 3.30 at night from Khar police chowki!' he said, rotating his neck now towards Hiranandani. 'Asking if I knew some character by the name of Bharat Morwani. I told him I didn't know any peacock.'

'And I got five missed calls from him at around 6.20 in the morning.' Pawan Hiranandani produced an iPhone sleeker than the width of a coaster.

'That's five minutes before the time of the crash,' I said. 'The cops told me . . .'

'I spoke to Panth,' he grunted, raising his back ever so slightly. 'Just before leaving for court. Even Lalith here had a word with him.'

'That's right.' My boss shook his head in affirmation.

'MVT, right?' I asked, even though I knew the answer. I just wanted to rub it in, given their field of concern.

'That's right,' Hiranandani wheezed. 'He came down to the showroom today morning to have a look at some of the merchandise.'

'He seems to think you had something to with it,' I bluffed.

'Pranav!' Lalith Mangharam suddenly shuddered, turning the steel back of his chair around to finally face me. The eye contact only enabled a flurry of unspoken signals, easily ignited by my supposition.

'I'm telling you . . .' I assured them. 'That's what he said to me. That you're a thief, and that half of Bandra says so.'

One of the formally-dressed flunkies started to motion towards me.

'Ehh . . .' Pawan Hiranandani agitatedly suppressed his movements with a graceful swish of the hands.

The guy moved aside and let the proprietor speak his piece.

'I don't know what the hell you're talking about, smartypants,' he spat, this time into an abandoned coffee mug. He leaned over from the sofa to point a finger at me insinuatingly. 'You're trying to brew up a fracas over nothing!'

'I'm not,' I promised him. 'That's just what I heard.'

'That's not what I heard.' He stiffened up his lazy posture with a jerk. 'You want me to call him up right now? I know him from before. He'd gotten in touch with me a couple of months back regarding the Lexus sale. The Abu Dhabi dipshit who's crowding us right now with his imported attorneys had filled his head with some kind of second-hand information about the transaction. I told him to think nothing of it and that in a fortnight, I'd have the requisite documentation to account for the sale.'

'That's not what I heard,' I persisted.

'Pranav!' my employer shrieked again, in defiance of my claim.

'Shhh . . .' Pawan Hiranandani silenced him. 'Let the mouthpiece speak what's on his mind.'

'Ohhh . . . I'm more than that,' I said. 'I'm a practising expert on all matters that concern the legal welfare of a human being. Animals and companies, I can't service.'

'I see that right well . . . considering how you carry yourself.' He sat almost upright for a moment, or maybe it was just a mirage. 'You know, it takes a lot for me to get up from this sofa. Even more to take me down to the courts.'

'I can see that right well, too.'

'Pranav!' My employer was going to be hit by apoplexy any minute now.

My impertinence was beginning to bleed into every bit of sense I could salvage from this forsaken discussion.

'Point being,' I said. 'I could help out.'

This had even my employer calmed. Mateen Lakdwaala's chair rotated to a halt. Pawan Hiranandani gradually froze as he shifted sideways to receive a box of tissues from the guy who had gone out with the Sinarest.

'My client happens to be well-acquainted with DCP Panth. A bit of a familial connection, you see.'

'Ohh . . . ours is more than that . . .' Mateen murmured.

'Shhh . . .' Hirandandi bent a finger at him, waving it back at me to proceed. 'Go on . . .'

'Well . . . uh . . .' I continued. 'DCP Panth even told me that he's friends with his dad. You know what tends to happen with familiarity like that. With them, it's personal. With you guys, it's strictly business, a kind of an arrangement, if you know what I mean. You wouldn't care if the other person got hit by a truck, let alone a murder charge, just so long as it didn't affect what was going into your pockets . . .'

'Murder charge?' Pawan Hiranandani suddenly sat up.

'What's this guy talking about?' Mateen grimaced.

'I'm sorry about this, Pops . . .' my boss apologized on my behalf, without my asking him to.

'I have nothing to apologize about, sir . . . I'm speaking the truth. Or at least what I know to be the truth. If it is the truth, that is. My client's dad and DCP Panth are friends. And worse still, they're *good* friends. They happen to know each other from a long time ago. He has an alibi for where he was at 6.25 a.m. and is still sitting there. That's about as airtight as it gets. He hasn't moved, you see. And his dad is probably on the phone with the MVT unit as we speak, pulling whatever strings he can to get his son off the hook . . .'

'So?'

'The way I see it, the . . . uh . . . partiality resultant of that dynamic has managed to manipulate the direction the investigation has decided to take today . . . and it . . . uh . . . seems to have landed right at your doorstep, or front seat, more likely.'

'It was bound to,' Hiranandani slurred. 'He purchased the car from me, didn't he?'

'But the fact that the cops have found out that it's an unregistered vehicle?'

Hiranandani blew his nose into a handful of tissues. 'How'd they find that out?' he sniffled.

'They ran a check on the vehicle last night when Moolchandani brought it to the station.'

'Why the hell did he do that!?' Hiranandani howled.

''Cause of my client.'

'And the reason you're here right now is 'cause of your client?' Mateen Lakdawaala inquired.

'That's right. He's the one who's gone and brewed up a fracas over nothing. The only thing is, this time, it landed his adversary on a slab in Holy Family.'

'Who's this Morwani guy?' Mateen finally asked Hiranandani.

'How the hell should I know!?' Hiranandani gargled. 'Probably just one of the hundred loudmouths that roam around Bandra, trying to use your name every time they get caught by the cops.'

'You think he knows about the road?' Mateen wondered.

'I doubt it!' I said. 'He just bumped into him at the Reclamation signal.'

'And what was he doing before that?'

'I don't know, probably cruising the streets.'

'This client of yours,' he scratched at the plaster on his right elbow. 'Is he a real racer?'

'Usually doesn't cross one-twenty, one-thirty max. Hasn't got the guts to—'

'Where's he from?'

'From here only. 15th Road.'

'Well, I don't know this guy from Adam!' Mateen Lakdawaala got up.

'Sit down, Mateen!' Hiranandani's already-irritated expression deteriorated further into a frown.

I gave the metallic chair with its back turned towards me a slow sideward shift, making enough room for me to wriggle onto it, and placed only half my weight on the spherical edge. I was now seated right beside my employer, where I should have been placed all along.

'He's not speaking on behalf of the Chamber.' Mr Mangharam trembled. 'This is just to inform you.'

'No worries, Lalith!' Hiranandani serenely nodded his head. 'I'm not going to hold this against you or Mangesh.'

I looked towards Mateen Lakdawaala. 'I take it you are occupying that chair in an administrative capacity.'

He flicked a look at my boss and then obliged, as if he were addressing the press. 'Mr Hiranandani and I are in an alliance. A sort of business arrangement, actually. Our interests tend to coincide from time to time.'

Midnight Freeway

'And maybe ours might this time,' I offered. 'As they did, with the late-lamented Yogesh L. Moolchandani, only I hope I don't end up on the wrong side of a one-way toll road.'

I turned to my left and noticed that Hiranandani had already dialled a number on his phone, while I was shifting about in my chair. 'Hello . . .' he hollered into it. 'Narayan? Hi, Pawan Hiranandani speaking. I'm sorry to be calling you at this hour, but I'm currently seated with my legal team, and they have a couple of questions for you . . .' He held the phone up diagonally for the chemist to pass over to me. Once it came into my hands, I offered it first to Mr Mangharam, who refused to touch it. I spread out the phone against my chest and said, 'Before we commence, sir, may I just say that it is indeed an honour to be referred to as a member of your legal team.' Mr Mangharam rolled his head in disbelief and started to look away.

'Hello sir,' I spoke into it. 'Pranav speaking.'

DCP Panth's voice started to scatter with a passing wind. 'Hullo . . .' he crackled.

'Hello . . .'

'Haa . . . who's this?' his pitch rose up a notch at the end of the inquiry, the way it tends to do with curiosity.

'Pranav Paleja. You were at my house this morning, remember?'

'Ohh . . .' his voice came clearer now. It sounded like he had stepped into the inside of an automobile. I could hear the 'THUD' of the door slamming soon after. 'What are you doing with Pawan Hiranandani?'

'I'm here with my chief, Mr Mangharam. Would you like to speak with him to confirm I'm still with the Chamber?'

'Ehh . . .' Mr Mangharam started to back away from me. He rose up from his chair and collected his briefcase from the table. 'As I said,' he reminded the gathered company. 'He's not speaking on behalf of the Chamber in any capacity.'

'Naa, I've got someone else that can do that for me,' Panth replied. I could hear the phone change hands.

'Pranav . . .' Nalini's voice came in loud and clear. 'There's been a bit of a development . . .'

'You going from Altamount Road to Bandra police station in a matter of hours. I'd say that's more than a development. It's a leap.'

'About the case, I mean . . .' she stuttered, swiftly regathering her vocal cords to speak audibly. 'We're not at Bandra police station. We're in Khar. The . . . uh concerned party is currently inside giving their statement, minus the concerned individual, that is. We've just taken off to look for him.'

'You mean, his parents?'

'They just showed up to collect his car, when all of a sudden the mother broke out into hysterics when I tried to question her. She nearly hit me over the head with a water bottle. They plan to have him sent for a two-week treatment period to a provisional nursing facility in New Bombay. It's a kind of reform school.'

The engine itched noisily before it rumbled on. Scattered voices in Marathi rung out from all corners of the car interior. She soon asked them to be silent, so that she could conduct her end of the conversation over the phone without having to shriek like a banshee. 'SHUT UP!' she shouted. 'Everyone! Please . . .'

Midnight Freeway

A firm command from DCP Panth blasted out in return, forbidding all talk while she was on the phone. His deafening call for silence made more noise than all their jabbering put together.

'Where are y'all going?' I asked.

'First to this pool parlour on Linking Road called CrackJack, and then to check Sheesha.'

'He's not at either of those places.'

'How do you know?'

'First, you tell me how you got involved in all of this . . .'

All eyes in the room spun towards me.

'I can't get into that right now . . .' she mumbled.

'Then at least tell me what the development is . . .' I said.

A swift silence ensued, broken only by the blabbering of some hawaldaar evidently admonishing a passing pedestrian to get out of the way.

'Well, according to a night patrol van that was doing the rounds on Reclamation at about 6:15 in the morning,' she spoke, quickly camouflaging her speech in a sudden conflagration of sounds, only one of which was a honk. 'They'd spotted a silver Volkswagen Jetta on the highway, heading south towards the Sea Link—going at nothing less than 150, and followed all the while, every inch of the way, by a gang of speeding bikers . . .'

'Wait a minute, let me have a word with him . . .' DCP Panth demanded his phone back, on hearing certain snippets of precious details. 'You're draining my battery, miss,' he told her. 'I haven't opened up a PCO for everyone to come and chit-chat for as long as they please. If you don't mind!'

'Sure . . . sorry, I was just . . .' I heard her hand over the phone to him.

'Hello . . . Paleja . . .' he barked into it, causing my ear to recoil from the speaker and register not very long after that I, too, had been speaking on someone else's talktime. But then again, opening up a PCO for everyone to come and chit-chat for as long as they wanted was precisely what the owner of the device had envisioned, at least for the showroom if not for himself. 'You know anything about these bikers?'

'Nope,' I responded.

'Have you tried Bharat's number?'

'Have you?' I asked back, feeling no need to reaffirm the obvious.

'The phone is ringing, alright, but there's no answer,' he informed me like it was news. 'I heard some talk of Mateen Lakdawaala last night at the station. I've got five eyewitnesses, including two senior constables and Sub-inspector Saawant that say his name was mentioned by both parties. Did you know his number was one of the last ones dialled on Moolchandani's phone prior to the crash? His and Mr Hiranandani's. That's why Ms Hegde came down to the station to have a word with me. But what's this business about Mateen Lakdawaala? I want to know why his name came up! How does Bharat know Mateen Lakdawaala?'

'He was just gassing. Of course, he doesn't know . . . pardon me . . .' I bent over the phone to address the other side of the desk as if requesting permission. 'Mateen Lakdawaala.'

What turned out to be two of Mateen Lakdawaala's cronies from the white-shirted lot, began to circle my chair on registering that utterance. One of his eyebrows lifted involuntarily.

'Then I want to know why his name was taken last night,' DCP Panth insisted. 'After all, it's not the kind of name to take lightly.'

'You know Bharat and his friends, officer! They're just a bunch of kids that like to talk big. He even took your name, I told you, didn't I? He was smashed. 'Look,' I said, nearly about to hand over the phone. 'I've got Mr Lakdawaala right here in front of me. Would you like to have a word with him?'

'No-no-no-no . . .' Panth's voice suddenly shrivelled up. That was the first trace of uncertainty I had detected in his manner all this while.

'He's saying he wants to know why your name was brought up last night!' I put the phone against my chest to tell Lakdawaala directly, without the slightest consideration.

Mateen looked to Pawan Hiranandani, who was downing a glass of water with a Becosule capsule. That was one flavour that jibed with his tastebuds. 'Heh?' he retorted.

'Mr Lakdawaala's name has cropped up in the investigation.' I turned to him.

'Cut the call . . .' he gulped the last lot before placing the glass down on the floor between his sandaled feet. 'Now!'

'Okay . . .' I said, raising the phone back against my ear. 'Uhh . . . officer Panth, may I call you back in around half an hour or so . . .?'

TEN

'This doesn't look so good.' I joined the tips of my fingers into a triangle upon the glass tabletop of the acrylic desk, blocking Lakdawaala's shifty eyeballs and my employer's twitching sideburns that more than once startled my peripheral vision—presenting a far graver case than I had been a party to. I didn't mention a thing about the bikers, or Moolchandani doing 150 on the highway right before the crash. All I had to stress was that we were in trouble; if I was indeed, as the lift suggested—a member of their showroom, whatever that meant. Right now, I'd just crashed my way into their conference and made myself right at home without as much as being asked to take a seat. I'd occupied an entire desk while they weren't looking. There was no way they could have heard what was spoken from the other end of the line, and any indications to the contrary didn't show in their confounded stares masked with solemnity.

'He's pointing the investigation right in your direction,' I announced.

'Who?' Lakdawaala asked.

'DCP Panth,' I addressed Hiranandani instead. 'He's saying since the two of you were the last dialled numbers, and the car in question was purchased from you, with Mr Lakdawaala's name being brought up by both the concerned parties: The only leads they've got thus far happen to be, the two of *you*!' I pointed at them both.

'Wh-wh-wh-what are you talking about?' Hiranandani blubbered, suddenly swelling up with concern.

'I'm telling you, ask DCP Panth.' I threw him back his phone. He caught it with a lobbed drop at one of the sofa legs, and inspected the screen to see how long the call had lasted. He proceeded to dial his number and then spoke to him over the phone for the next five to ten minutes in Marathi.

Lakdawaala looked expectedly bewildered to have heard his name mentioned as often as it was. 'What were you saying about me?' his left hand clasped tightly onto the edge of the armrest and stiffened up into a claw. He slowly lifted himself out of the chair and side-stepped over to my end of the desk. 'You want a smack on the back of your head?' he flattened the palm of his left hand across my cheek.

'Naa thankss . . .' I backed off, pushing his hand away.

He suddenly swung hold of my chair and yanked it out from under me with nothing more than the use of his left arm. His entire sling tore open from his right elbow with the force, and he started to shriek in pain, countered stealthily by his fuming advance. He lifted up the chair and let out a roar—'Aaaaaaarghhh!' Whether it was anger or agony, it would take a rocket-scientist with the power of clairvoyance to figure out.

I ducked as the flat-back flew halfway across the room and smashed into a glass case containing a horse-shaped trophy of some sort from the Mahalaxmi Race Course.

'Some Bharat Morwani?' Hiranandani drawled into his phone, unfazed by all the commotion.

Both of Mateen Lakdawaala's cronies grabbed hold of me by the arms, and started giving it to me, one-by-one, taking turns at the abdomen. My employer scarcely lifted a finger to stop them. He probably thought I deserved it, and I probably did, but not for the same reasons he thought so. When Mateen fell to the carpeted floor in a pitiful collapse, my employer immediately leapt up to tend to his right arm and re-tie the sling, but his efforts only yielded more cries to the contrary. My head was thankfully spared, but my legs took a walloping. They were rubbery by the end of it and barely managed to kick-start the accelerator when they had to. I thought twice about using what I'd brought along to use, on account of my boss being present. In other circumstances, I would have gladly put it to good use, probably blown a set of holes into all those indelibly assembled high-end automobiles and reduced them all to rubble . . . all those Mercs and Beemers, and SUVs and sports cars.

But I could get fired from the law firm, possibly even disbarred; I'd be unable to practise anywhere in the state of Maharasthra for flashing a firearm without a permit.

'Haa . . . he's here right now . . .' Hiranandani went on, referring presumably to me. 'He's a bit busy at the moment, can't talk to you right now.' I could barely comprehend him, but being somewhat fluent in Marathi, I was able to grab bits and broken phrases through blows from his more than thorough interrogation of DCP Panth. But when belted in the stomach, I almost heaved and failed to catch up with any more of the laboured communication between the two of them.

The last sensation I recalled was one of nasal numbness—a shockwave of neurons spanned all sight and smell when punched once accidentally on the nose. An entire network of arteries pulsed through my face. The pain of the punch mangled the guy's knuckles, and he suppressed a shout, flapping his palm in the air to relieve the neural shock. The heavy-set guy wearing the safari suit, who occupied the post of official bodyguard, had announced his return with a whack to my solar-plexus. He smacked me across the face three times, I could feel my cheeks starting to go red. Then, a backhanded slap landed on my lower jaw to warm up his knuckles. Once he had a fist raised, he wondered whether or not to use it. He could put my lights out, or worse still, give me brain damage. But he went with a kick instead—the least determined yet firmest of human gestures; at least in these circumstances, it amounted to something like charity.

I'd probably blacked out for about eight to ten minutes, while the words danced across me, over and about—'*Bharat Morwani . . . Yogesh Moolchandani . . . Khar police chowki . . . silver Volkswagen . . .*' Spilling out of Hiranandani's mouth like a comic book bubble blown out as if from a child's mouth through a ring attached to the ceiling fan. His entire bloated aspect over the sofa was beginning to swell into obnoxious patterns; his face started to get fuzzy, like cable static had encroached upon the naked eye—his head started to balloon out of shape—for a moment, he appeared almost animated or in black and white.

I was tossed out by the back of my hair and shoved into my car semi-conscious by two of the big guys in white shirts and black trousers, whatever reason they were wearing them for.

The engine gargled a few times before it came on. I jammed my rumpled copper-brown alligators onto the accelerator once some strength presented itself, and shot out of there before they had the chance to note down my car number.

The road was dark, and smirched black with fresh tyre tracks. The street lamps on this side of 4th and S.V. didn't seem to be working. Some honking illumination swept by on and off, but the white stripes darting before my eyes at the centre of the road began to blur into the other. I eased my foot off the accelerator and brought it down to the second. I was going at less than twenty and squinted furiously through the high beam, trying to decipher where I was headed.

There's a patch of night, in between the cracks of the clock, when time stands still—and hangs suspended in the air; the pendulum halts somewhere in the dim no-man's land between a.m. and p.m., all eyes are sealed and all ears out of reach—the sole sound tearing through the stillness, that of a gnarled engine gliding across the moonbeam. At times, a distant vehicle blinking away from the sprawling expanse can assume almost the aspect of an unidentified flying object, to those possessed of an excitable fancy.

Now that sight was somewhat restored, I rolled my window down and stuck my head out to survey the approaching signal blinking at me from up ahead. I took a right once my turn came so as to bask in the leathery landscape of Linking Road, with its blinding flashes of tube light and tawdry neon-sprinkled lettering; managing there, to fetch an unsealed bottle of Bisleri from a nearby panwaadi, which made me somewhat regain my bearings, at least temporarily.

Khar police station was only a hop, skip, and one-legged jump away. I would arrive there in my tattered condition to present to Nalini and DCP Panth, who had returned from CrackJack in the next lane not a moment ago, the weary spoils from my encounter with the esteemed Pawan Hiranandani and his associate, the notorious Mateen 'Magarmach' Lakdawaala, a noted underworld operator, and ex-youth minister of Bandra.

Bharat's parents had by now entirely deserted the settlement, and all that the authorities were left with was my statement regarding the details of all that had transpired at Pawan Hiranandani's showroom; of all that I had witnessed and overheard, and perhaps even of a certain *road* Yogesh Moolchandani was said to have owned, that, as rumour has it, Mateen Lakdawaala had been scheming to acquire.

ELEVEN

Bharat's smashed-up Civic still sat by the front entrance in the same position, not having budged an inch since that night. There was a line of Yamaha RX100s, KTMs, Pulsars, and Splendors parked inside the compound, with no helmets dangling from the twisted side-view mirrors. Nalini was inspecting one of the engines. DCP Panth—flanked by two constables on either side—waved at me from the front porch of the police station, almost out of protocol. He was dressed in a pink shirt and a pair of navy blue trousers, stomping a pair of Sparx floaters to get some dirt off his soles. Greeting the DCP with amicable nonchalance, I tossed one of his constables the car keys so that he could park it for me.

'Park it yourself,' DCP Panth growled.

I got back in and swerved ahead a few metres to place it at the culmination of a line of slumbering autorickshaws and tempos.

The two constables followed me out, studying the vehicle in front of them with acute attention. They started to encircle the car, gathering whatever observations the encroaching visibility of a passing headlight afforded them.

'If you want it, you can keep it,' I said, holding up the keys for them as I beeped the auto-cop.

'Come on inside,' one of them grumbled, grabbing me by the arm. I wasn't used to being manhandled, especially not by the police.

DCP Panth looked down at me from the porch, fidgeting his eyebrows at the constable that dragged me in.

'Grey Ford Ikon. MH02E93756,' the constable reported.

'Put out a notice,' DCP Panth instructed him.

The constable's grip tightened around my arm in affirmation.

'What happened to you?' Nalini spun around from the Yamaha to face DCP Panth, as if he had the answer to that question.

He rotated his right shoulder blade in a sort of inadvertent opening bowler's warm-up, then running its hump along the side of his head, put his hand in the direction of the entrance, leading me in. 'I'd like to have a word with you inside in private if it's not too much trouble.'

'Not at all,' I assured him.

The three of us (DCP Panth, Nalini, and myself, that is) strolled in; the two constables stayed put at the front entrance, slowly slipping out of the premises to inspect my car. Dinner-time was only half an hour away; what better way to kill time. The station was in its usual state of dormant chaos, temporarily sedated by the rivers of chai and small talk that crowded the waiting room. There weren't more than the usual numbers for a weekday. It was fairly empty compared to the times I had previously been there this early at night. It took till about eleven to get the place really packed. That was when business was booming! After one, it was nothing less than the most happening spot in the area to hit on a Tuesday night right before the bare-footed walk to Sidhivinayak to wash away the night's revelry.

A scraggly bearded Khoja electronics repairman was dismantling the magnetic press of a Hewlett Packard printer. Occupied Wipro desktop computers adorned each desk, their CPUs and UPSes beeping furiously in protest as the lights momentarily went off. Two hawaldaars stood outside the P.I.'s cabin, trying to glance in through the opaque glass frame mounted on the door. A middle-aged Sindhi aunt, beside two female constables, waited on the bench right outside—head tilted slightly sideways, hair trimmed into an uneven fringe, feathery tufts of brown branching out into a shoulder-length gold-dyed fall—an arch of anticipation lifting her brow up as if awaiting the next hand of rummy at a kitty party. She even wore fake eyelashes, and had a sequin-blotched purse resting on her lap that was doing cartwheels with the reflections off the tube lights.

'The bereaved party!' DCP Panth informed me, sticking out a thumb in her direction, as we crossed her from a yard's length.

'Moolchandani's partner's missus.' Nalini then whispered into my ear when we were out of range. 'Mrs Murpana.'

DCP Panth walked us till the sub-inspector's cabin, exchanging wisecracks with the various juniors that passed us by. They were a young batch of new recruits, fresh out of IPS training. They didn't even have the requisite moustaches or the slouch to account for their uniforms. One of them was slightly younger than the rest, and had a sort of rheumatic skin condition, blotches of white scattered like constellations all across his cheekbones. He sat leaning on his 'lathi' with a slouch, his head tilted up in the irregular posture of a vulture.

A horde of biker boys stood alongside the duty officer's desk; maroon-haired, soorma-eyed spring chickens from Kurla and Bandra-East, terrorizing the streets, and zig-zagging through the traffic quicker than a Wasim Akram reverse swing. One of them was humouring one of the hawaldaars till he got a smack on his temple.

'Ehhh!' the hawaldaar snapped. The guy tilted his head down, caressing his own forehead from the blow. From what I could gather, their names ranged from something like Romik 'Ragda', Taahaa, 'Mendak', Hassan, to even Sufiyan, Pakiya, Popat, and Marker. The hairstyles grew more flamboyant with prominence. The head of the pack had practically a mohawk reaching for the ceiling fan from his scalp. The second-in-command—a wiry thin chap of not more than twenty-two—had his hair hued a fascinating fluorescent green. Vivid shendis (ponytails) adorned the back of each neck, in varying degrees of ornamentation. As we stopped by the water cooler for Nalini and DCP Panth to grab a sip, I caught some of their banter; it was a totally different dialect from the 'Bhantai' language I had grown up with. It was even a higher-pitched tone, and somewhat raspy and nasal, certainly more rhythmic. Their preferred term of endearment was 'Bachi' instead of 'Baa' as it had once been to us. They stretched out the ends of each of their syllables, in marked contrast to the way I'd heard the centre of each sentence emphasized by the likes of, say, Mateen Lakdawaala and his sort. But then again, these guys were the newly appointed Hell's Angels of Vakola, not the ultimately far softer four-wheeler brigade that had more muscle than actual common sense.

Those who live by night have their own set of laws and customs. The night has its own compass, its own alarm, its own whistle and its own stick. The cardinal rule of the night is silence. To make noise is to commit sacrilege . . .

That's where all those black spewing mufflers and 1.8 Turbo Charge engines wore out, compared to the stealthy manoeuvres of a Yamaha RX100 that had spared its silencer. *At night, it was truly the bikers that owned the streets. If you messed with one of them, you messed with the whole herd, and they wouldn't let you out of sight until they had it settled. If you drove alongside them with respect, then respect was what you got. If you didn't, then God only help the imbeciles that actually took the trouble to find out.* They existed outside the bounds of law and order and occupied those narrow cracks of the clock, when time stands still and just lingers for whoever takes the trouble to breathe it. Even a high-alert security check post couldn't stop them from zipping right through and tearing past their cast-iron grip.

Pakiya knew how to speak Marathi, so he was the one doing most of the talking. I recognized one of them in an instant. A fellow who was hiding behind one of the bulkier boys with a Jansport backpack strapped onto his shoulders. It was Shakeel Nathani, affectionately nicknamed 'Bada' Shakeel. Most of his acquaintances would do him the honour of referring to him only as 'Bada' or 'Bade'. He liked being called that; probably made him feel big. Not a nice guy to know. Had even been tadi-paar at one point. Multiple offender. Had done time for everything from petty larceny to assault and half-murder. Had been accused and tried for extortion, kidnapping, smuggling, arms dealing, drug trafficking, had even got a terrorist charge slapped on him when he'd been caught with a shipment of custom-made cartridges for sub-machine guns, assault rifles, AK-56s, sten guns, and Excaliburs. He was supposedly in hiding, fresh out of prison on parole. He'd just completed a three-year stretch for money laundering, and had two to go. He'd been caught with a crore in cash by a patrol jeep on the old Bombay–Poona Highway. I always figured the less I had to do with him the better it was for whomsoever concerned. He was the one who had paid me back in kind. Even though he'd covered most of his payment by gifting me the 9mm, he still owed me about four grand more. I had helped him out on his last case. That was the least I could do for him. Terrorism and racketeering are way out of my league; money laundering is more my cup of tea. He knew all about me, how I operate, and he'd always relished the opportunity to collaborate with me on some occasion. It just had to be the right matter.

He evaded eye contact, knowing full well that I knew why he was doing so. And it wasn't because of the four grand. What I didn't know was, why he was riding with a bunch of loafers significantly younger than him, who certainly would not be aware of the gravity of this guy's police record.

'These punks were on the highway last night!' DCP Panth informed me, as he wiped his mouth and drew on a quenched breath. 'They'd scraped a certain someone, and the guy handed them a mouthful.'

'You mean the deceased party?' I asked.

'Don't take his name out here,' he murmured, swiping looks here and there. 'They started to surround him on the open-stretch, circling him as he sped up.' Here he began to demonstrate with a little pantomime he put into play with his fingers acting as motorcycles, and the suspended air being assigned the open road. 'He couldn't lose them.' Now he was in the dinky shaped forward motion of Moolchandani's Volkswagen. 'They wouldn't let him go until he nearly smashed into the fence on the side of the flyover. At least that's their statement.' The curve of his right palm careened into an exaggerated crash.

I turned to Nalini's eyes for at least some kind of verification for such a lurid claim. She just rolled her pupils and hid them under the black frames of her spectacles.

The usual fun and frolic of the police station wound on to a narrower corridor than I had seen before in a suburban chowki. It twisted on towards the back of the station, attached to the staff sub-quarters, where some of the junior hawaldaars were either housed or put up for the night—and evidently led to where the sub-inspector's cabin lay.

Inside, Sub-inspector Naresh Saawant was busily going through an assortment of files stacked up on his desk in order of area. The server was down, so he had to browse manually through the records of both Bandra-East and West.

'You hurt yourself?' He turned aside to notice me enter.

He didn't ask if I wanted a cup of tea as I took a seat, how I was, how I'd been since I'd seen him last night, *nothing*—not even a smidgeon of guarantee that we'd once arrived at some kind of an understanding not so very long ago and had hoped never to see the other's face as long as we rode the district.

An empty glass of water sat on a coaster right at the edge of my side of the table. He filled his glass up from a steel jar that lay on his side, yet I hesitated to ask him to fill mine, knowing it had just been used. It had some someone else's fingerprints on it. I could even detect the faint scent of strong cologne; the kind people usually apply to wash away their sins.

'His business partner Mr Avnish Murpana was just here.' DCP Panth mentioned, just in passing. 'He's inside the PI's cabin . . .'

'Yaaa . . . I can smell him . . .' I said.

'There's someone that would like to meet you.' Saawant stroked the spotless surface of his table.

The rumble of a flush sounded from a distant toilet, and DCP Panth's deputy Naveen Kenkre emerged, wiping his hands on his uniformed waist.

'Evening, officer,' I greeted him, rising from my chair in respect.

'Evening.' He tipped his hat at me. 'What happened to your face?'

'You know, I've been thinking about that ever since we met today morning.' I swallowed some spit, leaning back in my chair and placing my elbows steadily on the armrests.

'I could fix it up for you, real nice,' he suggested.

'Naa, thanks! If I need a hairstylist, I'll be sure to give those boys outside a call,' I murmured with my mouth full.

'You know them?' his eyes tightened on me.

'Only by engine . . .' I almost turned around to spit, when my mouth crinkled up realizing I was indoors.

'Where did you go last night after we let you out from here?' Saawant took a long pause, leaning back in his chair. DCP Panth took a seat next to him on a steel stool. Saawant instantly offered him his chair, but he put his hand up, signalling him he was alright.

'I went home,' I told them.

'I see.' Saawant got up from his chair, turning his back and hobbling a few steps over to face a large shelf placed elaborately behind his desk. He took out a green box-shaped folder, and slammed it on the table, slicing it open in one jerk. He turned slowly from the shelf and bent down low to read from it, his reading glasses by now adjusted in place—'Last dialled number on the late Yogesh Moolchandani's phone was Pawan Hiranandani.'

DCP Panth tossed the Motorola Razr onto the table. Just then, Nalini wordlessly took a seat on the empty armchair beside me. She had her strategy set, and wasn't going to say a thing until she was in the presence of, what certainly now appeared to be, in all seriousness—her client.

'Funny, he didn't mention it when I was at his showroom just now . . .' I smirked.

'I guess his fists were too busy doing the talking.' Kenkre sneered.

'We rounded up those boys at CrackJack,' said DCP Panth. 'They all know Bharat well. His whole crew. And they claim they had been paid by one of the guys to tail Moolchandani last night on the highway until he went out of control and crashed and killed himself.'

'Well . . .' I hummed. 'That kind of . . . uh . . .' I turned to Nalini, 'changes things for our client, doesn't it?'

'Your client?' Saawant snorted. 'Is this guy here to represent Bharat Morwani or Pawan Hiranandani?' he asked Nalini.

'Both,' I said. 'Well, that certainly gets Mr Hiranandani off the hook, doesn't it?' I stirred from my seat. 'I guess you won't be required any longer now, Nalini. You can leave.'

'What do you mean?' she clutched hold of her purse.

'Unless you want to stay here and help me represent Bharat. Hiranandani's legal team has no more worries as far as this particular case is concerned, isn't that right, officer?' I gestured towards Panth.

'Uhmmm . . .' he coughed. 'That's right, ma'am . . . we'll keep you updated with the progress of the case, and will be sure to get in touch with you, if the last dialled numbers turn out to be a bone of contention, which they probably won't and aren't, to begin with, but you know . . . it's better to be safe than sorry . . .'

'Well . . . you can dish out those platitudes to a second-hand lawyer at Zaveri Bazaar!' she finally snapped. 'I'm not going anywhere until this case is settled. If you'd like Mr Hiranandani's statement regarding why he might have possibly tried to call him, then I can get it for you now . . . in *writing*!' she stressed.

'That won't be necessary for now, madam!' DCP Panth wagged his finger left and right.

'If it's just a missed call,' I began, 'that connects Mr Hiranandani to last night's proceedings, then . . .'

'This morning's,' Kenkre said.

'Ahh . . . but that's where you're wrong,' I reminded him. 'The key to what happened today morning lies in the events of last night. You say these boys were tailing him on the highway . . .'

'Today morning,' Saawant said.

'Not last night?'

'After you left from here.'

'Ahh . . . I see . . .' All expression froze from his face at my realization. The thought suddenly flashed right before my eyes—'That certainly means Moolchandani's death was somehow indirectly engineered by Bharat and his friends, if it were a direct result of their fight, going by the testimony of the bikers. And that obviously whilst in motion, Moolchandani had been frantically trying to reach Hiranandani for some kind of help. Hence the last dialled number, which belonged by all accounts to Pops Hiranandani.' But, when I spoke, something like this came out—'He was . . . uh . . . trying to reach Mateen . . . uh . . . Lakdawaala too wasn't he?' I tried to divert their train of thought once the notion struck me.

'Ahh . . . but that was earlier . . .' Nalini frowned. 'At 3.30 p.m. Before he left from here. In fact, he called him from the police station.'

'That's right.' Saawant nodded. 'I heard him speak to some big shot on the phone, he even offered his mobile to me to have a word with someone who supposedly knew my senior. I, of course, refused to do anything of the kind.'

'You said those boys outside,' this I directed to DCP Panth, 'had been paid by one of Bharat's friends to tail Moolchandani on the highway and see to his demise?'

Midnight Freeway

'That's not what the boys said . . .' DCP Panth declared. 'They just said they had been paid by one of Bharat's gang to chase him about and have fun with him . . .'

'By the way . . .' Kenkre cackled. 'They claim they still haven't received their pay. All they got was a phone call when they were crossing Khar police station at 6 o'clock. They didn't specify who. They had the car number, and just tailed him. They were promised five thousand.'

'Latest is,' Saawant spoke. 'that it's some guy by the name of Yash Gabba. Resident of Union Park. We tracked his mobile number.'

'I know him . . .' I said. 'Bharat picked him up from his place right after I dropped him home . . .'

'Well . . . then it seems clear to me beyond all doubt,' Nalini stated. 'that Bharat Morwani and this Yash Gabba fellow hatched this plan to simply muck about with Yogesh Moolchandani and it resulted in disaster.'

'That's just what I said.' I nodded.

'There's nothing more to it,' she insisted. 'Certainly, nothing that implicates my client.'

'Ohh . . . so he is your client, now?' I caught her.

'My boss's . . . clie . . . I'm . . . uh . . . here to speak on behalf of Pawan Hiranandani right now.' She corrected herself.

'That's right.' I tapped at the table, backing her up. 'She's been given complete power of attorney by our client . . .'

'Wait a minute . . .' Her elbow shoved mine. 'He's not representing my client . . .' she told them. 'He's here to speak on behalf of Bharat Morwani right now.'

'I'm here to speak on no one's behalf but Mr Lalith S. Mangharam, right now,' I said.

'So am I . . .' She banged her fist on the table.

'Well then, I'll race you to the hearing . . .' I made a number one sign with my finger, and swept it in the air.

The three cops just looked at us as if we were daft, or just inexperienced, which we certainly weren't, at least not her.

'Okay, how 'bout we plead guilty for vehicular smuggling?' I suggested, partly in jest.

'There's no *we*, you idiot.' She tapped me on the back of my head.

'It'll save us from culpable homicide,' I said. 'They can write it off as an accidental death . . .'

'Wait, wait, wait . . .' DCP Panth shook his hand sideways. 'You're getting wayyy ahead of us, here . . . no one said anything about vehicular smuggling or culpable homicide. You're the one that brought it up!' He pointed at Nalini. 'Ms Hegde, I have you as my witness.'

She didn't acknowledge this.

His face turned crimson with confusion—'You heard what he just said . . .'

'Mr . . . Paleja,' she informed them, 'is given to flights of fancy. He tends to lapse into spells of unreliability from time to time. In other circumstances, as I told you, he's quite good at his job. But I don't think you should take anything he says off the record quite so seriously . . .' She collected her belongings from the foot of the chair and arose abruptly. 'I'll be back with my client . . .' she turned about and started to walk back out in a sort of retaliatory stride.

'And . . . I'll be back with mine . . .' I told them.

'You know where he is?' DCP Panth jerked his head back in alarm.

'That's client–advocate privilege.' I got up from the armchair and started to head out. No-one stopped me. At the door, I turned my upper torso around to tell them—'I'll be back with him in about half an hour. By then, you'll probably even have gotten some concrete details from the boys outside. Keep them here till I get back!'

TWELVE

I caught up with her at about the outside porch. She waved her hand pointlessly at an auto stuttering past the front gate, whose rickety exhaust cast him way out of earshot.

'Which way you headed?' I asked.

'None of your business,' she mumbled, digging her head into what was less like a purse and more like a carry-bag. Shuffling through indiscriminate folders and plastic sheets, she frantically unearthed a manila folder with the Hiranandani Horsepower logo.

'You see this?' she presented it to me.

There was a silver postage stamp attached to the top right-hand corner. She opened it. Inside was a form scribbled with rows of information specifying bank account details, postal address, residence and office landline number, as well as mobile number, below which lay a column of signatures, and above which hovered a conspicuously vacant square compartment for the passport-size photograph. It was what appeared to be a rather authentic reproduction of a balance sheet.

She pointed out a Y.L. Moolchandani's name from among the list of account holders.

'Why don't you let me give you a lift to the showroom?' I suggested.

'Forget it, I'm taking an auto. Plus, if they see me there with you, I might even lose my job . . .'

'I'm not trying to snatch this job away from you. I'm just hoping to partake a part of the pie. Wet my beak, so to speak!'

'Bullshit, Paleja!' Her face crumpled in disbelief. 'I know what you're up to. You're playing both sides against the other! You came here as Bharat's lawyer to get him in the clear, so that you could walk out as Pawan Hiranandani's lawyer. I know these tactics. I've seen other small-time lawyers trying to dig their claws into big-time clients. They'll go to any lengths to get a gig this size, even if they have to commit the goddamn crime themselves.'

'Well, I'm not of them . . .' I said. 'And I'm not hoping to stay in the small-time for too long either. But as far as Hiranandani goes, I tried to present a rock-solid case in his defence right now before the cops, you saw that!'

'Yaa . . . just so you could get me out of the room and have them to yourself.'

'That isn't the only "why". . .'

'Then?' She stopped fidgeting with her purse.

'Okay . . .' I took a breath, thinking long and hard about what I was about to put forth. 'Right now, it's all in on Bharat. How about we place a bet? If the investigation turns, I'll give you double the salary I'm receiving from Bharat if you let me take Hiranandani. If it stays on Bharat, you can have Bharat for whatever he's worth. Take him to the cleaners.'

'Forget it . . . I'm not a "juaari" (gambler) . . . my older brother did enough for the entire family.'

'No . . . Nalini . . . don't you get it . . .?' I clenched my teeth. 'I'm trying to make sure that the two of us benefit from whatever direction the investigation takes. Can't you see that? I'm covering all sides, all chances. Right now, the odds are all against Bharat. But not for long. There's something about these bikers being here with such a clean-cut testimony that doesn't look so right . . .'

'As in?'

'As in . . .' Just then, I caught a flicker of DCP Panth and Naveen Kenkre trickling out of the corridor from afar. 'Let's go . . .' I caught her elbow and shuffled out.

I could swear I saw a bright red Honda City sipping off a stray street lamp on the other side of the divider when we got out of Khar police station. It looked like it had been sitting there for quite some time with the occupant reclining. My ignition took a couple of rounds of unscrewing before I could get it chugging. The battery squeaked a few broken noises of complaint; there was barely any petrol left. My needle was on E.

Nalini took the passenger seat. 'You wanna have a word with one of the bikers?' she asked.

'Looks like you already did . . .' I said, pointing at the Yamahas she had been busily inspecting when I'd showed up battered and bruised. The Honda City's lights came on.

'Oh yaa . . .' she took off her glasses. 'Romik.'

'What'd he say?'

'Nothing of any consequence.'

'You ever hear of a road the late Mr Moolchandani owned in New Bombay?' I asked her once we'd cleared out of the line of stationery three-wheelers in front of us.

'What road?' she asked, rolling down her window.

'A private two-and-a-half-kilometre stretch . . .' I gave the AC button a jab.

'How d'you know about it?' she asked, in a decided change of tone, turning one of the blowers in her direction.

'Mateen Lakdawaala told me about it just now.'

'Well . . . it's just a place where people go . . .'

'People as in . . . you mean? Uh . . . necking couples?'

'Not exactly . . . usually stags, except on weekends, then they take their partners along. That's when the drag races happen, or at least they used to when I was in college.'

'Drag races?'

'Yaa . . . they'd chip the speed breakers. My brother used to go . . .'

'Used to?'

'Yaa . . . before he was broke . . . when he still used to drive a C.'

'I didn't know that . . .' I said, resignedly.

'These bikers came from there too . . .' she said.

My gaze nearly fell off the road. 'How d'you know?' I scattered my sights.

'Romik told me. I promised him I wouldn't tell the cops.'

'They know the guy they claim to have nearly killed owned the strip?'

'Well, uh . . .' she gazed around, taking a humming pause, 'now they do.' She smiled.

My head twitched away from the windscreen I should have been looking at. When it reached beside her, she spoke before I could search for what to say.

'You still wanna bet on who the case is going to land on, Paleja?'

'What do you mean?'

She didn't spill a word.

'Wait just a minute.' I let go of the steering wheel. 'What was all that about Bharat and his friends telling them to tail him on the highway?'

'That was what I told them to say.' She bobbed her head up and down lightly.

'What are you talking about?'

'I cut a deal with them. Told them that if they sold out Bharat, they'd get fifteen months for aiding and abetting, if they took the name of the actual party that had asked them tail Moolchandani on the Sea Link . . . then . . . uh . . . God only knows what kind of sentence they'd have in store for them.'

'I see . . .'

'So, you see, Paleja, you should probably fold up your bets on Bharat while there's still time. No point backing a lame horse.'

'That isn't so, Nalini. His dad knows DCP Panth well. He's been sitting at his friend's place since last night. Hasn't moved. I can show you right now. There's no way a frame-up is going to work.'

'It's not a frame-up. It's fool-proof. You don't understand, do you?'

'What?'

'Last night after you dropped your client home, he called up Sub-inspector Saawant from his friend Yash Gabba's phone, because his battery was dying.'

'Whom he had just picked up.'

'Right. He picked him up from CrackJack where Gabba had indeed been hanging around with those bikers. The guys all saw Bharat driving his dad's CRV, unable to control it. Their statement is on record. He was inebriated beyond repair. He was slurring over the phone to Saawant, telling him that he was going to talk to Panth in the morning and get him transferred to Khopoli. Saawant will be more than glad to hang it all on this guy. He doesn't exactly like him, you see.'

'So?'

'So . . .' She leaned back in her seat, and finally put on the seatbelt. 'It looks like circumstances have conspired to put your client entirely in the wrong. Even though he may not have necessarily precipitated the incident, he happened to fall right in place. The little run-in he had with Moolchandani just so happened to prove profitable for someone else.'

'Who are you talking about, Nalini?'

'Who do you think?'

'Mateen Lakdawaala?'

'You saw "Bada" Shakeel Nathani hiding behind the bunch. Didn't you know he used to work for Mateen and co.?'

'I'm afraid I'm not entirely understanding . . .'

'I'll tell you what . . .' She turned around to face me. 'Let's place a bet. Try taking Hiranandani now and I'll take Bharat. Let's switch sides. If the investigation turns on Hiranandani, I'll give you double of what I make off Bharat while it stays on him.'

I thought about it for a moment, vaguely considering the proposition. 'Bharat's a lost cause . . . you said his parents aim to have him put into some kind of sanatorium.'

'In New Bombay . . .' she specified.

'New Bombay?'

'Somewhere off the map. It's not exactly a sanatorium; it's more like a rest house, a kind of resort or township actually, outside of Bombay city proper. Mrs Murpana will tell you all about it. She had them sold hook, line, and sinker. She was even asking me right now if I had any relatives or younger siblings who were troubled and prone to getting into fights, or had anger-management problems.'

My phone tittered as I turned onto S.V. Road.

'Bharat's mom,' I said, quickly spinning the steering wheel and asking Nalini to put it on speakerphone.

'Hello . . . beta . . .' her voice rippled through.

'Hi, aunty . . .' I said, raising an eyebrow at Nalini, who raised two in return.

'Hi beta . . . any word from Bharat?'

'Yes, aunty, he's at Bobby's house.'

I could feel Nalini make a mental notation before mouthing—'Bobby?'

'We're having him sent for a two-week treatment period to the L.K.L.M. Provisional Home for the Medically Ill in New Bombay.'

'Uh . . .' I didn't know what to say. 'Are you sure you'd want to take such a drastic measure?'

'We just got back from the police station,' she said.

'I know aunty . . . I . . . uh . . .' I gestured at Nalini furtively with my head. 'My colleague met you there.'

'Colleague?' she inquired.

'Nalini Hegde. Lady in specs.'

'Oh yess . . .' she recollected, not too fondly though. Her voice grew sore at the reminder. 'Ahh yes . . . beta . . . she wanted to know Bharat's number.'

Nalini snapped shut the speaker. 'Hello . . . ma'am.' She put it to her left ear, so it was well out of my reach. 'Yes, ma'am, Nalini speaking. Things aren't looking so good for your son, ma'am. Apparently, he and his friends caused the accident . . . I'm sorry to break it to you like this, but . . .'

I could hear muffled shrieks of what was said out in reply.

'Ma'am, you can come down to the police station and have a word with DCP Panth, yourself. Ask him, please . . . yes even I was just with him!' Her pitch grew sterner and certainly less cordial. 'The police are currently looking for your son. They've put out notifications all over Bandra and Khar. Right now, I suggest you please try and find your son for his own good.' She cut the call.

'Now why would you go and put the old lady's head full of worries like that?'

She tossed the phone back onto the dash. 'I don't know.' She kind of smirked, an evil glint danced in her uncovered eyes. 'Better to keep people on their feet . . .'

133

I called back Bharat's mom once the phone was within my grasp and assured her that my colleague had just had a long day and was tired. We were currently trying to resolve who would represent which party in the case. That was the prime concern at present. She had nothing at all to worry about as far as her son was concerned. I was just going to collect him and escort him personally to the facility in New Bombay myself.

'Can I come with you?' Nalini wondered. 'I'd like to get in a word with him.'

'You can talk to him for as long as you like at the station.' was my reply. 'And I can talk to your client?'

'Deal?'

'Deal.'

We shook on it before either of our minds had the chance to flutter.

'Where's this place, by the way?' I asked her. 'Any idea?'

'Which place?'

'This L.K.L.M. sanatorium his mom was talking about?'

'It's not a sanatorium, more of a rest and recuperation facility, actually. A state-sanctioned medical institute devoted specially to the care of offenders who might be afflicted by behavioural disorders that may categorize them outside the realm of regular offenders.'

'Where?'

'It's located within a new colony of 18-storeys in Navi Mumbai. Avnish Complex. An abandoned set of buildings constructed initially for residential habitation, but the plot was condemned due to a property litigation dispute.'

'Avnish Complex? Any relation to Avnish Murpana?'

'It's owned by him and Moolchandani. At least on paper.'

'Now, isn't that justice?' I remarked. 'Moolchandani winds up dead and the guy who supposedly caused his death lands up in an institution owned by none other than . . . wait just a minute . . .' It occurred to me. 'No connection with the road, is there? After all, the plot is in New Bombay.'

'If you intend to go and find out about that road Mateen Lakdawaala was telling you about, I suggest you don't . . .'

'Why?'

'Because . . .' She looked through the dust-speckled windscreen. 'It's the road where people go to die . . .'

THIRTEEN

I dropped her a good hundred metres away from the showroom. She walked the rest of the way, saying she didn't want to be spotted with me by any of Hiranandani's security guards. She had her own equation with them, and didn't want my brief dust-up to pollute it.

The road where people go to die . . .

Hell of a way to leave a sentence. I let the thought slither into the angled road curving down to Bobby's building like a snake through the shrubbery, which was wobbly as all hell! Ravaged with potholes—as if someone had sat on it with a pickaxe and hammer to try and chisel away some prophetic design.

I tore my eyes from the rear-view mirror once I stopped bouncing up and down on my seat, somewhat certain of an absence behind me. I'd caught a flare of red somewhere on the way down in my windshield, but it could have been anything, even the refraction from some distant red-light. Now that I'd slowed down and the coast was clear, I searched outside the windows to scan the locality. I crawled to a halt to ask a seated watchman. 'Sheetal Residency?'

He flapped his palm in the air, a firm 'No'. I asked an adjacent dairy before they closed their shutters entirely on me.

'Sheetal wha?' The baffled banyan clad keeper's mouth split apart.

'Sheetal Residency . . . Residency . . .' I specified, leaning out my window.

'I don't know any Sheetal Residency, there's a Sheetal Vilas in the vicinity, somewhere or the other, right down the road from here, take a left from there, I think.' He directed his hands up and down the streets and whirled them around somewhat indistinctly, implying it could be anywhere from here to Nariman Point.

A seated coconut seller chimed in, 'There's no Sheetal Residency out here. Only Sheetal Vilas and Sheetal Palace. Sheetal Palace is on 15th Road, near Shiv Sagar.'

'Sheetal Residence?' Another argued.

'Sheetal Residency . . .' I repeated for the nth time to a stationery cyclewaala.

One of the bouncers outside Khar Gymkhana finally obliged and came to my rescue.

It was nicely tucked away behind a wall of bungalows. I was pretty sure they were still there, at Sheetal Residency: Bobby's residence, that is. From what I remember, Bharat was out there playing cards and not likely to leave before he had broken even—a mighty far-fetched prospect, but nevertheless, his persistence ensured his unshifted presence.

They were all at Bobby's house, the whole lot of them— him, and Yash Gabba, maybe more. It was that light grey 12-storey at the downhill turning of Ambedkar and Khar

Gymkhana, near Bharat's speaker shop. Built in the spring of '98 by Pops' wife Sheetal Hiranandani, who had been from a builder family of some repute.

Sheetal Residency was one of those buildings that used to be fancy, but as the years rolled by, it began to look more and more like a second-rate emporium. The once pristinely white marble had now wasted away into a perplexing hue of grey laced with maroon. Many unpolished footsteps had washed away its God-given opulence.

I parked the car outside the building next to what I recognized to be Bharat's dad's CRV. There was no damage along either of the bumpers, not even a side-view mirror out of place. Thankfully, it looked like it had lain there for at least a night and a half. There was crowshit painted all over the windscreen, dried leaves strewn across the bonnet, and enough mud and dust in the wipers to jam them into a coma.

'Which floor is Bobby on?' I asked an un-uniformed gatekeeper snoozing in the watchman's cabin.

'8th.' He drew out three fingers on his left hand, one of which wasn't there, and held out a five with his right.

He didn't appear to reserve too selective a discretion for whomsoever entered the building. It was probably getting out that was the tough part. Either way, Bobby had declared it open house to every buddy of his within a five-mile radius, and no one could complain just so long as they didn't disturb the peace, which, of course, they pretty soon began to do. I could hear them berate each other from the elevator on up.

The backside of the compound, visible through a narrow slit at the back of the lobby, was remarkably free of vehicles—

as if all the owners had resolved to protect their windscreens from leaping cricket balls—with a small patch of garden next to a water tank, sloping down from the walls of the adjoining building.

The elevator doors parted open, revealing an ostentatious front door to a king-sized white flat. There were about five per floor with door frames, each more intimidating than the other, and plaqued surnames scattered about in almost alphabetical order. Some had opulent diyas and candlestands adorning the doormats.

Once I got off, there burst out from a distant apartment, a muffled echo of cackles—mostly falsetto celebrations of ridicule that at once scorned the sedate surroundings, yet strangely seemed to revel in the economic esteem it afforded them. I rang the electronic front doorbell to the flat from which the sound seemed to be emerging. '804,' it sounded off a sing-song announcement in 8-bit beats. Bobby opened the door, recognizing me and not looking too pleased about it.

'Oh . . .!' he exclaimed. 'P.P.?'

'Is Bharat in there?' I asked.

'Yaa, he's in here.' He moved aside from the doorway, letting me in.

'What happened to you?' He noticed my shirt untucked, the ends of my coat crumpled beyond recognition, the derelict outlines of my entire attire; my hair ruffled up, a faint reddening of the nose. Not a patch on the way Bharat looked last night. Couldn't hold a candle to the beating he'd received, and probably would again if he continued that way . . . this time, maybe even from me.

I had to compose myself when I caught a glimpse of my battered reflection in the bronze-framed full-length mirror hung on the wall of the vestibule.

'That's what I've been trying to find out . . .' I answered.

In the living room of a 3-BHK, 12,000 square-foot flat, which looked like it had been decorated by a Swami from outer space, stood a long glass table at which sat a pack of young men, all dressed for a Saturday night, sweating in the blast of two over-helpful 12 megaton air conditioners. Two of them had removed their oversized work-suits and hung them on the backrest of the longchairs that had left marks on the marble when dragged up to the dinner table. A bright red carpet covered the seating area in front of a 32-inch plasma TV that had the India–South Africa one-day match on, blaring away as background noise to proclamations like—'What a hand! Well played. Good one!' punctuated by a violent handclap.

'YOU IDIOT!' one of them wailed, as someone dropped a catch.

Bobby took his place at the head of the table, and Gabba, who was dressed in an Adidas windcheater and a pair of bright white sneakers, was busy fixing drinks on a bar upon which rested an array of fake imported liquor.

As I entered the living room, one of them let out a sigh saying—'Damn, I thought it was the delivery guy from Sahibaan.'

'What did you order?' Bobby asked with ignited interest.

'Three chicken Szechuan fried rice, two plates of chicken lollipop and one Hong Kong spring roll.'

'And in gravy?'

'Hunan chicken.'

'Did you call for the Shanghai sizzler?' Bobby inquired.

'What about the chilli paneer?' another one added.

'Oh damn, I think I forgot to call for that. You can have the spring roll, it's veg.'

Hiteish checked his watch. 'Call that idiot. It's been over half an hour. What is he doing? Laying the eggs a'what? I told him I want eggless fried rice.' He slammed his fist on the table.

'Evening, boys,' I announced, taking the liberty to step in and join the congregation.

Bharat didn't look too keen to acknowledge that I'd crashed his card game, but then again, he didn't have much of a choice. I was there in the flesh, and he had to account for my presence in some way or the other to save face.

There was Bobby and Gabba, and that Mateen Lakdawaala's brother-in-law Rishabh Taahilramaani a.k.a Raptor; also, the two brothers Hiteish and Lokesh from Band Stand sitting beside Gagan 'Sardar' who was dealing the next hand. They all looked at me, seemingly displeased at the prospect of having to accommodate another player. Of all the guys, I knew only Bobby and Yash Gabba personally; the rest I had only heard of socially or seen around the area, like that punter Loku and his blaring bullock cart he liked to call a Lancer. Even that Sardar from Almoeda Park, and the rest of the road ragers—toppling friends' R8s on a drift, driving the elder brother's City till they moved on to something more substantial, sorting stag entries at a nightclub that was tougher to get into than the Rashtrapati Bhavan. A Ganpati-shaped key hanger nailed in next to a makeshift agarbati altar carried an assortment of autocops, each arranged in order of status. The keys to an S-Class occupied the most prominent position, and practically elbowed out the lesser Honda and Toyota car keys dangling just under it.

'Yo, P.P.!' Gabba barked out from the barstool. 'How you doing?'

'I'm doing good, Gabba,' I said. 'What about you?'

'I'm good . . .' He poured out a stiff one. 'So far, so good. Win some, lose some, you know how it is.'

'I don't,' I said. 'Where you been?'

'I've tho been yer only . . .' he said, sort of spitefully, as if stating the obvious. 'Where you been?'

'I've also been here only . . .' I said.

'You been yer?' He plucked out an ice cube and dropped it gently into the glass.

'Yaa I been yer . . .' I sort of threw my arms lightly about in an indefinite motion, fumbling with what else to talk about. 'I've been around.'

'You been yer haa?'

'Ya, I been here. How you doing, boys?' I said, keeping a warm track on the pulse of the room. There were nine of them, including that dimwit Saket, and weakling Ricky Tejwani.

'What are you guys playing?' I asked.

'Started with teen patti,' the Sardar spoke, shuffling the cards quicker than a cash counter. 'Now we're on variations.'

The living room itself was in no apparent disorder— no cigarette stubs or ash engravings left by on the marble floor, a small makeshift wastepaper basket containing Magic

Masala chips packets, arranged attentively to tend to the trash emanating from so protracted a sitting. The eight or nine kids sat there mildly distracted by my presence, yet also slightly indifferent to it—staring on blankly into the glass table, on which the fate of their night rested.

'Who is this guy?' Raptor stuck his thumb in my direction. He was the smart-alec of the bunch, with a chip on his shoulder the size of a landslide, given who his brother-in-law was. He was flying on his name, and his name alone—and probably had been since he had learnt how to crawl.

'Ahh, no one . . . just a friend of mine . . .' Bharat explained.

'Ahh, I'm more than that, Bharat.' I laughed, grabbing hold of an empty stool and settling down next to him.

'What happened?' he asked, as I patted his back and put one of my arms around his shoulder.

'Your mom told me you borrowed five and ten from her in quick succession,' I said out loud for everyone on the eighth floor to hear. 'You move fast, Bharat.'

'I didn't . . .' he began.

'I don't care what you didn't,' I said, letting go of him. 'It's what you did that counts. You're eight and a half grand short in my books and don't bother to pick up the phone. You've got some nerve sitting here gambling when you owe me that kind of money.' His friends all looked at him like he had horns on his head.

'Tell me something, Bharat,' Raptor contemplated. 'You always bring your friends to the place a'what?

'No, no . . . it's not like that,' Bharat shook his head. 'You're getting it all wrong, Raptor!'

'No, no . . . I'm just asking!' Raptor went on. 'You always bring your friends to the place like this a'what?'

'Like what?' Bharat asked.

'Like this!' Raptor looked at me coldly.

'No man . . . Raptor, it's not like that.'

'Then what's he doing here?'

'He just came like that only, to play.' Bharat tried labouriously to justify my presence.

'That's right, Raptor, just here to join the game.' I nodded.

'Why do you owe him eight and a half?' he asked Bharat.

'He's my lawyer.'

'Oh . . .' Saket coughed. 'You think I could call my dentist? I have to give him half a peti for these wires he's installed in my mouth.' He opened his gab to reveal a pair of braces.

'I'm afraid we're not going to be able to fit you P.P.,' Bobby told me. 'We're already ten. We're taking turns with the rounds. After this, we're playing poker. Rotating each game. Not all of us are playing, you know.'

'Yaa some of us are just here to watch the match.' Gabba turned his head from the ice tray, both hands occupied with scotch glasses half-full.

'That's right!' Raptor nodded, stacking a deck of chips from a metallic poker set lying on the floor with all the cash. That was the bank. There were chips scattered all over; three decks of recently-purchased brand new cards, as well as UNO and some sort of sporting trump cards resting atop a Reebok cardboard shoebox bulging with banknotes that doubled up as the side-bank.

'Look, P.P.,' Bharat quaked. 'I told you I'd have it for you in a week.'

'I thought you said two–three days?'

'Listen, man . . .' his mouth started to tighten up. 'I told you I'd give the money. Just leave me alone.' His entire head now started to shake vigorously. 'I'm in the middle of a game. Do you mind?'

'You wouldn't want me to go to your parents about this?'

'You piece of shit!' he exploded, in a pronounced change of tone, evidently stricken with embarrassment. 'Scum, you're scum!' I'd gotten the fireworks going. All it took was a mere mention of his folks.

He pulled out a wad of notes from the box next to the bank, and started counting them swiftly with a bank teller's ease. He pulled out 8,500 from the rubber band, in 500-rupee notes, and threw them on my face.

'Here!' he yelled. 'Take this. This is my one day's petrol money. I throw this on your face, you cheap bastard.'

'Here, take this.' I picked up the fallen money and threw it back at him. 'I don't want your rotten money.'

Bobby shot up from his stool, his shoulders flaring in a mediatory pose. 'Come.' He flicked his head in the direction of the doorway, picking up the scattered cash from the floor. All heads spun around as he guided me out. Once we were outside the living room door and on our own, he discreetly counted the money and handed me back the cash.

'How much is it?' I asked.

'8,000.'

'Cheapskate, when he throws money on the face also he doesn't count and throw it.'

The hand carried on as I started to count the money myself. Texas Hold 'em was underway. I could hear a cook snoring in the kitchen. I went back in to remind Bharat that he owed me another 500, but my demands got lost in the raucous banter, laughed off teasingly and shrugged aside as if I was some cheapskate crying over a buck. The guys were loud and boisterous, with nothing banal about them. They all had a manner which was strictly business, and that included even friendship.

'Rockets!' one of them yelled. 'The bastard's sitting on pocket Aces.'

'How much?' Gabba asked, counting a building of chips.

'20,' another one mumbled.

'Call 20, and raise you by 80.' Raptor tossed in four twenty-rupee chips. 20 was just the small blind.

'Call 80, re-raise 100,' the other guy expressionlessly drawled, one eye pointed in the direction of the silken sofa resting just beside the television.

'Call!' an accented NRI announced, throwing in another stack of chips. Turns out there was another guy in the bathroom I had missed earlier. If it was a five hundred buy-in, then that meant there was fifty grand minimum between them.

'Yo, Roko . . . want another buy-in?' Raptor inquired. 'Looks like you're out.'

'Naa, thanks man. I'm good.'

'You have to give me 15 from before.'

The NRI reached for his wallet. Raptor spoke with the incomprehensible Sindhi mumble as he collected the cash. 'Haa-much dya wan?'

'Gi-him 20,' Gabba instructed.

'All-in, 220.' The NRI dragged everything he had into the pot.

Raptor started settling the accumulations. 'Side-pot 600,' he calculated. 'Loku, wanna call?'

'Naa.' Lokesh shook his head. 'Fold.'

'What do you want?' Raptor noticed me again.

'P.P. . . .' Bharat began, evidently agitated at my return.

I brought out the wallet from my side-pocket and started to pack the notes into it. The 9mm now had space to breathe. 'There's another five hundred that's due,' I informed Bharat. 'But I think I'm just gonna settle for the bank!'

As I swung out the semi-automatic from my pocket and revealed it to the gathered company, he let out a shriek— 'WHAT THE BLOODY HELL!!??'

'Shhh . . .' I instructed them. 'Be quiet.' I put one foot behind the other to back a few steps away from the dining table and pointed the gun at Bharat's face. 'Nobody move a muscle, and no one gets hurt.' I retreated towards the television set, making sure I had everyone covered. Bobby's mouth dropped open. 'Those are the rules to this hand,' I continued. 'Is that clear?'

'As ice.' Gabba clenched his teeth, taking a sip of neat whisky.

'Hands on the table,' I yelled. 'Everyone!'

The ten of them froze, not knowing if I was serious or if this whole thing was a prank.

'Yo, Bharat, who the heck is this guy?' Raptor asked again, his mouth barely open.

'He said he's his lawyer,' Gagan 'Sardar' blurted out. 'But I think he's his friend.'

'Bullshit!' Bharat countered. 'I barely know this guy.'

'I said, shut up!' I repeated. I started to scan the table. 'Gimme the briefcase,' I ordered Raptor.

'What briefcase?'

'The poker set. The bank.'

'You gotta be out of your mind!'

'Do as I say.'

'Listen, buddy, you might not know . . . but . . .'

'I said hand me the bank!' I was trying to keep calm, but I could feel my nerves threatening to get the better of me. I took a slow breath as I repeated the instruction. 'Hand it over.'

Bobby thought about it a second. 'Give him the bank,' he decided. Raptor threw it on the floor by my feet, nearly chipping a tile.

'Okay . . .' I steadied myself. 'Now toss me that shoebox.'

'Listen, man . . .' Raptor finally got up, exasperated.

'Sit down!' I shrieked.

'Just do as he says, man . . .' Bobby trembled, his eyes squirming in their sockets. 'He's got a goddamn gun pointed at us, you idiot! Can't you see?'

Raptor kicked the cardboard shoebox from under the table with a neat marble slide that arrived right at my feet.

I bent down to pick it up, the barrel of the gun still planted in place, my finger on the trigger all set to blast off the second anyone decided to make a move. I hastily emptied all the contents of the shoebox into the steel poker set, and clicked shut the case to lift it from the floor. All eyeballs stared back at me, bulging beyond all comprehension. They collectively gaped on at me like I was half-mad as I started to motion towards the door, collecting the poker set and walking backwards a few steps to make for the exit with the gun still tilted in their direction. Just as I grabbed hold of the doorway to the living room to slip out the main door, the bell rang.

'Who is it?' My head snapped to the side.

'The delivery guy from Sahibaan,' said Gabba.

'Tell him to bounce.'

'Bullshit!' Hiteish shouted. 'I want my fried rice.'

The bell rang again. A servant who was asleep emerged from the kitchen in a moment and opened the door, clearly unaware of the gravity of the situation. Once he entered the living room with the plastic bag containing the food, and caught a glimpse of the 9mm, the fried rice fell from his fingers, leaving a splotch of Szechuan sauce on the polished marble floor.

I slowly started to back away from the living room towards the front door. No one moved a muscle. They just sat there still, knowing the watchman downstairs would take care of me. Just then, I felt a spasm of sickness enveloping all my faculties . . . all those calmly calculated states of composure that had often proven susceptible to an untraceable encouragement of irrational fancy in the most undesirable of circumstances.

Sometimes I'd find myself talking to a perfectly well-mannered stranger and feel an uncontrollable urge to put his lights out, for no rhyme or reason other than it was the least appropriate thing to do.

At such instances, my mind could be entirely out of my control, or more accurately—what it chose to consider or meditate upon was a matter outside of my psychological jurisdiction.

What if I were to spray bullet-wounds all over their well-fed faces, nourished with home-cooked food and cold coffee served on a stainless-steel tray—brought up on marble flooring spick enough to slide on. The poison started to pulse through my veins. 'Noo!! Stop it!!!' I banged my own head against the open door to the drawing room. 'Don't! No!!!' I now started to whack my head clean of all these unwanted notions that decided to descend upon me all at once, of their own volition, entirely uninvited by my own thoughts. The guys now started to look really worried.

'Bharat, you're coming with me,' I ordered softly, regathering my powers of speech and thought.

Bharat shrugged at first, but was told by Raptor to follow my orders lest anyone got hurt.

I shoved the poker set into my arms and dragged him past the stunned delivery guy down the lift by his collar, one hand on the semi-automatic—the poker set clutched tightly between my elbows. The watchman downstairs didn't know what to make of it. He started towards me as we exited the lift, but I told him to back off, or else Bharat was going to be limping home with one leg in a cast. I threw him into the car, still holding the gun out in case it was required. He rose from the passenger seat in a second and began to scream all kinds of hideous profanities at the lobby in description of all that had occurred.

I started the ignition and kicked at the accelerator, hurtling the car out of sight. From my rear-view, I could see Bobby and another watchman tumble out of the building, looking on into the darkness of the direction I was headed in. Once I climbed up the slope to Ambedkar Road, I took a sharp left turn at a hairpin bend and disappeared from view into a side lane that took me back to the main stretch of Linking Road. I went as fast as the road would allow, dodging oncoming vehicles and overtaking slowpokes, grazing a parked sedan and flying past a stationery autorickshaw parked in the middle of the road. Bharat kept getting thrown about in his seat. I instructed him to wear his seatbelt. When he refused, I showed him the gun.

I knocked open the poker set once I turned off into S.V. Road and adjusted the rear-view mirror in place to make sure no one had followed us out. A bright red car was trailing behind me before the signal, but for all I knew, it could have been nothing more than a coincidence; that he was heading to the same side of town as me, on the way back home from work just like myself. There was close to a lakh of rupees resting inside the case. I put the gun back into the registration folder and enclosed it within the glove compartment. I wiped the sweat off my jaw and shoved my foot down on the accelerator across the intersection of Khar and S.V. Road, heading towards the police station.

'What the hell is wrong with you, you son-of-a-bitch!' Bharat wailed, once the road flattened out, and he managed to stay still in his seat with the aid of the straphanger just above him.

'Just take it easy, Bharat!'

'What do you mean, take it easy!?' he shouted, mangier this time and with less coherence. 'You just robbed my poker game!'

'We did . . . you see . . . we'll split the proceeds 50–50!'

'What the hell are you talking about . . .!?'

'Like I told you, Bharat, we're one and the same, remember? Client-partnership. A joint venture. I represent your best personal interests, at all times, at all costs!'

Bharat was by now nearly beginning to cry. His drunken agitation tore open into a half-formed tear, easily extracted by the widening of his mouth. 'Are you out of your mind!?' He slammed his hands down on his thighs in despair.

'Far from it, Bharat. I'm in complete command of what I am about to undertake. I take full charge of your responsibility. As a matter of fact, I've never felt better in my life. You know . . .' A thought struck me as I tapped at the poker set. 'Come to think of it, I did have kind of what you might call a rough day, but this right here has made me feel a whole lot better. It's lifted my spirits.'

He started to settle into his seat.

'You should have seen me a couple of hours back.' I tugged at my collar, emphasizing its rumpled condition. 'Was in no shape to handle any matter. Got the shit kicked out of me!'

His eyes grew dazed as they settled on me.

'That son-of-a-bitch Lakdawaala and his goons . . .' I proceeded.

'Eh-eh-eh,' Bharat's face shrunk at the mention. 'If you're getting in deep with Lakdawaala and into his bad books, then count me out of it, please! I happen to know his brother-in-law. He'll talk to him on my behalf.'

'That's my job, Bharat. As a matter of fact, I got my ass kicked doing precisely that.'

'What?' His jowls wobbled.

'Talking to Mateen Lakdawaala on your behalf. Trying to get you out of his bad books and into his good ones. We're in this together, you and me!' I reminded him. 'I was feeling a hell of a lot worse then, I can tell you, but I'm sure feeling a hell of a lot better now. It's amazing!' I laughed. 'The way the mood spins. I guess this is what the doctors refer to as an upliftment of the spirits through natural means. Without the aid of intoxicants. Through the toil of activity, not some morbid anticipation of sitting on a couch and looking for laughs at the bottom end of a beer mug. In other words, a kind of treatment. Self-designed and self-prescribed, of course. But God's honest truth is that . . . Bharat . . .' Here I tried to reach for his understanding in a desperate attempt at igniting some kind of empathy. 'I have a kind of condition that requires me to break the law in order to be at peace . . . or at least at ease. I don't know why. It's just a small sacrifice, you know, considering how much I otherwise do to uphold it.' But anyway, forget all that!' I smiled. 'The happiness boys are back in business! You know what, Bharat, I think I enjoy stealing more than anything else in the world.'

Bharat was only now beginning to detect the bullshit behind my smarmy blood-pressure taker's manner. From the look in his eyes, it was apparent beyond all doubt that he had lost all hope in my discretion altogether. I was no longer the helping hand he had once taken me for. The friend who would land up without hesitation at a moment's notice to straighten things out for him.

'Why did you do this, P.P.?' he moaned.

'I don't know, Bharat . . .' I said, slowly bending the wheel over to face Khar police station. 'I guess you never really know, do you? You never really know, you know . . . I guess there's no sense to it at all! No logic in it either. Why one swings or hoots or howls into the wind? Why the madman sings, scrabbling on the street-corner for the rubbish from the floors? Why the dirt collects? Why do birds crash into windowpanes? Where are murderers born?'

'What the hell are you talking about, P.P.?' He spun out his mobile phone in alarm.

'Aha!' I snatched hold of it in an instant, confiscating it with the ease of a schoolteacher. 'Caught you trying to be fancy there. Don't get any funny ideas about the gun in the glove compartment. I know you won't. As I said, Bharat, you have absolutely nothing to be worried about. It's all gonna be fine . . . I'm there to take care of you . . .'

'Take care of me?'

'Yes . . . you see, your parents aim to put you into some kind of a little resthouse. So, I've been appointed as your escort, to see you off in a sense.'

'Where?'

Midnight Freeway

'In New Bombay.'

'Look, P.P., . . . why don't you just take the money and drop me home . . .?'

'Ahh . . . it's not so simple, you see. Your parents are gonna be pissed. There'll be a lot of handling to do of the situation, which has already been aggravated beyond repair thanks to your miscalculations.' I pulled up outside the gate of Khar police station.

'Where's my car?' Bharat demanded, gathering a glimpse of the vacant parking space outside the entrance.

'Your parents were here.' I looked around. 'But they didn't take it. Your mom was quite worked up from what I heard.'

It was evident from the two white Gypsies I had seen earlier at the courthouse, parked diagonally before the front porch, that Pops Hiranandani and Mateen Lakdawaala had arrived well before us. A couple of the bodyguards were fraternizing with one of the bikers when he noticed Bharat.

'Eh, Bharat!' The biker called out to us as I led him by his hand into the station.

Bharat turned around to notice that it was Shakeel. I noticed him too, but obviously, he didn't notice me, or at least, he pretended not to.

FOURTEEN

'Listen . . . Bharat . . .' he panted, before finally acknowledging my presence with a wink. 'Something horrible has happened, man . . .'

'What?'

'Come here . . .' he took us back out the entrance to the sidewalk, all kinds of bracelets and chains dangling from his neck. He was lanky, wide-eyed, and dazed, like he had been hit in the head with a hammer and never quite recovered from it.

'P.P.,' he now turned to me, 'I don't think you should take him in there. The boys all took your name,' he said to Bharat. 'I swear I didn't have anything to do with it.' He joined the tips of his thumb and forefinger onto his adam's apple.

'Don't lie, Shakeel!' I interrupted his vows. 'That lady told you to do it, am I right?'

'Yaa . . .' he admitted. 'The lady told us if we said you guys had paid us to follow that Volkswagen on the highway, we'd get a lighter sentence . . . probably even a non-punishable offence if we're lucky and she manages to talk us out of this.

I had to go along with it, man. You know how it is; I'm out on parole. If my jailer Baale Rao finds out about this, I'm dead!'

He was trying to give me the impression that he was still an able-bodied employable man. I knew he didn't stand a chance to turn straight and get a real job. When I picked him up from Arthur Road on his release, the first thing he wanted to know was what the score was. He had placed a substantial bet on the India–Australia One day. The honest buck had no place in the torn compartments of his fake Gucci wallet.

'Listen, buddy . . .' Bharat stiffened up. 'Just what the hell are you talking about?'

'Listen . . . P.P., just get him out of here.' He flicked his fingers off into the distance, pointing towards my car. 'Mateen Bhai's inside with his lawyer.'

'I know . . .' I said. 'I happen to work for that lawyer.'

'Oh . . .' Shakeel stopped. 'I thought you were working with Lalith Mangharam?'

'That *is* Lalith Mangharam inside with him, and the lady is his solicitor, Nalini. You mean to tell me she's going to represent you? Are you outta your mind!? She's making a fool out of you . . .'

'Well, that's what she said . . . otherwise I would have called you only . . .'

'I'm glad you didn't . . . right now I've got my hands full.' I grabbed hold of Bharat's arm and began to guide him back inside. 'I don't have time for you right now, Shakeel. Call me tomorrow if that lady can't get you out. I'll try my best.'

'Wait just a minute . . . who is this lady?' Bharat asked Shakeel.

'She cut a deal with these guys to stick your neck into the oven,' I told him. 'Just so they could get Mateen Lakdawaala off the hook.'

'Is Mateen in there?' Bharat's eyes lit up.

'Just came.' Shakeel turned aside.

'Mateen was the one who paid you guys to follow the Volkswagen on the highway, wasn't he?'

'Well . . .' Shakeel murmured. 'Not exactly. You see, we had been following him a while.'

I looked at Bharat. His forehead started to form odd sorts of shapes and writhing patterns in the shadows. He looked back at me like I had nightblindness.

'As in?' I nudged Shakeel along.

'As in . . . we'd caught up with him in New Bombay . . . listen, don't tell anyone about this, but . . .' His tone suddenly tensed up. 'The guy who was driving the Volks runs an illegal go-karting complex off Palm Beach Road. We discovered it one night, and his security guards chased us out of there. There were these kids riding out there, in the middle of the night in floodlights. Some of them were on freakin' dune buggies. Crashing into each other and scraping through the fence of the racetrack. Smashing into lamp posts and banging into bundles of tyres. It was utter demolition! Complete carnage and mayhem. Worse than any of us are capable of. Even the worst bikers have some sense of civil decency. But this was a bunch of kids gone wild. The security guard told us they were a contingent of students from the nearby institute, but we didn't buy it. Something seemed off.'

'Where is this place?' Bharat asked.

'Uh . . . it's tough to locate. It's an unmarked lane. Listed on the map as Avnish Complex. Practically halfway into the mangroves.'

'You ever hear of that road of his?' I asked Shakeel.

'I know what that road is,' he paused, starting to shake, 'it's just that I hadn't gone there for many years, at least, ever since I went in. I had no idea what it's turned into . . .'

'And what's that?'

'A freakin' illegal amusement park.'

'What are you talking about?'

'I'm telling you, that's what I saw. I wouldn't be surprised if some of the kids didn't make it through their laps.'

'What road?' Bharat asked.

'We used to go racing there back in the day,' Shakeel said. 'But after a couple of people died out there, it became kind of spooked. No one wanted to take a chance to go there in the middle of the night. It became a kind of motorway Bermuda Triangle. Apparently, there's a ditch out there in the stretch of road that caves in, every once in a while, swallowing any passing vehicle in the ooze of the swamp just below it.'

'What nonsense.'

'At least that's what people say. No one wants to go there anymore, though. It's considered haunted. There was an incident of a crash in 2003 when it had just been built. There was this guy who was driving a Yamaha RX100 at top speed. He came in collision with a speeding Cielo, which was coming in at 120 on the return path. According to the injured driver who miraculously managed to survive the scrape, the biker flew halfway across the scenery with the impact. His body was never recovered.'

'Did you know that Moolchandani owned that plot of land?'

'I knew that Mateen Bhai had wanted it at one point. So naturally, when I informed him what had become of it and what I'd witnessed there, he was no doubt astonished. He told me to keep an eye on a silver Volkswagen Jetta roaming the compound, which we spotted last night at the track. We followed him all the way from New Bombay. We were crossing the Maheem Creek, when all of a sudden this Honda Civic starts chasing him on Reclamation. Turns out it was you.' He pointed to Bharat. 'We waited outside Khar police station. It took so long, some of the boys went over to CrackJack next door. But we kept up with him all the while, until he stopped to register us. He finally managed to overtake us towards the Sea Link, and obviously when we saw the crash, we scattered. I don't think the CCTV even picked us up; we were way behind. He just cruised right into the tollbooth.'

Nalini's number sprung up on my touchscreen. I immediately put it on silent. We slipped off a little further on out of Khar police station, all the way up to my car.

'What about the missed calls then?' I asked Shakeel, putting my phone away.

'Missed calls?'

'Don't you know,' I told them both. 'Moolchandani had frantically been trying to get in touch with Pawan Hiranandani for some reason or the other. Right before he crashed, he gave him five missed calls.'

'Well . . .' Shakeel giggled. 'Yaa, I heard about that. One of the bodyguards told me that . . .' He looked over and about both shoulders. 'Okay, now this is strictly between the three of us, alright?'

We both nodded.

'Well . . . the guy, Ganesh, out there said that Moolchandani had just recently purchased this Volkswagen Jetta from his "seth" (boss), and that it was a bit of a faulty piece of equipment.' He cupped the hollow of his fist around a cough. 'And Hiranandani knew this. That's why he sold that particular model to Moolchandani. He suspects it had something to do with the car. At first, he thought that maybe it was the brake pads or the power steering that might have snapped or something, but then on thinking about it, and testing out a feature on another piece of the same make, he arrived at quite a different opinion.'

'Moolchandani was going at 200 on the opening to the Sea Link.'

'I know,' Shakeel admitted. 'Not a great car to go in if you want to go at 200. There's a feature in it . . . though that Ganesh there had encountered similar troubles with . . .'

'Similar troubles?'

'I can probably guess what must have happened.' He bowed his head, like he had something to share that was strictly off the record, provided I didn't press it.

'Really?' I did.

His downcast eyes now slowly lifted into mine. He hesitated for a second, reckoning it was best for me to mind my own business and him his, but he proceeded anyway.

'There's a feature, which, if I'm guessing correctly, may or may not have been partly responsible for what happened this morning on the Sea Link.'

'I see . . .' I shook my head. 'And exactly what feature are we talking about here?'

'This thing called cruise control. You heard of it?'

'Sure.'

'Well,' He took a deep breath, 'the way Ganesh sees it is that apparently, the car was on cruise control.'

'Cruise control?' I repeated.

'That's right.' He crumpled his chin. 'You just leave it be and sit back and enjoy the ride on autopilot. Who needs a driver?'

'I know what cruise control is, dummy!' Bharat spat.

'Maybe Moolchandani was worried that it wasn't switching out of cruise control and that it was picking up speed without him being able to do anything about it.'

'So?'

'Maybe he was calling for help.'

'Help?'

'Don't you get it?' he finally lost his patience. 'It's the car that killed him. It got stuck in cruise control. Kept accelerating. Wouldn't stop no matter what.'

'A vehicle can't be held accountable for murder,' I said. 'It's an inanimate object. It can't be tried.'

'They don't have to put the car in jail; that's just the way it happened.' His incisors glistened a neon white which had by now grown into something of a trademark. The entire city had at one point expressed the urge to take a swing at those shiny white teeth.

Midnight Freeway

'I see . . .' I slowly drew back from him, and caught hold of Bharat's arm.

Nalini came out the gate. I ducked as she turned to catch sight of Shakeel.

'Eh . . . Shakeel . . .' she yelled out. 'Come here!'

Shakeel went trotting up at her command. I swiped Bharat into the corner of the brick wall that covered the front of the police station. We both hid behind a bush.

From the branched fringe of the overhanging foliage, we could see their shadows communicating in silhouette. I swept a glance across to the other side of the road to check for the red Honda City. It was gone.

'Easy now . . .' I said to myself. Bharat looked at me from the corner of his eyes, kind of strange.

As soon as the shadows cleared out of the gateway, we leapt into the car and made a dash for it before anyone on the inside caught sight of us.

'Whooo . . .' I let out a gust of relief once we swerved out of there. 'That was close . . .'

'Where are we going?' Bharat groaned.

'There's just one place that's safe for you right now, Bharat,' I said. 'Just one place that can keep you out of jail, provided you're admitted into their facility. The L.K.L.M. Provisional Home for the Medically Ill in New Bombay . . .'

FIFTEEN

We filled up some petrol at a truck stop before the Mahim Darga. Bharat was tallying the total from the loot in the poker set when I clipped shut the case, reminding him there was a CCTV installed at the petrol pump, and that if any of the staff were to get wind of what was lying in the passenger seat, they'd surely notify the nearest checkpost. He still emptied out a bundle from the silver-plated side of the set so that we could pay for the petrol.

I'd by now switched off my phone, swarming as it was with missed calls from Nalini and Lalith Mangharam, even a message from DCP Panth informing me that my client's presence was being eagerly waited on by all assembled at Khar police station. The dawn was beginning to approach over the scattered clouds. The time according to my watch was 5.45 a.m., the time I had dropped Bharat home the previous morning.

Bharat resumed his calculations once we hit Reclamation. '10-20-30-40-50 . . .' he muttered to himself, flipping through the notes. He began to divide the notes from the poker set into bundles of 2000s and 500s, fetching a packet of rubber bands from the glove compartment and arranging them tidily into wads of ten and twenty thousand each.

It's amazing the slimness with which an amount like that will stack up between the fingers. I always imagined twenty thousand to take up a handful. It weighed less than electronic money in the larger scheme of things. I'd pick a bundle that could fit easily into a chest pocket over 20 GB worth of notifications from the bank, any day.

'I'm much obliged, Bharat,' I said to him. 'That you're taking the trouble to do for me what I wouldn't have done for you. I was never particularly good at math; you see, economics was never my forte. I tended to excel in the humanities. But either way, I'll be glad to hear your count of the proceeds.'

'As in?'

'As in, everyone has a different count. We're not computers, you see, merely human. When I count that same set, I'm gonna come up with a different figure from the one you're heading towards. It's kind of like an interpretation. Everyone has their version of the facts.'

'Pass the Thums Up!' he gestured at the frost-speckled can we had picked up from the petrol pump, resting under my seat.

I shrugged about in my seat, trying to reach for the reclining lever and told him—'Save it! It's for the road.'

He threw himself back on his seat, and raised the window to gaze outside through half a layer of tinted glass.

'Pass the poker set,' I said.

Putting two and two together can sometimes be an unrewarding process, especially when the figures just add up to a jumbled set of associations that confound rather than clear up one's apprehensions.

'I can have your share transferred to your account,' I offered, concealing the metallic case under my seat in case the car was searched.

'Huh?' he grunted.

'Where you're going, you aren't gonna need it!'

I thought about what the night patrol jeep crossing the same spot we were on had witnessed heading south on the highway that morning. I guess being a night patrol cop isn't any different than working all night at a call centre, or rushing to Khar police station at 1 a.m. in your spare hours. You tend not to notice the more discreet happenings that would otherwise raise your antenna.

As we veered onto the flyover swooping past Mahim Creek, I thought long and hard about whether I'd missed anything on Moolchandani last to last night at the chowki. What he was up to, where he was going or coming back from, maybe New Bombay, considering the spot he ran into Bharat on. He was taking the turn from Reclamation to S.V. Road, possibly to head back to Mahim since he lived in the town, that much I was certain of, as was Bharat. He pointed out the exact spot where their vehicles had met. He was coming back from the highway, as he was on the opposite end of the much-contested signal.

If he was in any way responsible for a road where people went to die, he probably met with a just end. It was AI's way of imparting justice. Maybe his GPS had killed him, knowing where he had just been. I'd never heard of the automated mechanism of a car being responsible for the death of its driver, maybe a passer-by or pedestrian or an idiot kid crossing the road chasing after a cricket ball, but not the very entity in whose command its operations lay. That was about as close to a self-destruct mode the wizards that came up with these fancy notions had probably set in store, like the car itself felt like committing suicide. Some people think machines have a mind of their own, and aren't entirely incapable of errors of judgement in a human capacity. Somehow it made it feel all the more sinister as if the car itself were guilty of having been shipped illegally and had provisions for what to do in the event that its owner broke the law. Shut down—that's the only kind of justice AI knows, which in human terms, translates to death, if there is such a thing for machines. What happens to machines after they die or get discarded? What happens to those purposefully prefabricated electronic souls? Now that's a thought worth considering.

SIXTEEN

The Western Express Highway was empty at sunrise.
Not a tyre scraped its crumbling tar; its potholes all filled
with municipal cement, half mixed with God knows what
material. In the Monsoons, the roads would go all to
hell. The morning twilight was starting to show over the
grey horizon, with the fishing boats all making their way
out over the rumpled waters. The weather was cool, the
glimmer of a slight nip in the air—the sea wind blowing in
my face as I pulled the window down. Once we picked up
some speed and the engine purred along steadily, I had to
roll the window back up because of the thumping sound
the air makes, especially if only one has been left open.
It's deafening; feels like a piledriver in the eardrum. The
white stripes at the centre of the road darted drastically
before my eyes, flickering faster and faster as the car sped
up. The long, desolate stretch of sunlit highway wound
on indefinitely ahead towards the Bandra-Kurla Complex.
I could see the Sea Link from afar in my rear-view mirror—
the broad expanse of Bandra retreating behind me.

I placed my phone at the speedometer, and put the radio on. It was scrambled. All I could hear was the weather report in Marathi. The road was quite clear save for a few 12-tyre axle trucks, cement haulers, and water tankers that roared by on and off. I hadn't slept in over 48 hours, had taken a beating, a day in court, and a night at the police station. I took out all my withering annoyance on the accelerator, speeding up more than my capabilities or my car would allow.

'Can you pass the Thums Up!?' he yelled over at me.

I couldn't. Everything in the car was still as a snowflake, the ashtray kept wobbling about in its holder, and the sun flaps kept hitting the windscreen every once in a while, but neither of them succeeded in stifling up the composure of the atmosphere. We could bask endlessly in the cosiness of its enclosure. The interior of the Ford Ikon was like a tent, protecting us from the vast expanse outside.

Passing the Vashi toll was a welcome sensation, traversing the serpentine procession of vehicles stacked immaculately along the preceding bridge leading up to New Bombay. The spiralling flyovers criss-crossed over gleaming vistas of marble and glass, skyscraper monuments erected in honour of some obscure establishment peddling thermal plants and hardware manufacturing units. Navi Mumbai is altogether quite a different animal from the rest of the city, which seems entirely to have been shredded out of bewildering masses of concrete and beams of banal bricolage. Empty plots of a hundred square metres promised all the miracles of civilization. There were parts that were rapidly deteriorating into squalor and decay. All the teachings and prayers of the good old rural pilgrims had degenerated into a fistful of radio ramblings and a half-worn-out sign with a portrait of the promised land. There were signs of hotels, amusement parks, resorts, institutes, and townships, but no one had ever witnessed their existence or even anticipated their arrival.

An endless row of electricity poles branching out of a baroque electric substation flanked the onward path, as if in watchful mediation over land and sea—their network of wires entangled overhead, and trespassing onto the murkier innards of the dense vegetation just beyond.

Locating the Avnish Complex was not as arduous a task as I had anticipated. After shuffling past the vast housing colonies of CBD Belapur and bypassing Palm Beach Road, we arrived at a secluded industrial wasteland; a sort of anomaly on the map—a dead end in the winding no-entry lanes we had encroached upon, beyond which lay the mangroves—cordoned off from the residential sprawl—littered with debris, crooked girders, unused wrenches, and broken struts and rivets sinking dismally in the muck. We manoeuvred bumpily in through an opening in the vegetation that disseminated into a network of dirt roads, walkable pathways, and barely motorable routes up an incline, then past a grey water body (an inlet of some sort from the neighbouring creek), some five hundred square metres of entangled foliage, and finally through a brickyard to culminate at the foot of an enclosure of a gargantuan plot.

The emergence of this spectacle of engineering must certainly have puzzled many of the local administrative authorities. Who knows? Maybe the construction site had been sanctioned by the State Infrastructure, Industries, and Energy

Division, which was currently undergoing privatization. Yogesh Moolchandani had then probably contracted this work out to some infrastructure development firm or an industrial corporation like Larsen & Toubro, maybe even some other builders of considerably advanced significance.

The construction site must have caused plenty of inconvenience to all those sparse shanty-towns, jhopad pattis (ramshackle dwellings), and bandaged hutments that had the misfortune of having settled around it: the shriek of drills exceeding tolerable decibel levels, the pile-drivers thundering away day and night, the roar of interminable machinery, the dusty particulates encompassing all—every breath a cacophony of hammering, chiselling, gyrating sounds that grew more incessant with the intricacy of the activity, robbing many of their hard-earned slumber.

The sound was deafening . . . like the cast iron wind that accompanied it. The nights must have gotten louder; no one must have been able to sleep with the racket. They must even have tried to do something about it. Get it shut down, for God's sake. Give back the people their peace of mind. But no one heard their cries and tormented howls. All we could hear was the sound of those engines.

No one seemed to know what the work was for or what they were building. But the site appeared to be growing more ominous in its outer structure as the work churned on, stretching beyond its aluminium-clad boundary. I parked the car at a stray clearing in the mangroves and asked Bharat to hand me the 9mm from the glove compartment.

There were corrugated aluminium casks that had been conjoined into a miserable excuse for a perimeter or boundary wall, which was 12 feet high and ran along the entire property, preventing anyone from looking in. At the entrance of the premises, through an inconspicuous gap in the metallic fencing, there entered a series of trucks, JCBs, cement haulers, yellow XCMG cranes, and other large-scale transportation vehicles carrying dismantled hardware and motor equipment towards an adjacent excavation site, curtained by the haze it was so fiercely emanating. A whole lot of construction workers were all at it with their picks and shovels. A delegation of officials had been sent to inspect the ongoing work at the site. One of the supervisors was ranting out orders in Marathi over a loudspeaker. A siren went off as all workers were rounded up for a medical examination at the Control Office.

Bharat just looked on at this site of industrial mayhem and marvelled at the ingenuity of an engineering enterprise of this magnitude, trying to make sense of all the ongoing development around him. Next to the Control Office lay the contractor's shed, behind which were chained a line of rusty cycles, mopeds, and Kinetics in haphazard postures, all blocked by a red Mahindra three-legged tempo double-parked alongside what appeared to be Bharat's maroon Honda Civic, sinking tyre-deep in the muck.

He at once checked the number plates, visibly startled. I circled the shed to poke through a half-open window but caught nothing but the spin of a table fan blowing all sorts of papers and documents off an empty desk. Then, all of a sudden its autocop beeped, and the locks spun open. We both gathered around it, our necks twisting sideways, and our eyes leaping to and fro. There was no sign of anyone in the vicinity that could have pressed that button, even the door to the contractor's shed blurted out but a phantom stir, a faint creak that sparked my apprehensions into motion.

From afar loomed out, in large blue lettering over the archway of a three-storey warehouse, 'VIMAL S2K MOTOR REHABILITATION PLANT'.

'I guess this is where cars come to die . . .' I mumbled, half to myself.

'Wha?' Bharat's mouth slid open.

As we proceeded slowly along the aluminium perimeter, I wondered why the enterprise was being conducted in such acute secrecy.

Beyond the five indistinct sectors that the construction site had been divided into, lay a taller and more incongruous boundary wall, separating the centre of most activity from a deeper corner of industrial mayhem, that was being carried out more discreetly, but with a more prominent deployment of manual labour. Due to the large and overbearing structure of the enclosure, this section was not visible at once to the general public. It was situated on a more singular terrain that lay below sea level, surrounded by the shadowy slant and crest of two converging hillocks which merged into the peripheral marsh that lay ahead in the distance. One would have to climb the hills to a more elevated altitude in order to peep over the calculatedly concealed boundary wall.

After having strolled about considerably in the hopelessness of our predicament, we decided to satisfy our curiosity by climbing up the hill to find out what it is that they were building.

173

Some of the personnel from the construction site had taken notice of this intrusion, and tentative form of trespassing.

'What about my car?' Bharat inquired as we made our way up.

'You can forget about it.' I sighed, not out of sympathy, but out of exertion.

'You mean I should just leave it lying here to rot and die?' he huffed.

'That's exactly what I mean. Right now, that car is hotter than a sack of burning embers. It's a vital piece of evidence for our case.'

'But I thought you said it hasn't moved?'

'Well, it hadn't,' I muttered. 'But now it has!' That shut him up.

After a long and troubled hike up the hillock, we reached the midpoint. I cusped the palms of my hands around my forehead in the shape of a pair of binoculars and tried to grasp what lay ahead, concealed by the hill, but alas, to no avail. We had another couple of hundred metres or so to go before we could cross over to the other side of the hillock in order to gaze into the concealed area. We crawled up the rocky paths and navigable walkways until we reached the peak. We halted a moment to catch our breath after the strenuous ascent, and proceeded steadily downwards from the opposite side of the hill.

We were now far above the level of the boundary wall, and could almost see the structure that was tirelessly being worked upon and had attained considerable progress. We walked further ahead, up to the point that provided a better view for us to gaze into the innermost reaches of this apparition. And there it stood in all its languid glory! In its grey gloom and guilt. The monstrosity that had been eagerly anticipated for by its builders and had stretched itself imposingly upon the horizon. A vast colony of 18-storey buildings, half-built and empty. Like a silent monster in the wake of its genesis. Innumerable cubicles had been proportionately carved out of its edifice. Uninhabited blocks of cement-lined cells, each the same size. Would-be homes of the nameless, faceless multitudes.

In the sole building of this colony that seemed inhabited, I identified at once what carried the insignia of the L.K.L.M. Provisional Home for the Medically Ill. We made our way down into the compound, sliding through a narrow slit in the aluminium fence. We swayed in past the vacant watchman's cabin at the slim shaft-like gate, and walked on towards the approaching lobby.

A Nehru topi-wearing, white-uniformed watchman was gaping into a CCTV monitor at the front desk like he was watching the 9 o'clock news. Another official was straightening his sideburns with a pocket comb in front of a gold-framed mirror, and doing his moustache with his pinkie while looking the other way from his reflection. None of the assembled security personnel paid us as much as a glance at first. Another chowkidaar in a watchman's outfit was busy lounging about and leafing through the newspapers stacked up on a magazine rack next to the mirror. They knew how to pass the time; they didn't need any help from us in that department.

As we headed towards the elevator, the white-uniformed watchman stumbled out of his stupor and stood up from his monitor.

'Yes?' he inquired, in a stiff tone of premature defensiveness. He pointed at a sign above the glass door to the stairway, which said 'STRICTLY NO VISITORS ALLOWED'.

'We're here to admit a new patient.' I pointed at Bharat.

By now, the other two had taken notice of us. The three of them started to make towards us as I retreated a few steps in the direction of the lift. 'By the name of Bharat Morwani.' I pulled Bharat along.

The three of them stopped. 'I see,' said the topi-wearing official. He took off his cap and straightened it out like a paper boat before placing it back on his head.

'First floor to your right. You'll find Dr Anusha Madam at the reception. Right this way!' The man pointed at the lift, going back to his desk and monitor.

We got into one of the elevators and decided to explore the first floor. The whir of the ascending elevator took longer than it usually would to climb only one flight of stairs. It seemed like a century before the elevator doors parted, and the bright tube-lit corridor before us resembled many of the hospitals I had visited over the course of my long and illustrious medical backlog.

I glanced into one of the clinics through a partially open door: a young man lay practically paralysed. He couldn't even wriggle his fingers. He lay prostrate on a bed with an ingratiating nurse taking his temperature, and a doc gaping into his half-shut eyes like he was a specimen of scientific significance—a bonafide nutcase. Someone to chuck into the garbage can with one hand tied to the lid. He was dressed in some kind of an inmate's garb. A pair of striped pyjamas and a white t-shirt that he probably wouldn't be seen dead in, in other circumstances. He had a distinguished look about him that carried the faint whiff of old Bawa aristocracy.

'He's coming to,' the doc declared.

I couldn't tell if he was conscious or in a swoon.

'I'd like to see my lawyer,' were the first words that escaped his lips when he was fully awake.

'What's his name?' A hazy light blinked at him from up above.

'Adv Ashok Singhania . . .'

'Contact number?'

'98452 . . .' the numbers started to scatter as he spoke.

The doc probably thought he was not in his senses.

'Why don't you just get some rest,' he suggested. 'The police'll be here any minute to take your statement.'

'The . . . p-police?'

'That's right. It's just a necessary formality. You have nothing to be worried about, that is unless, of course, you were under the influence . . . then there's not much we can do about that.'

'Under the influence . . . of what?'

'Of alcohol,' he chuckled, looking sideways at the nurse. 'What else?'

The nurse's shiny white teeth must have been too much to take. Almost like a Pepsodent commercial. The guy suddenly started convulsing at their appearance as if he was having a stroke.

'You don't know who I am . . .' was the next thing he said.

'Why don't you just lie back and relax . . .' the doc persisted.

'You know who I am?' he asked again, regaining whatever composure was left in him.

'What?' the doc's eyes narrowed. This time even the nurse leaned forward to comprehend just what the hell he was saying.

'Listen to me . . .'

'Listen, Zain,' The doc declared again in his calm bedside manner, 'Why don't you just get some rest . . .'

He grabbed hold of the doctor's collar and nearly strangled him, before he was restrained by the nurse, who did an efficient job of pulling him back. His arms fell all over the side of the bed, his lower body nearly toppled off of it. His eyes bulged out of their sockets like he was starting to see shapes and patterns in the overhead tube lights. Just then, I noticed the same sinister-looking Sindhi aunty I had spotted at Khar police station standing in the corner of the clinic, next to a glass window. She was studying the patient from afar with her arms ominously folded, and her eyes doing multiplications and subtractions.

'Eh . . . I know that lady . . .' Bharat pointed.

'Shhh . . . keep quiet.' I batted his hand away.

As we carried on past the clinic into the deeper recesses of the corridor to gaze at the other patients in the ward, it soon became apparent that we were in the midst of some kind of deranged procession of dormitories on either side: muffled shrieks and jungle cries rang out across the glass frames mounted upon burly wooden doors, consigning them to a state-sanctioned doom. Patients mummified in full-body plaster, dislocated shoulder blades strung up to brass bedposts, an endless array of fractures, concussions, haemorrhages, deformities, anatomical abominations of what could have only been the result of the most atrocious car crashes in motor vehicular history. There were all kinds of injuries in varying states of deterioration.

Once we got up to the end of the corridor, where the stairway slanted upwards, past another opaque glassy door, I noticed a pile of bedpans resting along the polished floor, containing relics of mucus long forgotten by the human bodies from which it had spewed forth. All windows were drawn shut, shunning all daylight from the outside. Artificial illumination seemed the order of the day in this settlement.

We gradually ascended the steps up to the second floor, escaping all notice; immersed as the officials were in examining their spoils. The varnished walls of the staircase reminded me faintly of my college—a building that did not like to think of itself as such, and wore the pretence of a Polytechnic campus or a renowned institution. Charts and childrens' drawings decorated the second-floor corridor on all sides. Green notice boards stretched on, carrying pictures of skin and mouth diseases; a pale improvement on those seen on cigarette packets of the day. From afar, I felt I could unmistakably hear what sounded like an old '90s Bollywood beat. A dance class was underway, conducted by an over-zestful, mullet-wielding dance and choreography instructor who was enacting upper torso exertions for everyone to follow. A gym and fitness centre lay next door, where a battalion of ward boys was admonishing agitatedly the convalescent youngsters entrusted under their care. A chap who looked no more than twenty was being made forcefully to run on a treadmill, the speed of which beepingly increased with the overseer's wrath. Shouts and dreadful implications were tossed about with the simian nonchalance of a military bootcamp. Most hideous of all horrors lay above on the third floor, where the droning buzz of medical machinery and the hum of a hand-fan breezing the endless corridor spoke terrible ruins of what was left of human life. Corpses were wheeled out on wide metallic food trays and stretchers by similar Nehru-topied, white-uniformed officials.

We were the only ones to be seen wearing casuals, and so being, we caught the attention of a nurse with yellowed hands, wiping the residue off her fingernails on a starched apron.

'Yes?' she asked, with an approaching air of dread, her eyeballs scanning the path we had taken to arrive there.

'Hi . . .' I greeted her. 'I've got a patient for you.'

'You'll have to go to the first floor. Dr Anusha Upadhyay will be seated at the admittance counter. May I see some form of identification, please?' her eyes still reached for anyone in the vicinity who could corroborate our presence.

'I'm afraid I left it in the car.'

She took us to the fifth floor via the elevator. We conversed briefly about the nature of Bharat's case, and I informed her that I was sent by his parents to deliver him to their care.

'Right this way, please,' she said, as we stepped out of the elevator.

Four men in white lab coats, their faces covered with surgical masks, filed out of an adjacent operating room and shoved past us, barely acknowledging the nurse. She guided us into an empty antechamber adorned with stacks of board games, puzzles, and video game CDs. A muted Sony LCD was playing 'Mahasangram' on CVO, and the explosions were still perceptible, even though they weren't audible. The set-top box perched atop it had a wire extension plugged into an input port on its back that stretched down to a PlayStation 4 resting at the base of the TV stand. It was wrapped with a wire which converged into a sort of locking device at the power button. An adjacent paper notice taped to the wall proclaimed: 'Authorized Playing Hours: 9 a.m.–11 a.m./7.30 p.m.–9.30 a.m.'

An Alienware desktop sat by the side of the antechamber, next to a half-empty bookcase. I started to admire a CD case balanced right at the edge of the side flap of the keyboard tray. The lock to its zip had been somehow unclipped. A rectangular GeForce 3 graphics card sat next to a mousepad as smooth as a baby's bottom. The entire CD case was filled from top to bottom with a wide variety of RPG first-person shooter games—Doom, Quake 3 Arena, Unreal Tournament, CounterStrike—car crash mayhem games like Midtown and Motor Cross Madness, Daytona, NFS 3: Hot Pursuit, Carmageddon, and Road Rash. It all started to come back to me—all impulsiveness of an absent-minded youth. The inadequacies of an impressionable personality type. *The one who'd rather simulate experience than live it.*

I slipped out of the rec-room to glimpse the adjacent operating chamber, where a red UV light beamed over a lone patient's swollen varicose-veined legs. He was strapped to a bed with the aid of two belt-buckle contraptions, one over his upper torso and the other pinning his thighs down to the mattress.

The nurse, who I had expected to see waltzing around outside the antechamber in a watchdog capacity, had vacated the dim, endless corridor. Just as soon as I started to move into the operating room, I caught the rustle of some movement from its toilet. Another lab-coated gent with a fluorescent green face mask emptied out of it rather roughly, barking out something or the other to the lad who lay on the bed.

The elevator dial blinked orange before its doors opened, letting out the Sindhi lady from the first floor, who wasn't quite as opulently decked to the gills as she had been last night at the police station. She caught me loitering about outside the antechamber and immediately introduced herself as Sharan Murpana. She then stepped inside to have a look at the new patient.

'I'm currently chief of operations at this facility while my husband is on leave,' she said. 'If I'm not mistaken, you were at Khar police station last night, am I right?'

'That's right,' I affirmed. 'I saw you there too, right outside the PI's cabin. I presume your husband was having a word with him in private.'

'That's right.' She sniffled. She didn't look like she'd slept a wink all night either. On noticing Bharat, she sat down beside him in a classroom desk-chair.

'How are you feeling today, Bharat?'

'Fine, miss, thank you,' he muttered.

Her eyes enlarged as she examined his dried-up bruises from the night before last. 'I had a word with your parents last evening at Khar police station,' she said. 'They seem to be extremely concerned about you.'

'What did they say?' his face grew still.

'Nothing in particular. Just about your general aimlessness and indiscipline. They're concerned about your future. You didn't complete your correspondence course from Mumbai University. The speaker shop, Nirmala, was robbed a month ago and hasn't picked up sales to remedy that fiscal disbalance. Do you have any concrete notions at all about where you see yourself in the next couple of years, and how you want to spend the prime of your youth? What do you want to do with this irreplaceable time?'

'Not really . . .'

'Well, that's where we come in.' She smiled. 'At the L.K.L.M. Provisional Home for the Medically Ill, we provide our patients with a wide variety of recreational activities to enliven their spirits. Multiple forms of invigoration, which, how shall I say . . .' She tilted her head back and reached for the sky. 'Uplift and exhilarate!' She spread her hands out in the air. 'By bringing youngsters that would have otherwise had rather normal lives, to encounter extraordinary circumstances. It can cure apathy of any kind. Give you a fresh outlook on things.'

'Is there a name for this treatment?' he asked, retrieving her from her reverie.

'There is . . .' she opened her eyes and widened them as she spoke, 'It's an international course of sorts. State-certified, and approved by the most renowned experts in neuro-therapy. "Re-schooling", we call it. You see . . . the attempt is to take the fully-grown individual to the childlike state, and first deconstruct to then rebuild. This way, the person has another chance.' She graciously bowed her head, producing the car keys to his Honda Civic and dangling them before his eyes. 'We're here to give you direction.'

'Where did you get a hold of that?' Bharat quaked.

'Career counselling,' she continued, 'The education that most of you missed out on due to callousness.'

Bharat pulled his nerves together and asked softly, with much courtesy. 'Ma'am, please tell me how you have the keys to my car?'

'You know, it's not actually your fault . . .' she went on, unhindered by his queries. 'Haha . . . I, too, never really paid much attention in class.' This change of tone somewhat startled rather than baffled Bharat. 'School and college years aren't the only ages for education. The human mind only starts to fully develop after graduation. It's never too late to start afresh. Give it another try. If you fail, pick yourself up and try again. Spend your days in a healthy and wholesome manner.'

'Just how exactly do you intend to go about all this?' I asked, from a distant corner of the rec-room, hearing every word with the keenest precision.

'Well . . .' she turned to me now as if addressing a lesser mortal, not one of any consequence, but who was there only in what might be categorized as a menial capacity, at least by them. 'As you know, this is a state-sanctioned private training centre.'

'Training centre?'

'We provide facilities out here that are unique and utterly inconceivable at any other public outpost.'

'Isn't this a private institution?'

'More like an institute. An installation of sorts. Why don't I give you a tour of the ninth floor? Show you both around.'

This time when we got into the elevator, some dispassionate muzak accompanied us on our way up. It was identifiably Yaani crossed with the Super Mario tune on an electronic synthesizer.

We arrived on the ninth floor to a sort of elaborate cyber cafe, replete with Xerox machines and colour printers, scanners, a wilderness of antennae, endless rows of circuit boards and byzantine networks of PVC electric conduits tangled around a crab-like modem, all kinds of tentacular wires pouring out of its sides. Spread out before us were a series of monitor screens on which Counter-Strike was being played by a bunch of guys on individual computers against each other in full vigour. Sounds of machine-gun firings, bomb explosions, radio communication receivers, and bullets reloading, rambled out intermittently at brief, abrupt, irregular intervals. The kids all looked like experts at the game.

Calls of 'FIRE IN THE HOLE!', 'Who planted the bomb!?' 'OH, SHIT!!!', 'You have to go to secondary equipment!', a sound byte saying 'COUNTER-TERRORISTS WIN' emanated sporadically all around us in fitful bursts of jubilation.

When she took us into the labyrinthine server room at the back, I asked—'Are all these kids survivors of car crashes?'

'Not all of them,' she explained. 'Some of them merely had close shaves, and are in perfect physical shape. You see, when this place was undeveloped, it was something of a notorious hangout for speeders, people on the lookout for reckless kicks. Yogesh had leased it out to some shady realtor in Thane, and he'd send all his biker boys to come and parade around the open stretches. It was even an attraction for some of the more affluent types known to haunt the roads at irregular hours. You know the kind,' she smiled at Bharat, 'who just keeping going round and round in circles through the city, and sometimes wind up off the map, finding themselves in areas and territories they never bargained for. Now come here . . .' She took us near the back window of the server room. She pointed out into the distance at a sort of depression in the surrounding landscape, a marshy crater circled by sparse green—inside of it dwelt only dark grey; a sludge of quicksand that could have easily doubled up as asphalt if one were crossing it with only the beam of a headlight. The quagmire formlessly disguised itself in a declivity on the road. There were mounds and swells and motorable paths branching out from all corners of the construction site, through unpredictable openings in the mangroves and adjoining hillocks. 'They call this the Bermuda Triangle of New Bombay,' she said. 'Cars are said to have disappeared, whole—without a trace within its muck, and drowned in the inland creek just below it. This is all,' she spread her hands out, 'after all, reclaimed land!'

She started to walk us back out, deciding we'd seen enough for one day.

'But sometimes you know . . .' she frowned, as we walked along, observing the mayhem around us. 'The vehicles are recovered—especially the more expensive and bulkier ones. There's a drainage pit some thirty to forty feet below the ground that travels through numerous channels to spill out eventually into the neighbouring sea. Those that manage to escape its whirling clutches find themselves offshore on the edge of the landfills, unscathed yet somehow changed by that baptism in the septic abyss.'

Bharat stared on, silent—his gaze traversing vast landfills and an infinity of subterranean sewer systems.

'And it was perhaps in light of that,' she continued, mischievously studying Bharat's bewildered awe, 'that some of the authorities, in conjunction with Yogesh, had resolved to set up a sort of rest and recuperation facility for the wealthier victims who were known to take steps, or sometimes drops, into the unknown. Some of these people have never gone back home after their trysts with destiny, reborn as it were. Some of them have been committed by their families in lieu of lightening up certain maladies that were proving to be fatal . . .'

'Such as?' I ventured to inquire.

'You can never really comprehend the mind of the adrenaline junkie!' Her eyes deadened, and the corner of her lip curled downwards unsympathetically. 'It's like the kleptomaniac or the trigger-happy madman. It's all a sensation that they're after. So we can provide that happily for them here, without anyone getting hurt. But . . .', here she turned and emphasized this, 'provided it is under our supervision and as per our itinerary.'

The elevator on our way down to the fifth floor was again empty. No one seemed to require its services as much as we did. The piano music, too had deserted it. She led us back to the antechamber where she hoped to leave us, as she probably had more pressing matters to attend to and had designated enough time for an introductory tour to a new inmate. Only, I stopped her once again with a query, 'And what are your rates like?'

She froze, absolutely still, and looked to Bharat. 'Could you please inform your lawyer that he is free to leave now, and that we will take absolute and complete charge of you from here on? Thank you!' She tried to fake a smile, but nothing formed but a frown.

I again stalled her at the doorway, 'Excuse me Ma'am . . . but how exactly am I to explain this to his parents?'

'Well, that is none of your concern!' she stipulated.

'It kind of is, you see. I represent the family interests.' I unnoticeably winked at Bharat.

'I've already had a word with them . . .' she restated.

'I can't very well tell them that this is a video game academy they're admitting Bharat to. I know it's a lucrative profession, I had a friend once who took part in a Counter-Strike tournament and won 2 lakhs from it. But I don't think any of the contents of this building are inclined in that direction. Firstly, they don't seem to need the money. They probably have the abilities and the will, but . . .'

'WHAT NONSENSE!' she bellowed, now suddenly overcome with indignation. 'This is much more than just that! You don't know what you're talking about, young man!'

'I'm not that young. At least, not as young as your inmates.'

'This is a medical endeavour,' she shouted, her cheeks wobbling ferociously, 'and partly psychiatric too, for your kind information. But thankfully, with the state's co-operation, what we're giving you here are the amenities of a cyber academy.

We have the fastest internet connection in New Bombay,' she boasted. 'A server that links all authorized networks into a recruitment base at the ground level.'

'A WHAT!?' Bharat nearly had a stroke with this news.

'A . . . uh . . . uh . . . degree of sorts . . .' she stumbled around her unwitting announcement, easily extracted by my insinuations. 'Internationally-renowned. Recognized world over.'

'You mean to tell me I'm going to have to sit for a course?' Bharat's eyebrows expanded. 'Give exams, attend classes . . . out of the question, Ma'am!'

'N-n-n-no . . . not exactly . . . you see . . .' she stuttered. 'It's much more fun than all that!'

'Fun?' he gasped.

'You're talking about a cyber cell!' I stated.

'Those with the requisite talents to engage in cyber-warfare, drone targetting, virtual combat,' she spilt out accidentally, and then realized shortly thereafter that she had done so. 'Don't you understand? The state has sub-contracted this out to a private firm, which happens to be us. Numerous companies have set up branches and wings all over Panvel and Thane. Don't you see the scope of the operation? The difference we're trying to make!'

'What are you talking about?'

'Gamers,' she smirked, 'racers, pool-hustlers, card-sharks, you know the sort. Those equipped with the geometric precision that determines a hit from a miss.' She spoke with something of the unmistakable precision of a schoolteacher or motivational speaker, or even a seminar conductor. Her articulacy baffled me. 'Calculating their scores for some invisible victory with the universe,' she continued. 'On cell phones, joysticks, and portable devices. The shadow talent that goes undetected by ordinary scrutiny. How else could our vast and endless variety of misguided youth be expected to provide some legitimate service to society without proper instruction? Without, of course, resorting to petty forms of criminality, that is. Sometimes it doesn't work. We have what you could refer to as terminal cases. No amount of counselling, explaining or even sermonizing can help salvage the decay within. But I know there's hope for some of them yet,' she said in reference to Bharat. 'There are always fighters!'

'And virtual commandos.' I laughed.

'It's never too late for a person to change their ways— even the ones beyond repair. The rectification and reform of a misguided individual is merely a matter of common sense and effort. If you can convince them that going straight and following the law is in their best economic interest, then you might have an argument that holds water with the wavering convictions of the criminal mind.'

'So, you aim to set up a network of affluent criminals?'

'Not always, you see. Their characteristics are determined by the technological appliances they've had access to during the course of their upbringing. Usually, this pertains mainly to those of a hereditary income bracket that might permit the purchase of a PlayStation, at the very least a car that's able to cross a hundred and twenty kilometres per hour. Any sort of destructive toy that can be yielded to produce a beneficial purpose in the long run, to society. Now, this is a special qualification and one granted only to those who've enjoyed a leisurely youth.'

'Who owns this place?' I asked.

'As I said, it's a state-sanctioned . . .'

'Who built it?' I specified.

'Ahh . . . my husband's late partner Yogesh, who I believe you are familiar with. That's why my husband is unable to be with us at present. He's currently at the crematorium seeing to his last rites. I couldn't make it due to some other pressing matters downstairs . . .' she coughed.

'You mean Zain?' I smiled. She didn't answer.

There was a gentle lull in the air, artificial as it was. The central air-conditioning of the entire floor suddenly stalled and then rebooted.

'Did you know that Yogesh was killed by his own car?' I asked her.

She didn't say a word in reply, only asked if we'd like any refreshments.

'Purchased by a renowned car smuggler of some disrepute,' I added, to convene her sparse attentions.

'Mr Hiranandani . . .' She took a long, deep breath, as if she'd answered the question a million times, 'is currently with my husband, seeing to the proper cremation and funeral services of the deceased.'

'Are they in business with one another?'

'I don't exactly know what you mean?'

'What does he have to do with this place?'

'He merely supplies us with second-hand automobiles from time to time for our activities, and also certain car parts, equipment, hardware, and machinery for the Motor Rehabilitation Plant.'

'And Mateen Lakd waala?'

At his name, she baulked. She didn't want to admit to his acquaintance, but nonetheless did when the room cooled down to her convenience. 'You see, without Mr Lakdawaala's invaluable participation while he was still in office, this project would have been practically impossible to administer and set into motion. Without his contributions, both legal and administrative, we would not have been able to obtain the state's more than generous donations to do the work that would be required to set up an establishment of this magnitude and far-reaching scope. You see,' this she addressed entirely to Bharat, 'The Central Social Welfare Board had conducted a survey back in 2015 on the number of family members per household engaged on a daily basis in recreational virtual gaming. Arriving at an estimate that far surpassed their wildest suppositions, they came to see the video game itself as serving a potentially utilitarian function. They found in its boundless precincts, a landscape akin to the church or collective grounds of daily congregation for enforcing obedience to a said set of rules; an effective implement for the transmission of certain therapeutic methods that could transfer the moral alignment of a human being. Just as yoga works to readjust the alignment of the bone structure and its intricate joints, so do our myriad techniques at achieving a harmonious development!'

'Harmonious development?' I demurred.

'That's right,' she turned back to me. 'The essential goal is the attainment of harmonious development in all facets of life. Geometric precision, exactitude, clarity, calculation—a single-minded approach to mathematical certainty. Particularly to those unable to achieve their goals through physical means. When one gives direction to the misdirected, you are doing not only a favour to their minds, but also to their souls. This, in essence, is the current objective of this initiative. Which is why Mr Lakdawaala and Pawan Hiranandani have helped to bring this enterprise as close to official status as the current predicament would warrant. We are, after all, looking at a looming landscape of unthinkable cybernetic complexity. This is only step one in a programme to build a force incrementally that can aid the state in its cyber capabilities.' She paused, and thought a while about that possibility.

'Then that's probably why they bumped Yogesh off,' I had the gall to speculate. 'To get his name off the property and manipulate the concerned paperwork to Mateen's advantage.'

She was no doubt alarmed at my insinuation.

'What did you say?' She squinted at me, her whole manner now stiffening up beyond the bounds of knowable courtesy.

'Nothing . . .' I played along, looking downward. 'I was just joking.'

'Excuse me, are you trying to suggest my husband had something to do with Yogesh's demise?'

'Well, what are you doing with Bharat's car keys then?'

This she didn't have an answer to yet.

'Considering that it should be in the possession of the police?' I added.

'I don't think you should pay much heed to his speculations,' she informed Bharat. 'We can even get you another lawyer if you'd like.'

Bharat quavered. 'Listen, miss, may I please make a phone call to my parents . . .'

'When there happens to be a dispute,' I said, 'between the builders of such an elaborate organization, there's just one recourse; state intervention.'

'It's only for the better,' she said. 'In some cases, the might of the state is the only desirable alternative to the incapacities of private management. They have, after all, supplied us with a team of specialists in the fields of both psychometry and neuro and nanotechnology. A department that schools students on the fundamentals of hacking and programming. Advanced strategists that will pave the way for a brighter morrow, and provide these children with a future where their assets are harnessed and put to tasks that would fulfil both a public and private function.'

'Wait a minute . . .' Bharat gasped. 'My parents would have never signed up for this.'

'Aha . . .' she coughed. An old woman's ruffled cough. As she cleared her throat, she spoke again, this time plainly and with no expression whatsoever. 'They claim you're suffering from some kind of disorder, the nature of which has not been brought to my attention yet. We shall commence your treatment by conducting a variety of tests. Rupesh!' she called out. An orderly crossing the outside corridor promptly brought the doctor from the adjacent operating room into the antechamber. He briefly lowered his green surgical mask and bowed his head at his madam.

'This is Dr Sarveshwar Roy. Chief-in-charge of our Neural-Response wing. He shall take three different sets of blood samples; one to check for any signs of chemical imbalance, the other for a platelet count, and also one to verify what sorts of intoxicants might still be floating about your bloodstream, so that they may be cleared out and we can provide for you a natural form of relaxation and excitement, possibly even adrenaline, if you're in good shape by the evening for our nightly detours.' She swung out his car keys again. 'That is why we are in possession of your personal automobile. It will be required for our programme.'

With that, she strolled out of the doorway in her Sindhi half-strut, like she was exiting a nightclub, in order to leave us alone with Dr Sarveshwar Roy. As the door clasped shut and the doc detected the irregular bulge on the side of my hip that started to take the shape of a gun, his eyes fell and he started to move back from it—but before he could exit the room, I pulled out the semi-automatic from my side pocket and told him to remain absolutely still and not breathe a word. I couldn't see his mouth move, so I couldn't tell whether he was tense or in command. His eyes concealed any anxiety he might have possessed in the flurry of the moment, they were deadly still—just as I had asked them to be. He now started to take two tentative steps towards Bharat, fully confident that he could take care of whatever the hell was happening right before his unbelieving eyes.

'I said, be still!' I repeated.

He didn't listen, and tried to reach for Bharat's unprotected arm. I immediately pistol-whipped him tightly on the chest and

195

he let out an 'ooooooooffff!'. His upper torso fell forward to the floor in an instant, and as I cocked the gauge and unhatched the safety, his left hand caught hold of my leg from beneath me. He started tugging at my leg with all the force that was left in him. He began to chew on my leg, biting hold of it, his teeth tearing into my calf muscle. It was worse than a dog bite contracted from a rabid Doberman. He just kept going for my leg, trying to pull me down below with him. Bharat just sat there expressionless, watching me drag him all the way around the antechamber, trying my damnedest to clamp down on a shriek that could escape me most urgently on account of this sudden burst of pain. I could feel the blood trickling down to my ankles. I grabbed hold of the PlayStation from beside the TV and smacked him three times over the head with it. The CD drive burst open, with cracked shards of 'Warcraft 3: Frozen Throne' spilling all over his hair. The final hardened plastic 'THWACK' put an end to his vigorous motions, and he finally collapsed, falling to one side and flopping over. I quickly darted out to check that no one had heard the struggle. There were some officials shuffling past the corridor towards the elevator, but they looked like they were in a hurry to attend to a far graver case. I immediately bolted shut the door from inside. Bharat still hadn't moved a muscle. He just looked at me practically zombified, his jowls drooping down to his chin, the whites of his eyes growing into a bulge, like I had done a terrible thing whose advantage he would want to refrain from making use of. I dragged the semi-conscious doctor to the bathroom. It was a handicapped toilet with acrylic bars spread out laterally across the commode. I took off his face mask and lab coat, quickly tied them on, and leapt out of the lavatory, leaving him by the wet floor.

I placed Bharat onto a vacant wheelchair that sat by the side of a sofa and wheeled him out of the antechamber to speed up to the elevator, which had just descended carrying the load of officials I had narrowly escaped. I pressed agitatedly at the lift button, trying to call it back up before it was too late.

'Where you taking me?' Bharat inquired from his chair.

'Home.'

The elevator doors cleared, and another, more authoritative nurse emerged from it, acknowledging my labcoat and surgical mask with a nod.

'Where are you taking him?' she asked.

'To the gymnasium.'

'Hmmm . . .' she approved. 'Bit of exercise would do him some good. Wouldn't it now?' She bent down, addressing Bharat like a two-year-old child.

Bharat kept stubbornly silent, letting out only a grunt in reply.

SEVENTEEN

The lobby was miraculously empty when we crossed it on the way out. The blokes we had encountered on our way up were probably *way* up by now. Possibly on one of the top floors. It was getting to be breakfast-time, and the staff canteen was said to be up above. Whatever obstruction that might have prevented our swift but definite exit seemed to be far, far away. As though the building itself were taking a brief nap. Even some of the lights that otherwise might have filled up a structure of this size appeared surprisingly diminished, as if they were trying to save up on electricity or something by switching them off after a few hours of use. As we stepped out of the lobby and I rolled Bharat down a luggage ramp, I gazed up at the monolithic tower above us to witness not more than five or six floors alight. White plastic blinds covered the windows above leaky air conditioner rears jutting out of the parapets. I could sense a sort of vibration from down below that grew into palpability the more one thought of it. Maybe it was just the effect of all the electronic equipment embedded firmly in the fabric of the building: the intangible ache one feels after having clutched onto a mobile phone for too long, or the imaginary radiation that pours out of a heated CPU after long hours spent in front of a computer. But as we proceeded on, I felt certain that there seemed to be some kind of a mechanical whirring sound emanating from the very foundation of the building. We made towards the exit point of the building, crossing a glassed-in meter room covering a block of electrical units with a sign on it reading, 'DANGER HIGH VOLTAGE'.

The watchman was again nowhere to be seen. The crackling of a mosquito-killing grill-lamp was the only sound that escaped the watchman's cabin from afar. While walking out of the building premises, I noticed a topless youth sitting on the muddy ground on the other end of the watchman's cabin, hiding himself in the folds of its shadow. We asked him for directions out of this place, and he softly obliged, pointing out into the distance of the heaps and mounds of rock and debris clogging the shambling landscape. Some of the construction work was still underway. From afar could be heard the thud of a bulldozer, or a JCB ploughing the earth in pursuit of progress. Smoke billowed out of a churning cylindrical tank and deposits of molten cement were laid out to rest before the yellow-helmet-wearing contractors' supervision. There were fewer labourers around at this hour of the morning; those on the nightshift had probably already clocked off from duty. Winding our way across the turgid terrain, the work grew louder and at times less shrill as we descended and then again scampered up some temporary ascent.

We started sneakily to scuttle across the excavation site once we had dismounted the hillock, our backs pressed firmly to the boundary wall. Bharat was by now almost about to collapse. The Chinese home delivery food he had been deprived of had taken its toll on his strength. I hadn't eaten anything either. We were both starving. I wondered if there would be a vada-pav stand anywhere nearby. Not even a peanut vendor had dared to venture into Avnish Complex.

'I'm not feeling so good.' Bharat sat down for a moment on the stony earth, his back resting against the seething aluminium perimeter. 'I think I'm about to hurl!'

'All that spurious Black Label,' I sneered. 'If you have to spew, make sure you don't make too much of a spectacle out of it! Try and keep it quiet, so nobody notices.'

'How the hell am I supposed to do that!?' he coughed, violently. His throat started to make a variety of sounds, which quickly began to draw attention even from afar, despite the ruckus the excavational artillery was making. It was a distinct sound of someone retching turbulently, and quite unlike anything the assembled apparatus was capable of emitting. Some of the construction workers started to look towards us. I covered Bharat immediately. It looked like even the Contractor had heard it.

'Just let it all out!' I instructed him. 'Nice and quiet.'

His eyes were watering profusely; his entire complexion had turned red. He tried to barf into the rocks beside him, but nothing substantial came out. The sounds grew more undignified as I kicked at him.

'There's someone coming here.' He hid his face once it stabilized.

I turned around. From the direction of the contractor's shed where Bharat's car was parked, a group of four to five men were heading determinedly towards us in official attire. Bharat recognized the one in a grey Armani work suit. It was Raptor, with his brother-in-law Mateen Lakdawaala leading the pack in his Keds, but with a black sports jacket wrapped around half of him to shield his sling. Only his left arm was in its sleeve. His white-uniformed lot was right beside him as they trundled along past ditches and patches of wet cement to effortlessly reach the section of the construction site where we had been taking refuge.

'This the guy?' Mateen asked Raptor, pointing presumably at me.

'That's him.' Raptor pointed right in my direction. 'He came to Bobby's house with a loaded semi-automatic.'

Bharat slowly got up. 'What are you doing here?'

'You Bharat Morwani?' Mateen frowned at him, flicking off his aviators to get a proper look.

'Yes . . .' Bharat hesitated, lifting his hand to a jitter.

'That's alright, Bharat,' I patted him on the back. 'Let me do the talking. I'm his mouthpiece.'

'We were waiting for you at the station last night.' Mateen straightened his back, placing his left knuckle on his hip. 'You were supposed to show up with your client. It doesn't look so good, you know. You absconding with your client and all.'

'I wasn't absconding. I was merely dropping him to the L.K.L.M. Provisional Home as per his parents' instructions.'

'Then why isn't he there now?' His neck turned uphill towards the proceeding elevation that shadowed the sunken plot of abandoned 18-storey buildings.

'Because we saw what goes on in there.' I shuddered, catching his glance. 'And I've already informed the Additional Commissioner of Police by way of text message,' I gassed. 'I happen to know him from before. I told him everything, about all that we saw, the dehumanizing confinements, the barbaric regimentation, the gruelling physical regimens inflicted on everyone, the utilization of immobile accident victims for cyber warfare, the human experiments.'

Raptor started cackling.

'Why are you laughing, man?' Bharat's face tensed up. 'You didn't see the shit we did man! If you did, you probably wouldn't be laughing as hard.'

'I know what goes in there, you dimwit!' Raptor stopped laughing, and squinted sideways at him, sort of mockingly. 'I happen to have been admitted there at one point in time.' He pulled up his shirt sleeve to reveal a caterpillar scrawl of stitches imprinted in the flesh of his left shoulder blade. '2018. The Ford Mustang incident.'

'It was even in the papers,' one of their cronies informed me.

'Forgive me for not being familiar with it.' I shook my head.

'It was Bobby and me!' Raptor reflected. We toppled Mateen Bhai's Mustang from the showroom on what was supposed to have been a test drive on the old CBD Belapur Bypass route. Here only.' He pointed out into the distance. 'Not too far away.'

'I see . . .' I lowered my head resignedly.

'Mateen bhai even had me committed to a two-month term in the L.K.L.M nursing facility as punishment.'

'I heard you helped bring this project about!' I said to Mateen Lakdawaala. 'The L.K.L.M Provisional Home for the Medically Ill, I mean. From what Mrs Murapana related, you seem to have been instrumental in setting this place up.'

'I want nothing to do with that place!' Mateen's mouth drawled, irritatedly. 'All I want is the road,' he thought out aloud.

'What's with that road?' Bharat asked, finally intrigued.

'It's a real estate goldmine,' Mateen mumbled. 'If they do decide to connect New Bombay to the city, and build an airport out here, a lot of the surrounding marsh is going to be reclaimed. It's going to be up for grabs. Have you ever seen the topography of this green belt from up above on an aircraft?' His eyes lifted to the sky as he spoke. 'It's a mystery. You don't know if your feet are stable on the ground you're standing on.'

I dug my soles into the grey-pebbled scrap earth of the construction site. 'Is that why you knocked off Yogesh Moolchandani?' I mustered up the courage to ask. 'To first make your way into his facility, then slowly make your way up to his road.'

His brother-in-law started to get shaky at the mere mention of this.

'You and Pawan Hiranandani, both,' I stated, 'sold him an unregistered vehicle that was faulty, that got stuck in cruise control, and wouldn't stop accelerating no matter what! That's why the five missed calls!'

Mateen's eyebrows began to writhe in thought. He snapped back on his aviators, and looked to his brother-in-law questioningly.

'Did you tell him that?' he asked Raptor, softly.

'Nooo, Mateen Bhai! Are you mad!?' Raptor gasped. 'Why would I do a thing like that?'

'Is that what you told him?' he pointed at Bharat with his functioning hand.

'Noo Mateen Bhai!' Bharat's cheeks wobbled. 'I didn't even know this until now.'

'Then who told him that?' he demanded from his cronies. They all shook their heads in bafflement.

'It doesn't matter who told me . . .' I said. 'What matters is who I've told! Once the word gets out, even if you decide to pop the both of us and dump us here in the mangroves—they'll be on your case sooner than you've shuffled your feet. Not even Nalini and Lalith Mangharam will be able to help you then.'

'Who told you?' Mateen insisted.

'Well, if it's any consolation, Shakeel told me, okay? Bada Shakeel. Nathani,' I specified. 'And you wanna know who told him? It came straight from the horse's mouth. One of Pops' bodyguards. Ganesh, I think his name was.'

Just then, Bharat's Honda Civic came sputtering up to us over this ruinous terrain. The engine sounded more full-bodied and ferocious than before. Shakeel's teeth flashed at me from over the wheel, and he soon stuck his neck out of the window to smile at us. 'Whaddyaa say Baaa?' He grinned from ear to ear, twitching his eyebrows to the tune of the engine. 'Can you hear that?' He raised the accelerator again for no apparent reason, just to demonstrate the larger diameter exhaust that had been fitted to the rear. 'You'll be able to touch 200 in this baby now!' he told Bharat.

Once he'd turned off the engine, and his eyes fell on the windscreen, his brains followed soon after. 'BLAM-BLAM!' Two loud shots went off from the left side of Mateen Lakdawaala's sports jacket. A splash of red in two separate smears hit the glass in butterfly formation, before anyone could even register the echo of the gunshots. Shakeel's head bounced back and forth over the steering wheel till his upper body rattled to a standstill. His neck fell sideways on his shoulder, twisted out of shape, a good chunk of it displaced onto the windshield in front of him; his silver chains, bracelets, and earrings still dangling tremulously in the stillness that followed, and half his hair thrust terribly out of its scalp.

'Duck, Bharat!' I shouted, when the next set of shots spun in our direction. One of the bullets got lodged in the aluminium perimeter above our cowering frames as we both hit the dirt. The metallic ricochet sent off a spark that hit Bharat in the eyes. 'Aaaaaahhh!' he caught hold of his eye sockets.

Before I could even produce the 9mm from my pocket, another shot hit a pebble right before my face. I recoiled from the ground in an instant, scrambling for the fence with one hand wrapped tightly around Bharat's right arm. I dragged him along with me, emptying four shots indiscriminately in their direction. Noticeably baffled at my possessing a firearm, they all hurriedly leapt behind the car to take cover. Mateen's henchmen, who only by now were beginning to produce automatic weapons, all hid behind the rear extension, with Mateen advancing gradually, step by step, to the front door. He poked his hand out from behind a side-view mirror and fired three consecutive shots—'BLAM-BLAM-BLAM'—one of which whizzed by my ear. He was firing with his left hand. This time I aimed, and took out the side-view mirror behind which he was crouched.

The two of us took refuge up ahead, around the elongated anatomy of a stationery road grader. The construction work churned on, not having batted an eyelid at the crossfire. No more shots followed us this time. Nothing hit the rusty metallic edges we were clasping on to for dear life. I again put my hand out to unload a last slug into the car. This proved impactful, as it caused them momentarily to stagger around its boot and shrink away. We took the opportunity to make a dash for it. I was practically running backwards, with one eye still planted in the direction of the maroon Honda Civic, which now had three bullet wounds scattered triangularly about its bonnet. The front entrance was still close to a good eighty metres away. If we sprinted, we had a ghost of a chance. Another shot smacked the ground as we began to retreat. Bharat screamed. The construction workers started running wildly about, having deserted their chores upon finally registering the shoot-out. In a matter of seconds, the entire place was in an uproar. Pandemonium burst out across the construction site. The labourers all started running for the exit. Forklifts were overturned, ladders thrown down, mechanical arms dismembered, and tools thrown about in utter panic. The contractor exploded, the machinery stalled in its tremors, and Mateen Lakdawaala was waving his hands maniacally about in the air, ordering everyone to get back to their jobs. He might even have fired off a couple of warning shots into the air in the fashion of landowners of yore. The next one, however, grazed my foot. Another round proceeded in the direction of the front entrance, where the workers were all swarming in alarming profusion. The front entrance was blocked; that seemed clear beyond all doubt. We immediately took a detour to a minute opening in the fence about thirty metres diagonal from us. Blocked by the rear of some mechanism planted firmly in front of it, it was scarcely visible from afar and only now presented itself as a possible exit point.

When we finally did reach it, I let out a sigh of tremendous, exhausted relief. Sweat was dripping from all pours, not to mention the dried-up blood around my feet, the torn anklets of my trousers kept getting enmeshed in some rocky protrusion on our expedition out of the construction site. I shifted the piping that occupied the visible outlines of the hole, barricading our only means of egress. When I cleared the space, I noticed in resolute detail, the dimensions of the mechanism obstructing the exit. It was a cylindrical incinerator for concrete-disposal, a sort of dumpster furnace, which extruded all extraneous material by means of a steel tube attached to its rear valve. A distant ricochet dispelled all apprehensions and pushed us right into the only available escape from the confines of Avnish Complex.

We tumbled out through the narrow oval aperture into a refuse pit some twenty feet below. Bharat and I were covered head to foot in tar, dried-up cement, ash, chunks of brittle rock, and debris. The mud we were neck-deep in began to disintegrate. We tried to swim through the mess of semi-solid waste, wading into yards of plastic wreckage, molten rubber, dispossessed wiring, dried-up generator fuel, an infinity of insects, excrement, moss, algae, metallic sheets, blankets of foil, sharp tin fragments, the thorny underbrush enveloping all—crushing us in its very palms, and throwing us downstream into a tiny rivulet curling away from the terra firma and the dry land into an endless mudflat that spread out under a swamp of some density. Clutching onto whatever stray branches of passing vegetation that were available, we floated along the winding rivulet that soon hurled us into its culmination; a foaming tract of grey quicksand, swimming with blobs of industrial garbage and throbbing with a thick, almost milky petroleum lustre on its sickening surface, to merge serenely into a creek some twenty metres downslope. Gravity being our worst enemy at this point, we were propelled mercilessly into its mush of black ooze, which failed to devour us entirely, opting only to throw us with its churning muck into the creek that yawned at us from down below. We were passing what seemed to be, in all probability, a drainage pit of unthinkable vastness and perpetuity, with a gradient almost akin to the form of a waterfall. Some of the thorny vegetation that swept by seemed almost to grow deformed or merged with the all-encompassing landfill, some of which emptied out through means of a partially buried hydraulic turbine into the creek-bed; its whirling sewage waters trickling further down into the blackest of all oblivions: the mutant sea that caressed the outer reaches of the mangroves, and that now assumed from a distance, to my diseased fancy, almost the aspect of the circling perforations of a drain, a swirling vortex of scatological purgatory. I imagined at once what swaying reeds and carcasses of oceanic scenery awaited us if we were to be sucked into the whirlpool of neither solid nor liquid mass; just an endless wilderness of two-headed eels and opaque slimy waters.

This thorny comeuppance, this reminder of infinite waste, re-generating and indivisible, both physical and mental, had somewhat revived Bharat from his airconditioned coma of unease and irritability. He was thrust for the very first time in his existence into the bowels of civilization and what that entails. I caught his hands through the ordeal, tugging him out of the current that nearly swallowed us, and paddled furiously to the slanting shoreline wedged with rocks and crawling branches, some of which provided support to guide him up to his feet once we were in the shallows of the creek. The vomit passed uninterrupted. I wiped the muck off his clothes, and pulled him out of the wetland that abounded all around us to step onto the firmer ground supporting the vegetation. We made our way out of that labyrinth of writhing, twisted vegetation and deceptive earth as if by some divine assistance.

Once we had made our way back up to the gravelled terrain that orbited the construction site, we did eventually manage to locate the car which I had parked at a singularly odd location. Bharat was practically paralysed with terror and exhaustion. I placed him in the passenger seat and jumped back behind the wheel. He still seemed to not have much to say about the whole thing. Maybe returning to his building on 15th Road would arouse some sensation. But it was a good hour and a half's drive of stiff silence till there.

He dozed off on the never-ending expanse of the Western Express Highway as the forenoon struck like a lightning bolt on the muddied windshield. He was gradually lapsing into a stupor. All the dreary remnants of the alcohol had withered away; the sole life-sustaining force for him. I wondered whether he would make it out to the other side alive. I wondered if I would. The thoughts were starting to come back to me, the paralytic neuroses that arise under pressure. Images of Yogesh Moolchandani's car crash started presenting themselves to me of their own accord. I knew I'd be fine if I just stayed in control of my faculties. If the paranoia started hitting me, I wouldn't be any good out on a highway with a client in the passenger seat. I'd crash into an oncoming vehicle, or worse still, find myself off-road, derailed like one of those automobile entombments that are a customary sight on most highways. I had to stay in control of what came and went upstairs.

First, it would be the tremors; a certain recoil, lapse of motion, sudden spasm destabilizing all judgement and sensation. Then, the *neurosis*. Then, the shivers . . . then, the calm . . . then, the associations and crippling plummet into the swirling vortex *where the mind should not go*! The caverns of the psyche, long dormant. Meditations on meanderings into the forsaken realm of probability. Then the *prayers*, then the harrowing itch! The rotten worm wriggling its way out of palpability.

Then, a sudden burst of wind, a vision freckled with astral fragments. Baffled features, flailing limbs, teeth digging into the socket of the jaw in command of speech. Then, the laughter and the gaiety. The *sickness* . . . then, the poison, then the antidote in reason, then the swoon, then the marrow bleeding visions of desolation. Then, the *thought*, then the speed, the accelerating greed, the need to dismiss feeling, and the discoordination. Then the breath, and the slowing of all thoughts innumerably growing. Then, the birth and the *death*! *Cyclopean vistas of waste*! Then, the joy, then the sorrow, then the chronic distillation of all sense into survival! Then, the steadiness, and the sweat. The hand stable, the forehead dry, the neck loose . . .

And then, the madness!

All of a sudden, as if the magical hand of fate had decided to ward off visibility, clouds started to gather seamlessly over the widening expanse of the highway, diminishing all available illumination and camouflaging the contours and unfriendlier stretches of the road. I put the headlights on full beam and needed every inch of light I had at my disposal. Suddenly, I felt a noise coming from the axle that sounded dauntingly like a flat tyre, but when I realized it wasn't, I began to see what it *was*; and it was worse than a flat tyre, that I can assure you . . .

Pretty soon, the headlights began to fade away, with the battery looking like it was going to pack up any second. It was almost pitch grey, with a thick smog encompassing all, and even as I twitched at the handle, turning it back and forth to switch back on the lights or flash the indicator, there was no sure sign of anything before my path. It was like a solar eclipse, or a mere visitation on my part. I couldn't see a thing!

All sight started to pack up with my thoughts. I could crash into a divider, and I wouldn't come to know about it before my head was hanging off its hinges. I was driving blind. Hitting 90, and not slowing down on account of the disadvantage. On the contrary, it only made me all the more reckless, knowing it was practically dark and that anything could happen, we could fly off the side of the highway for all I knew.

I pressed down gently on the accelerator, speeding up to an alarming degree. It wasn't the wisest thing to do given the circumstances, but I possessed a sleepwalking security that we'd make it out in one piece, even despite the blinding volcanic ash of uncertainty. The fate my client and I had in store was significantly worse than a quick and violent death.

I wondered what Nalini would have to say about what I had just done and all that had transpired. Or, for that matter, my employer, Mr Lalith Mangharam.

'Rules are for everyone,' he'd squawk. 'No matter how inconvenient. Even if it's a simple matter of putting on a seat belt, or waiting at an empty red light at 1 o'clock at night. We have to lead by example. If we don't follow the rules, what makes you think the client will?'

Unfortunately, I gave up following the rules pretty early on, just about the time I began to figure they don't really count in the long run; probably in junior college. You see, I always imagined one's academic credentials to govern one's onward prospects, but the more I studied and did what I was told to do, the less I saw in return. I had waited long and hard for my earnest smile and goodness of heart to pay off. When things didn't pan out according to my anticipations, I began to lie, steal, cheat in my exams, break the line—think of myself to be more equal than the others. I sold fake exam papers on the sly, hit another kid in the face with a rock, smashed my car into an SLR for the sheer sake of the exhilaration it gave me.

I'd never been in any trouble with the authorities, until I swiped a Walkman from one of my classmates. I was informed on by the college peon, who saw me listening to it in the restroom of the main foyer. I was suspended for three months and had to repeat a year. I was diagnosed as a kleptomaniac by our student counsellor, had to undergo mandatory counselling sessions. That was the last time I had been in any kind of scrape in an official capacity—the last time up until what was to follow.

Let me assure you that this is in no way an admission of guilt or a confession of any kind, but simply a testimony on my part, with myself acting as counsel to my conscience.

EIGHTEEN

I could go on looking at myself in the rear-view mirror without as much as a shrug so long as the well hadn't run dry. Once that was over, I'd be no good to anybody, let alone myself. Maybe they were right, I was a kleptomaniac; I couldn't follow the law if it were served to me on a silver spoon—but the confusion in my eyes lay not so much in whether or not I was a kleptomaniac, but in the fact that my far worse condition was comprehended in official terms as such. All the authorities could make of me was that perhaps I was a kleptomaniac, without taking into account the more inexplicable aspects of the pathology.

I'm no different from anyone else. We're all made out of the metal I suppose, but I don't know. The more I think about my predicament, the more I'm encouraged to label it as self-inflicted, and of my own making. Not saying my symptoms weren't genuine, but the disease had long settled, and the only thing that gave credence to it was experience, or in this case, lack thereof. It substantiated my syndrome into a legitimate affliction, most certainly of the more peculiar kind. But as far back as I can remember, my thoughts always seemed to race to the most catastrophic conclusions. Scarcely could I look outside a window without anticipating the apocalypse. Seldom could I cross the road without the fear of a garbage truck knocking me over. I'd take a look at a baby, a perfectly adorable bald-headed baby, and the first thought that'd come to me wasn't how beautiful it was, but instead, what it would be like if that skull were cracked right open. I'd be polite and gracious to the most kind-hearted, doting elderly and infirmed folks and wonder what if their throats were slit. I'd admire a handsome face and immediately get a flash of the nose being broken. I'd look at the most beautiful things in creation, great works of art, monuments, houses, colourful decorations lovingly assembled with great care and delicacy, and picture them torn down, battered, and destroyed.

Even after I'd dropped Bharat home, and had most of my worries settled financially, at least to provide for the stability of the passing moment, I still couldn't shake off the feeling that some doom was tailing me in the dim sunlight—of what form I could not speculate, I just knew there was a strange shadow following me, keeping track of me, hiding behind the curtains of the most reassuring familiarity, measuring all my deeds, and planning to impart justice as per his discretion. But, I guess it is kind of reassuring . . . knowing that any second there can come a thought that'll just wipe the smile right off my face.

When I reached home, I was sweating; drained, even though I hadn't lifted a muscle over the past half hour. It was early in the afternoon now—the entire morning had gone by me in a blackening mirror. By the time I was through counting the notes, I was certain I had enough to keep me going for about a year, maybe a holiday, or a brief stint out of town. It amounted to a total of Rs 3,45,000; probably one day's petrol money for the renewable residents of Sheetal Residency. I threw the remaining poker chips into the car ashtray, and dislocated the rubbery compartments and chip holders to stuff in all the notes I had assembled. I clapped shut the case, and sealed the lock with both hands.

I happened to glance over the side-view mirror as I was shutting the glove box. A couple of blocks behind me, a line of cars were parked outside the pavement of an opulent seven-storey building named 'Ambercroft'. It was perched right atop a hill, its compound slanting downwards. In between the two Innovas and a second-hand C-Class, stood the same red Honda City whose persistent presence I had first taken notice of at Khar police station. The parking lights were on, and an indistinguishable figure sat in the driver's seat, his face partially obscured by the blinding twinkle of the headlights. I instantly got out of the car, slamming the door shut with my fist, and started to head towards the neighbouring building with a slow, tentative walk.

It may have been the same red car I had noticed at Khar, or it might not have been, I couldn't say. I hadn't given it much thought. I had other things on my mind. His parking lights were blinking and the sun-flap in front of the driver's seat was pulled down, presumably to conceal the identity of the man behind the wheel. After parking my car and tossing my keys over to the watchman, I walked out the building to see if he was still there.

'Excuse me.' I tapped on the window of the Honda City. The driver was no doubt a bit startled on noticing me staring at him through the car window. As the window rolled down, I stuck my hand in to shake his. 'If you intend to follow me, I suggest you call it a day. You can come by tomorrow to pick me up at about 7.30 in the morning. That's my daily departure time. It'll save me the effort of driving or the expense of a taxi cab or worse still, the local.'

'Huh?' the guy mumbled.

'Don't kid around with me. I've seen you. I know you've been tailing me from Khar police station on. Plus, you can't park here all day. You better get a move on before the tow-truck makes a round. They'll bust you for vehicular vagrancy.'

The man stayed silent. He looked around the dashboard, turned off the battery, and stepped out of the vehicle. He was young, probably in his late 20s, healthy-looking, but a little drained of the colour youth normally endows one with. He looked like he'd tuned forward his body clock to his own specifications, and bypassed adolescence straight to middle age.

'My name's Kartik.' He introduced himself with a crooked smile. 'Aunty Bhairavi's nephew. I think she might have told you about me.'

'Bhoparai?'

'That's right!'

'I thought you don't exist. It's a privilege to finally meet you in the flesh. I've only heard of you on bank statements.'

'I just thought I'd show up and have a word with you.'

'At your aunt's behest?'

'At my own. If I have to pay a fellow over four lakh rupees, I'd like to have a look at him for myself, and see if he's worth it.'

'You had your fill yet?'

'I saw more than I wanted to.'

'What did you see?'

'You see, I followed you out from the sessions court last evening. My driver Santosh had been keeping an eye on you, and informed me that you were heading North. Anyways, then I followed you from there to Bandra, you took the Sea Link, which I thought irregular, considering it was evening and it gets real crowded at about that time. You got off at a showroom on S.V. Road. "Hiranandani Horsepower," I think it was called.'

'You've got a good pair of eyes. If I need to chart out a daily schedule, I'll give you a ring.'

'While you were in there, I was waiting outside, behind the line of cars parked at the entrance. I saw two white Gypsies pull up outside the showroom. A white-uniformed chauffeur got out from an S-Class which was parked inside, and went up to them. Two men got out the Gypsy,' he said, pointing in the direction of the street and making a two.

'What did they look like?' I asked, my head turning back and forth.

'They looked like bodyguards. One of them had a walkie-talkie. He handed the chauffeur a pair of car keys. Then I saw you get thrown out of the place soon after. It was kinda tough to keep up with you from then on. '

'Even in a City?'

'This thing's got no horsepower,' he said, tapping the overheated bonnet. 'No pickup. It's just a 1900cc engine. I used to drive a 5. Was taken away from me.'

'By whom?'

'Long story.'

Midnight Freeway

'Well, I got lots of time.'

'I don't.'

'You got enough time to spare on me, though. What gives me the honour?'

He let out a breath, bobbed his head up and down, and tried to speak, but couldn't.

'Did you know Ms Naraina's ex-husband?' I asked, 'the late Mr Gautam Bhandari?'

'I did.'

'And . . .'

His head stopped bobbing.

'What do you make of it?'

'That was my doing,' he said, without moving his mouth.

'I'm sorry?'

'I killed him; it wasn't her.'

'What?'

I looked around at the empty colony entrenched in its afternoon rituals, to ensure no one could hear what this idiot was letting spill right outside the front gate to my building. If anyone saw me with him, it could mean the end of my legal career.

'Look, maybe you wanna shift inside,' I insisted, taking him back inside the building and hushing him up all the way past the front lobby to the lift, which took longer than usual to arrive. I let him enter in first and pressed the button, staring blank-faced into the metallic parting. He stared into his phone all the way up.

'They say you can measure the status of a building by counting how many floors it's got stacked up,' I said, wondering whether or not he was in the market for any kind of conversation save the obvious. 'Ours has twelve.' I went on, heedless of his indifference, 'Deccan Peninsula has 24; it's the Deccan Plateau to our measly Western Ghats. Woodside Apartments, they call it!' I scoffed. 'There isn't any wood in sight for miles, scarcely a tree.'

'Mine has 14,' he boasted, as the elevator sprung open.

'Shhh . . . be quiet.' I opened the door with my house keys jangling out the keyhole. The newspaper was stuck in the door handle. I promptly unfolded it to behold what I missed.

There was the mention of certain strange occurrences in the Napean Sea, Valkeshwar area. Also, the disappearance of a 12-year-old, highly priced white Pomeranian from Marine Drive. It was said to be a case of kidnapping, that the said person's nephew was apparently holding the pet ransom and demanding Rs 14 lakh for its safe return. The Nepali housekeeper had been hijacked by a maroon Maruti van at the signal of C Road and Chowpatti. As I proceeded to read, and chanced upon the name of the person whom the pet belonged to from the corner of my eyes, I gradually became aware that it was none other than old Ms Naraina, my very own client. She had made the papers; it was indeed a moment for celebration. I decided I would send her a congratulatory message. The nephew's name was Kartik Bhoparai, resident of Mount Mary. The police are currently searching for him and the dog. Notices have been put out, photographs of the animal, and also missing signs all over schools and hospitals.

I tossed aside the newspaper and called her jailer to personally congratulate her on this exciting news and offer my services in any capacity if necessary, but he didn't pick up. Moti came charging up to us.

'Is that a dog?' Kartik asked.

'It's not a reindeer.'

'I'm afraid I don't like dogs . . . I'm allergic to them.'

Moti didn't like him either, and began to slowly drone into a growl, his bloodshot eyes trailing my new-found guest's every move.

'That's not the way it seems to me.' I laughed, tossing him the morning paper. 'According to this here rag, you seem to have quite an affinity for dogs, more so than is even considered healthy.'

'Look, that's a different story.' He casually shrugged it aside, not wanting to get into it. I didn't blame him. If I was guilty of kidnapping a helpless beast, I wouldn't have much to say for it either.

'I did it for the money,' he confessed. 'Same with Mr Bhandari.'

'All for the money, eh?'

'That's right. You see, I'm currently trying to set up a company that specializes in molecular cuisine and nutritional hygiene. Inedible foods—we're going to call it. We basically process and synthesize any organic material or substance into an edible form and serve it as food. So you can have Sandal Wood Steak, Cotton Kebabs, Pan-Seared Coconut Shell, a jam made out of banana peels, pencil-shaving pasta with a soft sawdust sprinkle.'

'Sounds like a million-dollar idea.'

'So you see . . . I needed some capital.'

'If that's what you've been tailing me around for, then you've got the wrong guy. I'm not your man. I haven't got enough bread to put pencil shavings on the dog tray.'

'That's not why I'm here.'

'Then pray, inform me,' I said, tilting up my wrist to demonstrate the time. 'I don't have all day. I work on a per hour basis.'

'Look . . .' the guy said, slowly taking a seat without being asked to.

'That's right,' I smiled, 'Make yourself at home . . . would you like a pina colada or perhaps a phenyl feni floating on the naphthalene rocks?'

'Look, man . . .' He started to shake. Now he was really tense; I could tell by the way his face had suddenly woken up as if revived from a coma. 'When I heard your name from Bhairavi aunty, I remembered I'd heard it before, or more likely seen it somewhere. Pranav Paleja. It's not the kind of name you forget easily.'

'I've always thought it to be quite ordinary.'

'Weren't you in the St Aloysius Reformation Centre for Young Adults?'

'I'm sorry?' This piece of news hit me like a rock the size of Gibraltar.

'I had spent six months there when I was only a kid, a teenager actually,' he informed me. 'I think I saw your name on one of the roll-call lists. I even remember once hearing it. People used to call you P.P. or Puppy. They used to make fun of your name and laugh every time it was announced in a headcount.'

Midnight Freeway

'Uhh . . . excuse me . . .' I rushed towards him, hauling him out of his seat. I yanked him up by the elbows and started to shove him out the door. Moti's growl had by now grown into a bark.

'Look . . .' he resisted, shoving back. 'It was many years ago, and I daresay you've changed since then. Become a fully rehabilitated citizen, working for the law.'

'I heard you're not doing so badly yourself.' My clasp automatically tightened around his arm as the words poured out. 'Got yourself a position as the owner of a company, I believe!'

'I do alright. Make ends meet, put food on the table, you know the regulars.'

'You mean inedible food.'

'I make enough to buy my way out of a scrap like the one I've gotten myself into.'

'You haven't gotten yourself into anything. As per the law, it's your aunt that's in deep. Not you.' I pushed him out the doorway, jerking him by his shoulders and holding him back with the door.

'Look please . . .' he protested.

'Shut up!' I snapped. 'Keep your voice down. This is a respectable housing society. What you're telling me amounts to nothing more than a confession.' I lowered my own voice. 'We decided to plead guilty, and apply for bail. Now I'll have to plead not guilty. I'd say for right now you let Ms Bhairavi Naraina be the guilty party. Don't make the mistake of telling anyone else what you just told me. Keep it to yourself.'

'When I heard it was you that was representing us . . .'

'Her . . .' I corrected him.

'Her . . . I naturally got worried.'

'Why so?'

'You know . . . uh . . . 'cause . . . uh . . . I had seen you there?'

'Where?'

'At the reform school.'

'What the heck are you talking about . . .?'

'Listen, don't play smart with me. I know all about you. What I did was worse, I'll admit it, but you've got a pretty heavy load on your chest too, my friend.'

'I have no idea what you're talking about, my friend.'

'Suit yourself.'

The edge of the door accidentally left my hands. I started to almost involuntarily back away from it. Kartik Bhoparai, standing on the other end of that doorway, was beginning to blur into the outline of the adjoining doors.

'You've been following me quite a while, haven't you?' I mumbled, snapping myself out of the momentary daze.

'Look, Pranav.'

'P.P.'

'P.P.,' he said hesitantly. 'I've got another lawyer, a Mr Akhilesh Goenka; would you mind if we could have the case transferred to him? I'll take the entire onus. I'll even own up and admit to the crime. Just please stay away from us.'

'Why . . . what's the matter?'

'Look, P.P. . . . please.'

'Puppy.'

'Pu-pup-puppy!' he gabbled. 'I don't want you near my house.'

I pulled him back inside without even realizing I had done so. I closed the door shut firmly behind me and latched the lever in place. It was locked, and there wasn't a chance he'd be able to figure out how to unlatch it without getting it stuck in the wrong direction. Moti started gnawing on his leg. He started to shake.

'P-p-p-pu-puppy,' he stammered.

'Puppy!' I told him.

'Puppy!' he repeated after me.

I belted him one in the stomach. He nearly heaved. 'Say it. Puppy.'

'P-pu-puppy . . .' he stumbled.

I punched him again, this time firmer and on the face. 'Say it!' I shouted. 'Puppy!'

'Puppy, Puppy! Puppy!'

I smacked him across the face, whacked him two or three times across the forehead with what the biker boys would have called a 'tapli'. I could have knocked him out flat with a single sock, but I settled for opening him up instead. I wanted to hear what he had on me. I sat him down on the same sofa he had been recently vacated from, pouring him a glass of chilled water, and apologizing profusely for going momentarily out of control. I served it to him on a two-by-two tray like any good host would, handing him a coaster to place on the wooden side table beside the sofa.

'I know all about you, Puppy.' He shook.

I sat down next to him, placing my hands on his knees as if to comfort or reassure. I nodded faintly, communicating to him with my rolled-up underlip that I understood. I knew what he was going through. Maybe I could help him.

'When you were studying in college . . .' he began. I didn't listen, or at least, pretended not to, but after a point, the words ceased to go in, almost like a human firewall blocking out a virus from a Pentium 4 Processor that couldn't cope with its illimitable malice. I looked over instead towards my Windows 7 desktop as he began to speak. The one that would rather simulate real-life experience than live it. That was my prognosis. Self-diagnosed, of course, the officials at the St Aloysius Reformation Centre had a different opinion.

'When you were in college . . .' he began again. It all started to come back to me—all those memorial corridors, and seminar rooms, all those trophies, all those boards of achievement, and endless lists, pillars of accomplishment, the placement cell with a neat little future in plan for all our students. All those maternal Mercedes and SUVs that came to drop off their darling little ones, to tuck them away into a safe haven where they were to be graced with eternal companionship as well as knowledge, in one swell package called youth.

'When you were in college . . .' Once I was in college. R.I.A.C., they used to call it. Royston Institute of Arts and Commerce—a swanky piece of real estate sitting in South Bombay with a 100-year lease; all the hip crowd flocking there right after the 10th boards; tough to get into, but not that tough to pay your way into—its administrative offices air-conditioned and airtight. Prestigious as they came, but not without its fair share of faults, one of them being the kind of cats they granted admission to: a rogue's gallery of rich kids and attractive acolytes of Ivy League aspiration. It was one of the few places in the country where you could get a foreign degree sitting on these shores, just like FLAMES in Pune. Before that, I had done my schooling from a place in Santa Cruz called Lady Harish Chandra Vidyarthi.'

'When you were in college, R.I.A.C.,' he continued. His words started repeating themselves. 'You drew up a plan single-handedly to take down the entire compound. They found sketches, fire, electrical and security maps of the campus. You wanted to commit a grand-scale massacre, Columbine-style. They found tapes, recordings, and even arms and ammunition. You had stocked up an armoury of bullets, some four handguns were found, three automatics, one regulation police revolver.'

'What about it?' I breezed past his account, trying to think nothing of it. Inside, I was thinking plenty. Only, they weren't the right kind of thoughts.

'At least that was the talk that used to go around at the reform school. That's why we'd all keep a one arm's distance from you, and leave you to your own devices, which in your case turned out to be legal textbooks.'

'What do you want me to do about it?'

'Look,' he quivered. 'Just forget about the whole case and leave us all alone. I tried everything within my power to get my aunt away from you, even offered to pay you your litigation fee before the trial concluded, begged Akhilesh Goenka to take the case from you, offered to pay him double your salary.'

'Well, that's the price he probably commands. You have nothing to worry about.' I smiled at him, I could feel my own eyes twinkling in the tube light. He started to go stale in the face with the same expression of trepidation he had been sustaining since he had entered the flat. The worry on his face began withering away into a drooping, lower-lipped roll. His eyes started to grow thoughtful. He nodded faintly with a barely detectable microscopic movement. Each alteration in his expression was minute yet calculated, perhaps to give me the impression that he meant more than what he was saying.

'Don't get any funny ideas,' he warned me, his left eye tightening up.'

'Well, you see . . .' I began, 'You don't have to worry about a thing. Nothing at all. At least as far as your aunt is concerned. I appeared in court for her trial on my own time, and free of cost. Call it social service or whatever the hell you will. I wouldn't want to waste any further time on her. But you, on the other hand, you—I could provide some help for. I could help you out in a way you never imagined, help clear up what's inside of you.'

'What do you mean?'

'Take a look at that dog,' I said, waving my hand towards Moti, who had by now spread out flat on the floor, resting his chin on his paws, listening as attentively as a jury. 'If empty vessels made the most noise, he must be the sole exception to that rule. He only opens his trap when he's got his mind full. Not too different from you in that regard, don't know about Fluffy. Haven't made her acquaintance yet.'

'It happens to be a he, by the way.'

'As expected.'

'What are you trying to say?'

I didn't know for sure myself, but still kept saying it—like it meant something—'What stops you from opening your trap anytime you've got plenty on your mind and feel like talking to somebody about it?'

'If that's what worries you, then you have my word . . . I will not whisper a word of this to any living being.'

'The cops you could go to, but I don't know if they'd take the time. Maybe the Reform Centre. Try them out. Or how about my boss, Mr Lalith S. Mangharam? I could give you his visiting card. Go and tell him all about me. That he's got a loose cannon working under him at the office that could go off any second the going gets rough. He'll tell you that you need evidence to substantiate these claims before they give me a notice and ask me to tender my resignation, plus he'll also mention that I have a spotless track record to boot. I've never broken the law, at least not legally, maybe in my spare time, but that's a different matter.'

I didn't know what I was saying or why I was saying it . . . but he just listened steadily, in calm thought.

'As I said, I will not whisper a word about this to anyone . . .' he repeated. 'Unless . . .' his speech jittered to a halt.

'Unless?' I hung off his incomplete rumination.

'Unless you decide to pursue this case for the pay. It is a lucrative case, after all. As I said, I will even pay your fees for yesterday's appearance in court if you wish . . . but . . .'

'But?'

'But . . .' He shook. 'As of now, I would just request you to relinquish all duties towards this case.'

'So, you can go ahead and spread all kinds of shit about me?'

'That's not what I said!' His eyes grew large and impatient. 'I said I would not, unless I have your word . . .'

'On what?' I joked. 'I want your word first. Only then will I consider giving you mine. I could just knock you off right here and now and be done with it, it'll save me a great deal of trouble.'

'I think I better leave.' He suddenly got up and headed towards the front door. Moti arose from his stupor on taking notice of this rather abrupt movement. He looked cautiously towards Moti and said, 'Wouldn't want to create an undesirable scene.'

'You've already done so,' I told him, holding Moti back by the collar. 'But you're right. I think you'd better. It's a pretty impersonal building. No one really cares what you do, just so long as you don't stoop to pry on what they're doing. If you keep to yourself and mind your own business, that's about as good a safety blanket as anyone can afford. It's an unsaid rule, an unwritten law. Keep your nose clean and love thy neighbour.'

I'd never done it before, you know, never killed a man with my own two hands, so to speak. I'd overseen it on multiple occasions and neglected to register it, but I'd never been the sole cause for it. I'd always been protected by circumstance, insured by goodwill, secured by reason.

I suppose it was kind of written in my destiny. Not saying a man's purpose on this earth is to send another to an early grave, but there is an odd symmetry to it: this was the next logical step—the culmination of all my wayward meanderings from the noble path I had set out so aimlessly to follow. To commit the ultimate crime!

NINETEEN

I suppose I just didn't have it in me to pull the plug and send him splattering into a couple of streaks across my white wall. It was the only thing I should have done to prevent what he then went and did to me. In the virtual realm, it seemed possible, probable even, and perhaps painless. To send a slug into a full-grown adult and wipe him out plain, put him out of commission. Perhaps that's what the L.K.L.M. Provisional Home for the Medically Ill in New Bombay was founded for; to encourage those kinds of impulses, and promise those behind the trigger that there was really no difference between blowing a hole into a building off the shores of Anzio in 1941 and actually plugging some poor sod that worked behind the desk at a 24×7, something I had indeed been capable of doing not so long ago, had circumstances forced me to. No real difference between playing Doom or Duke Nukem 3D out in the open in real life and committing what I had once been capable of in my thoughts. No real difference between skidding on the corners of NFS and actually running over a bunch of pavement dwellers while drunk in a BMW. And if the favour of the authorities were finagled by people like me, and if innocence could be bought, then *what's the real difference?*

I spent the first hour I had to myself, alone—spitting absent-mindedly into the washbasin in front of the bathroom mirror till I felt I was purged of the previous day's proceedings. Today was a new day. After having brushed my teeth for over half an hour and run an electric clipper along the side growth around my cheeks, I reached for a cigarette and a bottle of Listerine.

I started to get ready to face the day, after having served Moti his breakfast and rinsed his water bowl. I buttoned up a new off-white, 93 per cent polyester, red-checked shirt, and got into a pair of navy blue Gucci Boss trousers. I clipped on my belt, sprayed myself with cologne, snuck my feet into a pair of loafers, grabbed hold of my briefcase and headed out, closing the door shut. Moti was quite upset by my abrupt departure, and made his dislike quite apparent as I shut the door on him plain-faced. I shared the elevator with a delivery boy from Wimpy's. We didn't have much to say to each other so we stared into our phones on the way down.

A kid in a tricycle was wheeling himself up and down the lobby without adult supervision. He was liable to slip on the shiny white marble flooring we were graced with as compensation for the otherwise pretty standard accommodation. The delivery guy's scooter was parked outside the building right next to a 'No Parking' sign.

'That's a thousand-rupee fine now,' I murmured.

'I'm s-s-sorry?' he stammered, looking back at me.

'One thousand bucks, sometimes twelve hundred at the tow naka. For a two-wheeler, it's a thousand, I think. There isn't a parking spot anywhere for miles,' I told him. Outside, every spot was taken except for a rickshaw stand, and the spot he had just vacated. 'You're lucky the tow truck wasn't doing a round.'

I twirled my winged car-keys around my fingers like a revolver as he scooted off, and asked the night watchman who was cleaning cars to give my tyres a rinse.

'What's with all the keechad, boss?' he asked, spraying down the mudguards with a waterhose connected to a valve on the ground-floor pipeline.

'Moti went off and got himself into a fight . . . found him lying in the mud,' I said, splitting a match from the box to flick it alight. As I drew on a drag, I came up with a plausible story. 'Some internal bleeding.'

'Oho . . .' he mourned. 'Hope he's all right now?'

'Never been better.'

We scrubbed clean every trace of muck from the mangroves. I cranked down my window to gently hand him a hundred.

'Ahhh . . . what's this for?' he moaned. 'Just doing my job.'

'That's for doing a good job.'

'If every sweeper in town got an extra hunner for doing a good job, there wouldn't be any sweepers left around anywhere. It'd be them that occupy positions of high prominence, and all the saahabs would be reduced to cleaning out the privies.'

'That day isn't too far ahead, I guarantee you.'

'When that day comes, be sure to give me a call.'

'I'll probably be dead before that day.'

'Well then, when you meet our creator, be sure to tell him to get in touch with me.' He pocketed the hundred and picked up his bucket from the ground in astonishment, proceeding on to wipe out more windshields and open passenger seats to dust off all the leathery residue that accumulates on a commute.

It was early in the afternoon, but the kids were still playing cricket in the compound. They'd make an awful racket, sometimes even scratch my car. Once or twice, I regret to mention, I even gave them a smacking, but that was on account of a smashed headlight. Ever since then, the kid Mohit from the second floor would avoid eye contact whenever I crossed him. The kids all turned from their game as my engine roared. I blinked my lights for them to move aside and not get hurt, and waved out to them as I drove out the gate. I stopped outside to buy a cigarette from the neighbouring paanwaala. I had only 5 rupees in change and a tenner from before.

'One Marlboro Light,' I told the paanwaala.

He puzzled over the phone book that he removed from his chest pocket, folding and unfolding notes of tens and twenties. He looked at the fifteen bucks I handed him suspiciously, then folded them up neatly in between the pages of his phone book. Living next to the Bhabha Atomic Research Centre, it was probable that we had all been exhibiting the effects of nuclear radiation. Everyone in the colony was slower than usual. The paanwaala took his time giving me the cigarette, the watchman took his own sweet time opening up the gate, and the motorist parked in front of me took even longer moving his Kinetic aside to clear my path.

I got a call from a landline number just as soon as I turned the car key to raise the engine.

'Hello,' I answered promptly.

'Hello . . .' a gruff voice barked at me from the other end of the line.

'Yes?'

'Paleja?'

'Uh . . . may I know who I'm talking to?' I asked politely, trying to muster up that kiosk operator tone.

'Sub-inspector Naresh Saawant speaking, Khar police chowki.'

I turned the car off, rolling down the windows.

'Yes, sir?'

'Are you at work?'

'Yes sir . . . I mean . . . no sir . . . as in, I mean I am . . . going to work I mean.'

'Are you or aren't you? You making a round to the courts today?'

'I'm heading to the office.'

'Which side you headed?'

'Uh . . . I'm sorry?'

'Where you going?'

'Well . . . uh . . . I have some urgent . . .' I scrambled up what I was saying. 'At the moment . . . I have some work . . . I'm currently engaged with a client . . . I'm addressing a rather serious matter.'

'A matter, eh? What time do you go home?'

'I get done usually by 6 or 7 o'clock.'

'Why don't you swing by Khar police chowki on your way back from work? It'll be a bit of a detour if you're headed to Chembur, but I promise I'll make it worth your while.'

'Sure sir . . . uh . . . what is this regarding?'

'Come at 6 o'clock; you'll find out.'

It was only 1.15 in the afternoon, I couldn't wait till six in the evening to find out what he wanted with me. He had me all antsy, just the way he wanted it.

'Actually, sir . . .' I back-tracked. 'I just got a message from my client. He's just cancelled the meeting. The matter has been postponed. I've got an opening in my schedule from now till lunchtime. I can be there at the station pronto.'

'Sure . . .' I felt his smirk over the phone.

'I'm on my way there right away.'

'Most matters tend to disappear when there are more pressing matters to be reckoned with Paleja.'

Just then, one of the constables barged into the sub-inspector's cabin to deliver a piece of news recently acquired from the MSRDC control office: 'Just spoke to the authorities at the Bandra–Worli Sea Link. A Ford Ikon was seen passing through the Sea Link just moments before the crash.'

'Ahh . . .' Saawant sighed with satisfaction. 'Did you hear that Paleja?'

'There's a hundred Ford Ikons in the city,' I said. 'What makes you think it was mine?'

'The fact that you have no real reliable alibi to vouch for your whereabouts from the time you left the station to the time you entered the sessions court at 9.30 a.m.,' Sub-inspector Saawant declared.

'This is preposterous!' I nearly cut the call out of annoyance.

'Also!' His voice jumped to catch hold of me by the throat before I could disconnect. 'The maroon Honda Civic that we'd impounded was reported missing from the station last night.'

'So?'

'It's landed up now. And according to the party that delivered it, it was found in New Bombay near Moolchandani's construction site.'

'Well, we didn't have access to the keys. They were lying in your drawer.'

'Are you trying to suggest I had something to do with its disappearance?' he remonstrated.

'That's not what I'm saying,' I clarified. 'Listen, someone must have snatched the keys from your cabin. Who all were there last night?'

'That has nothing to do with it!'

'What do you mean?'

'Did you know that that car has the capacity to go up to 200 kmph?'

It was hopeless. The trap had been set; their plan successfully executed. The Vimal S2K Motor Rehabilitation Plant had deemed Bharat's harmless Honda Civic a deadly weapon.

'Okay . . . I have a confession to make,' I said, holding my palm on my chest. 'I have someone that can an account for where I was that night. Two people, in fact. One, a night clerk at a 24×7 on Turner Road, and the other—if you really wanna get down to it—my watchman, who will gladly tell you that I reached my building at 7.15 a.m., and was out of the house by 8.55 a.m.'

'What were you doing before that from 5.30 a.m. till 6.45 a.m.?'

'Well . . . uh . . .' I coughed, 'before that, I happened to have held up a 24×7 after dropping Bharat home.'

'You just happened to haa?'

'Perform a robbery all by myself. You can talk to the night clerk, he'll give you concrete proof. There's CCTV footage too. I even have a gun lying in my glove compartment with my fingerprints on it.'

Sub-inspector Saawant and the constable probably looked at each other momentarily confounded. No reply came immediately. I could hear a huff. Once their murmurs met, it became quite clear what they were thinking.

'You're admitting to another crime?' Saawant barked, 'Oldest trick in the book. You'll get a five-year sentence for armed robbery to save you from a twenty-year sentence for culpable homicide.'

'I'm not fooling around. There's concrete evidence to substantiate my claims.'

'There's concrete evidence to substantiate our claims as well,' Saawant said. 'A fellow by the name of Kartik Bhoparai just registered a complaint in Bandra police station about you. Claiming that you are a potentially criminal element. He said you were likely to endanger the welfare of his family. He called you criminally insane . . .' his voice suppressed a laugh. One of the other hawaldaars did the laughing for him. 'Said that you used to be with him in some reform school in Mount Mary, St Francis of Assisi.'

'No . . . that's not the one . . .' one of the constables corrected him.

'I know that guy. I happen to be representing his aunt. He owes me over Rs 4 lakh, which is maybe why he's saying all this stuff in the first place. To prevent himself from having to pay her legal fees. Did you ever take a moment to think of his motive? Wait a minute . . .' I stopped myself. 'What does any of this have to do with what happened to Yogesh Moolchandani?'

'That's what I'm trying to tell you . . .' Saawant raised his voice, 'We've got nobody else apart from you and your client who can explain this inexplicable occurrence on the Sea Link. We've ruled out suicide long ago. With the two of you, there's a motive, too. We've got five eyewitnesses that say your client had a tussle with him last night. You've all the reason you need.'

'Then I guess you'll just have to come along with me to find out, won't you?' I replied. 'We can go to the 24×7 right now. It's not far from where I am. It'll take but 30 minutes at this time.'

'Very well,' Saawant sighed, getting up from his seat. 'I guess I'll see you there in 20.'

TWENTY

I reached the 24×7 sooner than I had anticipated. The cops had arrived there well before me, owing to their proximity; not exactly walking distance, but still close enough to not be too much of a hassle. There were three of them riding in the sub-inspector's jeep, the two subordinates had tagged along. The shop was practically empty at this time of day. Two sardars were going over the drinks section in painstaking detail. An elderly couple was arguing over which cereal was a better alternative to muesli. An obese middle-aged man was out shopping for shampoo, soap, shower gel, and other cosmetics and beauty products, even bothering to use one of the shopping carts thanklessly piled up next to the cash register. He was dressed in a tattered college vest and a slightly scruffy pair of Bermuda shorts. He kept dropping all the contents off the shelves as his elbows brushed through the aisles, and then apologetically bent down in a half-hearted attempt at retrieval before one of the staff beat him to it, and picked up the fallen merchandise to place neatly back on to the shelves.

I noticed the same kid from the previous night, hidden in a crowd of four staff members busily conducting the affairs of the establishment from behind the counter. He didn't notice me, or at least, he attempted not to. The pharmacist was also there, a stout Maharashtrian woman in a white lab coat. She noticed us slip into the place and, getting a look at the uniforms, quickly told the head clerk to attend to their new customers.

Sub-inspector Saawant, followed by the two constables, placed his inquiries right at the counter, leaning forward on the glass, and almost resting his upper torso on it. 'This man out here . . .' he gestured, pointing at me. 'You seen him before?'

The head clerk shook his head, looking back at the pharmacist who was taking refuge at the corner most shelf.

'That guy,' I told him, pointing at the kid hiding behind one of the other clerks. 'He was there that night.'

The kid came forward and hesitantly placed his hands on the counter. 'Yes?' he asked, exceedingly polite and gentle, almost suspiciously so.

'You know this man?' his employer asked him.

'No.' He shook his head too, a firm, decisive 'No'.

'What are you talking about?' I protested, 'Don't you remember me?'

'I'm afraid I have no idea what you're talking about.'

'What about all the missing items? There was some Rs 10,000 worth of groceries and cosmetics that went missing. Don't tell me your books missed it, it can't be unaccounted for. I even have all the stuff lying at my place.' I turned towards Saawant. 'I haven't touched any of it, except for a bag of nachos and a can of ginger ale.'

'Are you sure this man wasn't here two nights ago?' Sub-inspector Saawant re-checked with the kid.

'Absolutely sure.'

'He's new on the job,' the head clerk informed us. 'It's a rotating shift. Our chowkidar has taken a sick leave, so there's no one else to mind the store at night. It's usually just a single person through the night. Day before night was his first night. You know how it is; he gets a little shaky on the night job, sitting all alone.'

'What about the CCTV camera footage?' I asked.

'The CCTV camera is currently not working. It's been disabled and is undergoing repair. Once, we had an instance of a crazed man trying to break in through the shutters because we weren't willing to give him the medication he sought without a prescription slip. Ever since that, we have been on the alert. Which is why we decided to update our security system. We're installing a new camera with better picture quality. The one we have currently is not of much use as you can see.' He pointed towards the CCTV monitor planted above the entrance under an agarbati altar. The lens was missing from the camera, and it just looked on at us like a dispossessed glass eyeball.

'What nonsense,' I complained, gesticulating aggressively at the kid. 'Didn't I tell you I'd offer you my legal services for base price in case you were blamed for the robbery? You have nothing to hide,' I assured him. 'It's alright, you can tell us. I'm admitting to my crime. I robbed this very store yesterday morning,' I proclaimed loud and clear for the entire place to hear. The two sardars turned back from the refrigerator and passed a casual glance over at us, pretending not to hear what they had just heard. The fat guy's head was buried in one of the bottom-most shelves.

'I'm . . . uh . . . sorry . . .' The head clerk smiled courteously, 'but there's nothing we can do for you. Our shop has not reported any loss from yesterday. As a matter of fact, I am happy to report that business is doing fine . . . despite the competition, I might add. You know how many 24×7s have opened up simultaneously all across Bandra. Nowadays, some of the shops even stay open all night illegally with the shutter pulled down or with a cloth-covering concealing the entrance. It's criminal. They're trying to put us out of business. But as of now, touch wood.' He touched the counter and then curved his index finger over his forehead. 'We're doing fine.'

The kid just stared on silently, avoiding eye contact and obediently nodding at his employer's comments.

'If we ever do have the misfortune of being robbed,' he continued, 'then I will be sure to inform you.'

'Sorry to have troubled you . . .' Sub-inspector Saawant nodded at him in acknowledgement, dragging me out of the store by the arm. One of the constables resignedly followed us out. The other one was busy going over the crates outside stacked with chips packets, asking the fridge attendant if he had change for a hundred.

'I don't know what to make of it . . .' I told Sub-inspector Saawant. 'The kid's just probably scared he'll get into trouble if he opens his mouth.'

'What do you suppose we should do with him, saahab?' asked one of the constables with his hands ominously folded.

I tried calling Kartik Bhoparai, but his number was not reachable. My phone battery died just when it was needed the most. The entire touchscreen folded up in a black glow, closing the curtains on the phone call neatly, without a beep.

The four policemen just stared blankly at me on the kerb of the road next to the HDFC ATM where I had parked my car the previous night. The ATM was back in service and fully functional with a line of three undergraduates waiting outside. There was no point in taking Saawant and his team over to the Kotak Mahindra branch across the road I had tried in vain to use. I had probably tossed the receipt with the date and time in the wastepaper basket for chewing gum wrappers beside the night-guard. The one who stood outside right now didn't look like he was on the same shift.

'What do you think?' Saawant asked the two subordinates on either side of him.

'I think he's talking out of his ass,' said one of them. 'God knows how many stories he's changed. What about Kenkre and Narayan Panth Saahab?'

'They seem to be certain,' said Saawant. 'According to them, when they showed up at his house, it was highly possible that he could have just returned from a crash unscathed. There wasn't any damage to his car. They say he had a nervous manner about him. He was smoking a cigarette, put it out and then lit up another as if he were trying to hide it from someone. Got aggravated at the slightest questioning. All the signs.'

'Saahab, what do you say we put him in lock-up for the time being?' the same subordinate spoke. 'Let's see what he says in a couple of days.'

'His statements deserve cross-checking,' mumbled the other. 'At least that's what I think.'

'I'll tell you what *I* think,' snarled Sub-inspector Saawant, his tongue lashing about on his teeth, and his hands placed firmly on his hips, 'He came to the 24×7 with a story neatly prepared in case it would work, and a phoney alibi to go with it which has subsequently ditched him, leaving him to face the music just when its services were required.'

TWENTY-ONE

I came clean about everything to them. Told them precisely the truth and nothing more or nothing less—that Moolchandani had actually copped it because his car got stuck in cruise control; a car sold purposefully to him by Hiranandani Horsepower with full awareness on their part of its defects. I told them all about my visit with Bharat to the L.K.L.M. Provisional Home in New Bombay, of all that we had witnessed there, and all the ways in which it concerned Yogesh Moolchandani, Mateen Lakdawaala, and even Pawan Hiranandani; that my boss and Nalini were working to engineer a cover-up.

'Even Bharat's car was lying there at the construction site!' I informed them.

No doubt they exhibited some apprehension with such a far-fetched claim. They seemed to have a considerable amount of difficulty in believing that an automobile could be responsible for a murder. They wouldn't have a case then.

They probably thought I was half-crazy by now, with a propensity for making up facts sooner than they could actually occur. But since this was the most substantial claim I had made thus far, it made more than a dent on them.

'You said you saw the Civic lying there in New Bombay?' Sub-inspector Saawant asked.

'How's that possible?' one of the paandus jumped to the answer even before I could open my mouth. 'It's been impounded!'

'How should I know?' I argued. 'It wasn't even there last night when I brought Bharat in to the station.'

'You brought him in?' The other constable laughed.

'I brought him in for a moment, but then, after Shakeel told me about the car, I took him back out.'

'You didn't bring anyone in!' Sub-inspector Saawant sneered. 'You were supposed to bring one Bharat Morwani in last night when you left the station with Nalini Hegde. But you failed to. You said half-an-hour, remember? Everyone was waiting for your client at Khar police station till five in the morning.'

'That was because I could see what was happening . . .' I exhaled.

'That's why we brought him in,' Sub-inspector Saawant continued.

'This morning!' one of the constables specified.

'Picked him up from his building. He's down at Bandra police station with his parents and Nalini Hegde. The family lawyer is engaged at present. She'll be representing him from now on. Seeing as you are a suspect in this case, it kind of disqualifies you for the job!'

If I was being charged with a crime, I'd at least want it to be for the right one. I stormed back in again to try and promise the assembled staff of what I had done with my own two hands. But none of them seemed too convinced. If only I had brought along the supplies from my flat in Chembur to corroborate my claims. I shrieked and wailed and generally made quite a nuisance of myself, telling everyone that these four walls had carried my presence not so long ago! That these very tiles had my footprints stamped on them, and could indeed be detected by a pair of reliable fingerprint experts.

'You're under arrest for suspicion, Paleja!' Sub-inspector Saawant snapped. 'Put him in handcuffs. A more thorough investigation will soon determine what you *did* and *did not* do. The investigation period is sixty days. Till then we will have the pleasure of your custody.'

The two constables did just as he said, and one of the clerks behind the counter lent more than a helping hand while they were clipping them on. He held me from the back, keeping my shoulders in place for them to grab on to. They made them just about as tight as possible without actually blocking the blood circulation. Their dragging me out stilled the sightless gasps and bewildered stares—not a usual sight for a sunny Tuesday morning in this locality.

I guess I was just neither here nor there. Neither cop nor criminal, just lodged in the centre like a cement slab, impervious to justice. Common laws of morality didn't apply to me, and on paper I wasn't capable of crime. 'I've got a 7-year-long track record to show for that,' I told the cops. 'Haven't lost a single case yet, have served faithfully and loyally with distinction. If that isn't enough of an alibi in my favour, then I don't know what is. Even the people I robbed don't seem to think I'm capable of crime.'

The same gatekeeper opened the door for us on our way out of the 24×7, greeting me this time, less spiritedly than before, probably because I was in chains and being dragged out like a convicted felon. I tried to fake a return smile, but nothing came together convincingly.

As we got into the jeep, Sub-inspector Saawant asked me the quickest way out of the lane back towards Khar police station. I told him to take it via Reclamation and not S.V. Road, as the early evening traffic at the Bandra signal was likely to be a two-hour affair.

Everyone in the car managed to keep in good spirits up until the Reclamation Fair grounds. The Jumbo Circus was in town and the road was jammed with tourists, Mumbai darshan buses, and school buses, autos, and two-wheelers all hurrying up towards Reclamation; the homeward crowd stuck in their late-afternoon revelry. School had just broken. We carried on towards Khar police station, homeward bound like most of the others, either falling asleep behind the wheel or banging our heads on it to keep awake. The nightmare circus that is traffic. It takes a toll on you—every day, the shrieking sounds cause wear and tear of the frontal lobe, the sights damage the cornea, and the air can be bottled, fit for an exhaust fan.

I was still sore that I'd been picked up for the wrong crime, and did everything in my power to regain at least that moral balance. It was later reported to me, in retrospect, that I had spoken eloquently in the long car ride to Khar police station with perfect map-like accuracy about all the sides of town I had recently haunted. That I had purposely taken them by the wrong route, knowing it would grant me more time to expound on some of the things that had been plaguing me for the past couple of days . . .

My reflections went something like this, according to the psychiatric authorities, Sub-inspector Saawant recorded every word:

'Thoughts are the only things that move quicker than the speed of light . . . you see, I wasn't born bad like most people think. I had the blessing and care of a loving family, the gift of a roof over my head and three-square meals a day that tasted unmistakably of contentment. Convenience—that real arch-enemy to conscience. I could have had it—a good life, and lived it the healthy way, the way someone like Nalini Hegde had managed to do without much complaint. A life full of joy and goodness, and kindness and consideration. A life that took others into account. A life without secrets, where the monster that lurks within is brought out under the lab lights so that we may poke its horns and tickle its nose, not let it devour us. *A life without secrets.*'

Apparently, I kept asking the two hawaldaars, 'Isn't that what we all want? A life without secrets?'

TWENTY-TWO

Why do these thoughts come to me? Thoughts of death and mutilation. Thoughts of things that could be, and shouldn't be or never should have been. Things the mind dwells on for the sole simple reason that it shouldn't. Is it the destructive impulse all animals possess, or is it merely the tame childlike cruelty that impels an innocent toddler to stick a twig into the tail of an insect and cut it right in half for the simple sake that he *can*. When everything starts out so right, how can it go so wrong?

I'm nearing the end now, not only of this account, but also of my stint here at the L.K.L.M. Provisional Home for the Medically Ill. Something like a year has gone by since my initial incarceration. I'm sitting alone in the sole examination ward. The creased heaps of flesh across the body make my movements sag, and the remaining strength is reserved only for insult.

The doors to my chamber creaked open only slightly ajar, and an orderly poked his head in to make sure he didn't have to put me in a straightjacket. I was one of the friendliest and least harmful of the inmates contained in this facility, yet they could never be too sure.

'You have a visitor,' he mentioned.

It was Nalini, wrapped up in some variant of a formal sari and conceivably alarmed at my appearance, but she disguised it at my half-hearted greeting.

'You don't look so good, Pranav!' she said to me as she took a seat, jittering in the steel chair that was colder than the AC blast we were subjected to in these rooms.

'Would you like anything to eat or drink?' I asked.

'Well,' she leaned back comfortably. 'I'm not a big fan of the Threptin biscuits; they probably pile on you in a place like this.'

'Hmmphh . . .' I let out a faint laugh. 'I always liked Threptin.'

'Parle-G?'

'We might be able to arrange a pack.'

She smiled.

'Nurse!' I called out. A young lady called Rajeshwari, who was new to the job, stuck her head in to ask what I wanted. 'Could you get us a packet of biscuits from the pantry?'

'Will do.' She made a thumbs-up sign and vanished into the corridor.

'They keep you well in this place?' Nalini asked, glancing around.

'About as well as they know how. It isn't all that bad. You kind of get used to it. Feels like . . . uh . . . I don't know . . . school. Minus the friends. I'm the oldest one out here.'

She let out a laugh, which developed into a cough and ended up as a wheeze.

'Got a bronchital condition,' she told me.

'We all have our cross to bear.'

'You like to speak in metaphors, don't you? You don't use plain language.'

'I was a lawyer, Nalini! It was my job to say as little in as many words as possible. I loved the legal jargon; it gave me a chance to ramble. Seldom would I let a sentence escape my lips that wasn't measured almost to the point of abstraction.'

'I happen to know that. I've read your legal briefs.'

'It's good to see you, Nalini, but I'm afraid there isn't much I can do for the Chamber of Mangesh & Mangharam now.'

'Ahh . . . I left it months ago. I couldn't wait to get the heck out of that flea-trap. Old Mangharam needed me much more than I needed that job. I went and got myself a legislative post in the high courts. I'm teaching part-time classes also at GLC.'

'A professor. I always squared you for one. You had a classroom manner about you.'

'So did you.' She shook her head confoundedly. 'Only, I couldn't tell which school you belonged to.'

'There's not much I can do for you in that department as well, Nalini.'

'You mean to tell me . . .'

'If that's why you've come here, it's a lost cause. I was a perfectly normal human being.'

'Normal?'

'Yup.'

'What's your definition of normal?'

'I don't know. What's normal? The wind is normal, the sand, the ceiling, the windows that look out onto a pleasant view. That seems pretty normal to me, at least that's what I know.'

'I've known all kinds of Pranavs in the course of my profession, but you don't seem to make much sense to anybody. There was this person by the name of Kartik Bhoparai, your client Bhairavi Naraina's nephew. He claimed you were mentally deranged, and of unsound mind. That you had planned to commit a grand-scale massacre when you were in college. And that it was common knowledge at a reform school that both of you had once been sentenced to. He even came and met with Mr Mangharam when I was in office.'

'Hah . . .' I almost laughed.

'Well . . . his aunt lost the trial.'

'I'm sorry to hear that.'

'The lawyer he got for her was not up to the job. Akhilesh Goenka. Was always a bit distracted if you ask me. So, she's mighty upset with him. Said he purposely sabotaged her chances by changing her lawyer, who had never lost a case in his life, for an older, less enthusiastic expert. But believe it or not, heh . . . the case has come to me. She's still alive and kicking and wants to take her nephew to court for blackmail, kidnapping, and also what she claims to be murder.'

I purposely didn't let her in on what Bhoparai had confessed to me.

'I can provide you no help on that particular front, Nalini!' I smiled.

'Why not?' One of her eyebrows lifted.

'I was convicted for the wrong crime, you see. Unless you can get that cleared up, I have no incentive, monetary or otherwise—except that to do with harmonious development.'

Her eyes stiffened. 'Harmonious what?'

'Development.' I blinked a while. 'Harmonious development.' Once my eyes opened, they circled the empty examination ward. 'The meeting of two planes into a single point, a dot on the map, a speck in the cosmos. The symmetry of a target, its simple perfection. They've had me travelling Nalini . . . I can tell you that, taken me places on the map I had no idea existed.'

'What are you talking about, Pranav?'

'You see, Nalini, before there was virtual reality, there was the church—where one could wander at will through a conjured landscape of alleged activity; and before that we were left with only the imagination. You see that's the whole point of this snake pit . . .' I whispered.

'Hmmm . . .' her lips crumpled up into a thought. 'You mean to tell me that there's something . . .' She played the piano with her fingers in the air, '. . . about this place.'

'That doesn't even begin to cover it.' I leaned on the backrest, letting out a deep exhalation. 'If you can get me out of this place, I'll give you every rupee I'm worth . . .'

'Well . . . now . . . Pranav . . .' She pretended to laugh. 'Come on.'

'I'm serious. I can have it transferred to your account first thing tomorrow morning. They've taken away our mobile phones, but we still have access to the computers.'

'That's not the point, Pranav! I don't want your money. What do you think I am?' Her features contorted in disgust. 'You?'

'Hah . . .' I glared up at the ceiling. 'I guess you're right. You're not me. You're you. But still, if money's not the only incentive, then how about charity?'

'Oh, come on, Pranav, you're embarrassing me now.'

'Morality?' I suggested. 'Doing the right thing?'

This mildly amused her. 'You think I'd be doing the right thing by getting you out of this place?'

'I'm a kleptomaniac, not a murderer. If you want, I can give you a list of all the things I've stolen in my life, but Moolchandani I never killed . . .'

'That case is still not entirely solved,' she said to me, sealing up her lips.

'Ooopss . . .' I coughed.

'I don't know whether you did or didn't do it. And I don't care. I had enough hassles with that case. Maybe they're right in what they said about you at the office after word got around that you were involved in Moolchandani's death. That you couldn't have hurt a flower, let alone a fly, if you'd wanted to. But I don't know . . . you do seem like a normal, even good, human being.'

'Good . . . heh?' I ceased on the word.

'Why not? We've all got a little bit of good hidden away in us somewhere. It isn't all that hard to find, or summon up, however you want to put it. Some like to stifle it right in the proverbial "bud", others make a living out of it.'

'I always took more of an interest in my client's moral compass than I did in my own. Which is probably why I have to go on serving the wrong sentence, and be punished for somebody else's crime. Even if it's a mechanism that committed the crime. A mechanism not capable of judging right from wrong, daylight from night.'

'Heh?'

'By all means, take a confession from me. I'll tell you everything I know about Moolchandani, but for god's sake . . . I didn't do it!' My voice rose to an alarming pitch. 'How about you take up my case, Nalini?' I begged her. 'It'll give me some solace. It'll lighten the load. Knowing that, in official eyes, I never meant to kill anybody!'

'Hmmm . . .'

'PLEASE!!! Nalini . . .' I went on.

'Get a hold of yourself, Pranav!' Her eyes flared up.

'After all, it is partly your fault that I fell into this trap in the first place.'

'What!!??' She nearly rose up.

'You and old Lalith Mangharam! The two of you toiled away on this case . . . waited till five in the morning that night for me to show up with my client, just so you could help Hiranandani and Lakdawaala get away with Yogesh Moolchandani's murder!'

'What are you talking about?' She sat back down, now more curious than before.

'This 2,50,000-square-foot private compound!' I grinned at her. 'Have you seen it? The builders cut a deal with the Central Social Welfare Board and got them to authorize the infrastructure to set up a sort of university campus for a special learning centre for the affluent and maladjusted. But have you looked around it?' I pointed to a corner of the distant wall. 'At the surrounding territory?'

'Hmmm . . .'

'The work that's underway, it's been under construction for years, is probably going to remain under construction forever perhaps, who knows!?'

Her eyes lurked outside the sole uncurtained window of the room. Like the vast expanse of highway allotted to the building of the Navi Mumbai Airport, this acreage was just lying—rotting, growing weeds, sprawling into endless fields of nothingness: waiting on unresolvable litigations that would accumulate over centuries to essentially blast all plans that gave seed to the endeavour in the first place; the very thoughts that had lifted marble and stone, to be stricken off the face of the earth for eternity, and all that would be left to show for it—a barren expanse of illegal enterprise.

'The proposed motor freeway intended to connect New Bombay with the greater Mumbai mainland over the Thane creek,' I proclaimed.

Now her eyebrows flattened.

'That's a myth . . .' she said. 'I know all about it. Just like the Bermuda Triangle of New Bombay.'

'Well, whatever it is,' I smiled. 'Yogesh Moolchandani owned the road that spilt out into that greyest of oblivions . . . and now he's well out of the way and long forgotten . . .'

The biscuits came in, so did two cups of tea and some soup that was near inedible. But she drank it out of politeness. She was a cordial and considerate person, and meant well; *a good person*. And so was I. I didn't know if she thought so, but I did.

We fell into one of those brief silences that occurs in between sips, where the other person thinks of what to say only to not bother because they're expecting you to come up with something that'll amount to a pearl of wisdom. I had none I could offer, only silver-toothed pronouncements of gratitude for her having taken the trouble and the time to have visited me in the first place. I only knew one thing—I was good. A good person, and I meant well.

'W-w-well . . .' I stammered, breaking her concentration on the soup mug she was blowing ripples into and trying hard to cool down. 'E-e-even if you don't wanna take up my case, that's fine, but . . . If I could say one thing . . . I'd just like to say I'm sorry.'

The ripples stood still in her mug; the vapours escaped it over her eyes. She didn't say a thing, just looked at me blank as always, this time cloaking some sensation in her eyes. She gently nodded her head, and closed her eyes for a moment.

'I'm a good person,' I persisted, nearly dropping my soup off the bedside table and scattering some crumbs of biscuit all over the bedsheet. 'I just want you to know that I mean well. I don't mean anybody any harm.'

She dangled one leg over the other and got up to place her mug on an adjacent bedstand. She took a slow walk up to the window and gazed out, and then back at me. I was lying prostrate on the bed, mumbling and muttering my worth to myself, and reminding her and all those that could hear, that I wasn't a bad individual. She didn't agree or disagree, just tried to study why I was saying what I was saying; even I didn't know. I just knew one thing—'I'm a good person. And I mean well.'

ACKNOWLEDGEMENTS

I would like to thank my brilliant editor Shreya Punj for her marvellous insights and for being a fellow crime fiction aficionado, and the fantastic copy edit team comprising Binita Roy and Nitin Sisupalan Jaya. I would like very much to thank Ahlawat Gunjan for his wonderful cover design. I would also like to thank my friends Trivankumar S. Karnani and Hasmit Trivedi for answering endless queries about the legal details, and Utsav Unadkat for helping me understand certain aspects of the automobile trade. Also S. Hussain Zaidi and Bilal Siddiqui for their friendship and encouragement.